RECEIVED

MAY 1 1 2010

D0397614

PRETEND
SHE'S
HERE

NO LONGER PROPERTY OF
SEATTLE PUBLIC LIBRARY

YA BOOKS BY LUANNE RICE

The Beautiful Lost

The Secret Language of Sisters

ALSO BY LUANNE RICE

The Lemon Orchard

Little Night

The Letters (with Joseph Monninger)

The Silver Boat

The Deep Blue Sea for Beginners

The Geometry of Sisters

Light of the Moon

Last Kiss

What Matters Most

The Edge of Winter

Sandcastles

Summer of Roses

Summer's Child

Silver Bells

Beach Girls

Dance with Me

The Perfect Summer

The Secret Hour

True Blue

Safe Harbor

Summer Light

Firefly Beach

Dream Country

Follow the Stars Home

Cloud Nine

Home Fires

Blue Moon

Secrets of Paris

Stone Heart

Crazy in Love

Angels All Over Town

PRETEND SHE'S HERE

LUANNE RICE

Scholastic Press / New York

Copyright © 2019 by Luanne Rice

All rights reserved. Published by Scholastic Press, an imprint of Scholastic Inc., *Publishers since 1920*. SCHOLASTIC, SCHOLASTIC PRESS, and associated logos are trademarks and/or registered trademarks of Scholastic Inc.

The publisher does not have any control over and does not assume any responsibility for author or third-party websites or their content.

No part of this publication may be reproduced, stored in a retrieval system, or transmitted in any form or by any means, electronic, mechanical, photocopying, recording, or otherwise, without written permission of the publisher. For information regarding permission, write to Scholastic Inc., Attention: Permissions Department, 557 Broadway, New York, NY 10012.

This book is a work of fiction. Names, characters, places, and incidents are either the product of the author's imagination or are used fictitiously, and any resemblance to actual persons, living or dead, business establishments, events, or locales is entirely coincidental.

Library of Congress Cataloging-in-Publication Data

Names: Rice, Luanne, author.
Title: Pretend she's here / Luanne Rice.
Other titles: Pretend she is here
Description: First edition. | New York, NY: Scholastic Press, 2019. | Summary: Fifteen-year-old Emily has six siblings, but she was also close to her best friend, Lizzie Porter, who died nearly a year ago, and she is still grieving; but Lizzie's family are also grieving, so much so, that they use Lizzie's younger sister, Chloe, as a lure and kidnap Emily, forcing her to dress, talk, and act like Lizzie, and threatening to go after Emily's family if she does not become the replacement for the daughter they lost—and Emily is caught between fear for herself and her family, and concern for Chloe, who she sees is also a victim of Mrs. Porter's madness.
Identifiers: LCCN 2018035371 | ISBN 9781338298505
Subjects: LCSH: Children—Death—Juvenile fiction. | Kidnapping—Juvenile fiction. | Identity (Psychology)—Juvenile fiction. | Bereavement—Juvenile fiction. | Mental illness—Juvenile fiction. | Sisters—Juvenile fiction. | Families—Juvenile fiction. | CYAC: Kidnapping—Fiction. | Identity—Fiction. | Grief—Fiction. | Mental illness—Fiction. | Sisters—Fiction. | Family life—Fiction. | LCGFT: Psychological fiction.
Classification: LCC PZ7.1.R53 Pr 2019 | DDC 813.54 [Fic] —dc23 LC record available at https://lccn.loc.gov/2018035371

10 9 8 7 6 5 4 3 2 1   19 20 21 22 23

Printed in the U.S.A.   23
First edition, March 2019

Book design by Baily Crawford

For Marilyn and Don Walsh

PART ONE

CHAPTER ONE

When you come from a big family, you're never alone—or at least, not often enough. That afternoon, all I wanted to do was walk home by myself. But Bea, my next-oldest sister—we were seven siblings in all—was crowding me.

"Are you okay?" Bea asked as we stood on the steps of Black Hall High after school.

"Yes! I'm excellent!" I said, injecting an extra dash of pep into my words to convince her to go on her merry way.

"You don't seem okay," Bea said.

"Just because I feel like walking home?"

"Well, you had that fight with Mom this morning. Also, your lips have been moving again."

"Uh, that happens when I talk."

"Uh, but there's no one there when you do it," she said.

"Do you have to point that out?" I asked, backing away from her. Bea and I shared a bedroom, a million freckles, and a ton of secrets. But when it came to anything involving my best friend,

Lizzie, my sister could be very intrusive, and frankly, it set me on edge.

"Emily, I know it's really hard," Bea said to me. "It's coming up on the anniversary, and you've seemed down, and I'm sorry—I'd just feel better if you'd let me and Patrick drive you home. It'll be fine."

"It *is* fine," I said, giving Bea my brightest smile. "Don't worry about me." I took a deep breath, because I knew I had to be convincing.

Bea was right—I'd been thinking about Lizzie more than ever lately. Three hundred and twenty-two days had gone by since my best friend had died. I was feeling *feelings*, giving in to my *moods*, as the shrink would say—and that's why I'd snapped at my mother that morning.

"Trust me, okay?" I said to Bea.

"Well, all right," Bea said. "But you're missing out. Patrick and I are stopping for fried clams. His treat. Last chance . . ."

I gave her a big one-armed hug around her neck and shoved her away, laughing. She patted my head in that big-sister way that was simultaneously patronizing and endearing. Then she headed toward the parking lot where our brother Patrick had the rusty orange Subaru running. The driver's window was down, and Patrick's elbow was resting on it. He and Bea looked exactly alike: dark hair and Atlantic Ocean–gray eyes. Unlike them, I was blond and blue-eyed. Patrick grinned and stuck out his tongue at me. I did the same to him—the Lonergan family salute.

I watched Bea get into the car. They drove in the opposite direction of our house, toward the fish shack. I had one brief moment of regret—my stomach growled as I imagined the tasty, crispy clam roll I was missing.

I spotted my friends Jordan Shear and Alicia Dawkins across the parking lot. Jordan waved. I was afraid she'd want me to do something with them, so I pretended not to see. I turned and started walking. Alone at last.

Fall was Lizzie's favorite season. She was everywhere. I felt her presence in the red and yellow leaves, the golden marsh grass, the diamonds of sunlight sparkling on bright blue Long Island Sound.

Hey Lizzie, Dan Jenkins texted me. Should I text back right away or wait till tonight? If people were looking at me, saw my lips moving as I hurried along by myself, they might have thought I was crazy—or learning lines for my latest play. Either way, I didn't care. Talking to my best friend made me feel like she was right by my side. And I needed that, especially now, because of the fight with my mom, because of how many days I'd been missing Lizzie, and because I honestly wanted to be going anywhere but home.

So maybe that's why I was barely surprised when I heard her sister's voice.

"Emily!"

I turned, and there was Chloe Porter, the former bane of Lizzie's existence, sitting on a stone wall across the street, as if she and her parents hadn't moved away last February. Had I conjured her? But no—she was there, and she was real.

"Chloe!" I said. In such a hurry to get to her, I flew across the street, snagged the toe of my shoe in a pothole, and just missed getting hit by a blue car. Its horn was still blaring when I dropped my backpack on the sidewalk, the better to hug her hard.

"It's really good to see you," Chloe said when we let go.

"You too," I said, scanning her face. She was two years younger than me and Lizzie, but she looked so old now—thirteen, a teenager. Startling emerald-green eyes, shoulder-length hair—unnervingly the exact same cut as Lizzie's, with a tendril that curled over her left ear, a brown so dark it was nearly black. I almost said that I didn't remember Chloe having that curl, and that her hair had been reddish-chestnut, not the dramatic and glamorous glossy black of Lizzie's. But I didn't. I just stared at her. It was almost as if Lizzie had come back to life. For real—not just part of my dreamy conjurings and imaginary conversations.

"Are you visiting?" I asked. Dumb question, because why else would she be here?

"Sort of," she said.

I tilted my head, waiting for more.

"My parents want to put flowers on her grave."

My heart skipped. It made sense. In forty-three days, it would be a whole year since Lizzie had died—on the day between our birthdays. I used to visit her grave pretty often. I'd leave weird things she had loved—twigs with acorns, a handful of moonstones collected from the beach, an iridescent bee's wing, a page of whatever I was writing, a cup of M&M's. Sometimes I found bouquets of roses and ivy tied with white ribbons, with notes attached from Mrs. Porter, so I knew she had been there.

"Want to come with us?" Chloe asked.

I almost said no, that I'd discovered the essence of Lizzie was nowhere near the cemetery, that she was right here with me as I walked along talking to her. But Chloe's face had turned so pale, her lips nearly blue, that I actually thought she might pass out. I got it—grief was not for the faint of heart. It was as physical as a stab wound.

"Sure," I said. "Where are your parents?"

"Over there," Chloe said, pointing at a white minivan parked up the street. Why did that give me such a pang? Maybe because it was yet another thing that Lizzie would never know about: that her family's old navy-blue van—the one she'd started learning to drive in—was long gone. The blue-and-white Connecticut plates had been replaced with white-red-and-blue ones from Massachusetts.

"I thought you moved to Maine," I said.

"Oh, we did," Chloe said. "But then we . . . uh . . ."

"Moved again?" I supplied, because she still looked so wobbly.

"Yeah." She swallowed hard. Then she gave out a laugh that sounded like a bark. "Sorry for being weird. It's just, the cemetery freaks me out. I hate going."

"I get it," I said.

We headed toward the minivan. There were her parents, sitting in the front seats. They gazed at me with such warmth, such familiar friendliness, that I choked up and wasn't sure my voice would work. The Porters had been my second family. It wasn't till that very instant, being in their presence for the first time in so long, that I realized how badly I missed not only Lizzie, but all of them.

Something crossed my mind, made me feel ashamed: In August, I had seen Mrs. Porter from a distance. I'd been walking my dog, Seamus, through the marsh. I'd glanced across the pond and I saw Mrs. Porter sitting on a driftwood log. I froze.

I hadn't seen Lizzie's mom since the funeral. Her grief at the gravesite had been so extreme. She had keened, a high, thin wail I didn't think a human could make, one that pierced my heart and made my bones feel ice cold. She had collapsed against Mr. Porter, and he and Chloe practically had to carry her to their car. As often as I'd thought of writing or calling her, just to say I was thinking of her, I was afraid that hearing from me would remind her too much of Lizzie and cause her more pain.

So that August day, instead of circling around the pond toward her, I'd gone the opposite way, toward the woods. At the last minute, I saw her notice me. She waved, called my name. I pretended not to hear and spent the rest of the afternoon feeling guilty. It made sense that she would have returned to Black Hall to visit Lizzie's grave, but I'd wondered why she was in the marsh—it was my favorite place to walk, but Lizzie hadn't liked the mud or the smell of low tide. She had preferred walks through town, past the church and the shops and galleries, up Library Lane.

Now, reaching the Porters' minivan, I felt tense, worried that Mrs. Porter would feel hurt that I'd avoided her that summer day.

Chloe slid open the back door. "Hop in," she said, and I did.

And all my fears were gone: Mrs. Porter turned in her seat, reaching to grab my hand. I hugged her from behind, leaning over to kiss Mr. Porter's cheek.

"Oh, my goodness, here you are!" Mrs. Porter said, still clutching my hand. I gazed into her eyes—the exact same green as Lizzie's and Chloe's—and noticed that her dark hair had much more silver in it than before, as if sorrow had bleached the life from it. Lizzie had inherited her mother's sharp cheekbones and wry smile.

"I'm so happy to see you!" I said, scouring her face to see if she was mad or hurt about what had happened in August.

"It's as if no time has gone by at all," she said. "No time at all."

"It's true," I said.

Mr. Porter was oddly quiet. He cleared his throat, as if he had a cold.

I stared at the back of his head—he had thick, curly brown hair, the same color Chloe's used to be. I remembered when we were really little, third grade or so, Lizzie would hug him, giggles spilling out, saying his hair smelled like spaghetti, as if that was the funniest thing in the world.

The minivan was already running, and Mr. Porter pulled away from the curb. He did a U-turn, and we headed down Main Street, past the big white church, along the narrow road lined with sea captains' houses and hundred-year-old trees.

"I brought juice packs!" Mrs. Porter said. "Chloe, in the cooler."

"That's okay," I said. "I'm not thirsty."

"Oh, but, sweetie—I always brought juice when I picked you up from school."

It jostled me to be called "sweetie"—that's what she'd always called Lizzie. But my heart was aching for Mrs. Porter. It must have been intense to be talking to me—the first time since Lizzie's funeral. And the juice part was true. Mrs. Porter and my mom vied for the title "Queen of Snacks." They never drove us anywhere without lots of juice and trail mix. My mom prided herself on making her own mixture of nuts and dried cranberries, but I wouldn't ever have told her that I preferred Mrs. Porter's because her concoction always included Lizzie's favorite—M&M's.

"Have some," Chloe said, handing me an ice-cold pack of orange-mango juice.

Perfect, I thought—Lizzie's number one choice. I slugged some down. A few drops spilled on the beige seats. I wiped them up with the sleeve of my green army jacket.

"How was school?" Mr. Porter asked, the first thing he'd said.

"Pretty good," I said. "I have an English test tomorrow. Lots of homework . . ." At that second, I realized that in the excitement of seeing Chloe, I'd left my backpack next to the stone wall. "Oh, could we go back a sec, actually, I forgot . . ." I started to say.

"Lizzie, English was always your best subject," Mrs. Porter said. "You'll have nothing to worry about. A poet, that's what I always said of you. My girl, the poet."

"Um," I said. "You mean Emily."

Lizzie wrote poems; I write plays. I couldn't really blame Mrs. Porter for the slipup, though.

"It's better we start right now, sweetie," Mrs. Porter said. "No going back, no being stuck in old ways. It's better just to move on from the start. You'll get used to it. We already have, haven't we, Chloe?"

"Yeah," Chloe said, looking away from me, out the window.

"Used to what?" I asked. I felt a tiny bit sick to my stomach— not the most unusual thing in the world. I was known to get carsick, but not usually right here on the sleepy country lanes of my hometown.

"Tell her, Chloe," Mrs. Porter said.

"You're my sister," Chloe said.

"True, we're just like sisters," I said. I looked across the seat at her, but she was still staring out the window. That's when I noticed we had driven past the cemetery. We were at the stop sign, about to turn onto Shore Road.

"Not 'like,'" Mr. Porter said.

Nausea bubbled up in me. I was going to be sick. "Please, could you pull over?" I asked.

No one replied. Mr. Porter just drove faster, past the gold-green salt marsh where I'd spied Mrs. Porter in August. We passed the fish shack. There were Patrick and Bea getting out of our old orange car. When I started to wave, Chloe caught my arm to keep my hand down. I noticed all three Porters avert their faces, and it hit me like a ton of bricks that they didn't want to be seen by my brother and sister.

"Stop," I said, feeling dizzy.

Mr. Porter didn't, though, and no one spoke. I saw the traffic light looming—once we went through we'd be on I-95, the interstate heading to wherever—and my head spun with the fact that these were people I loved, trusted as much as anyone, but who were acting so bizarrely. This couldn't be happening—I didn't even know what "this" was, but my gut was telling me it was now or never. This was my chance.

We stopped at the red light. I grabbed the handle and pulled, trying to yank open the door. Nothing happened.

Childproof locks, but I was nearly sixteen.

I tugged harder. The door stayed shut. My hand dove into my

jacket pocket, closed around my cell phone. I fumbled, starting to pull it out, but my fingers felt clumsy. I was getting really tired.

"It's better you relax," Mrs. Porter said. "We have a long ride ahead of us, Elizabeth."

"Chloe, say your sister's name," Mr. Porter said.

"Lizzie," Chloe whispered. And I felt her hand—cold and sweaty—close around mine and squeeze four times, just as my eyelids fluttered shut and I forgot every single thing in the world.

CHAPTER TWO

It was dark.

My mouth felt dry, the way it did after I'd been home from school throwing up from the flu. Now I had a streak of dry vomit on my cheek that made me realize I'd gotten sick.

We were still in a minivan, but now the seats were black instead of beige. The familiarity smashed into me—this was the *original* Porter-mobile, the one Lizzie had known, which I'd gotten a million rides in. Somehow the Porters had ditched the white van while I was passed out. Switching vehicles was some kind of terrible sign. We sped along a highway without much traffic. Then an eighteen-wheeler passed us, so close it made the van shake.

My stomach heaved, and I retched.

"Oh God, she's going to do it again," Chloe said in a high, thin voice.

Mrs. Porter turned around and jammed a bucket into my chest. I tried to reach for it and realized I couldn't move my hands. They were bound behind me with something so hard and tight it cut into my wrists. She held the bucket while I threw up until there was nothing left in my stomach.

"Gross," Chloe said.

My head lolled. I was so tired, and I wanted to fall back to sleep, but I forced myself to take some deep breaths of stale minivan air and try to clear my head. I was having a nightmare. That was all this was. It was just because I'd been thinking of Lizzie so strongly. I had conjured her family. An evil version of the Porters, but that's a nightmare for you: scary and horrible, nothing like real life.

Then Chloe said, "Yuck, it stinks," and opened her window. A blast of cold air knifed in, and I knew for sure I was awake and this was reality, not a bad dream.

"How much farther?" Chloe asked.

"Shush," Mrs. Porter said.

"I have to pee," Chloe said.

"If I have to tell you one more time to sit still and not think about it, you'll be sorry," Mr. Porter said.

"I have to pee, too," I said. My voice sounded raspy, and my throat hurt.

I saw Mr. and Mrs. Porter look at each other, their profiles silhouetted by the bright lights of an oncoming truck. With a furious sigh, Mr. Porter yanked the wheel to the right and we bounced onto the rumble strip along the side of the highway.

"Get out," he said. "Make it fast."

"Where are we supposed to go?" Chloe said. We were on the edge of a forest, tall pines growing straight into the stars. "Can't we find a rest stop?"

"This will have to do," her father said. Doors opened, and Lizzie's parents got out. Mrs. Porter took me gently by the arm and helped me out of the van. My head spun, and my knees buckled. She scanned the area, then led me onto a rough path into the pines. The air was cold. I could see the white clouds of my breath.

"Here?" I asked.

"Yes, sweetie."

I tried to free my hands but I couldn't. Mrs. Porter pulled down the zipper of my pants, and blood rushed into my face. I was so embarrassed that I couldn't go. I just squatted down, nothing happening.

"Think of running water," she said. "Pretend you're hearing a waterfall."

It worked and my bladder unlocked and hot urine poured out and splashed on my red shoes and the legs of my jeans. The sound was loud and went on forever and I was mortified knowing Chloe and Mr. Porter could hear. Then I stopped, and that was the worst part: Mrs. Porter was ready with a tissue.

My head was thick and pounding. I concentrated as hard as I could. I had no idea where we were, but all those pines and the chilly air—much colder than in Connecticut—and a distant sound of waves breaking made me think we were up north. If I ran into the woods, I could hide among the trees. My cell phone was still in my pocket; I felt its weight. If I could get away, I'd be able to call home. I'd circle back to the highway, and one of the truckers would stop and speed me away to a safe place where my parents could pick me up.

Was my family already looking for me? They had to be. They would have started as soon as I wasn't home for dinner. Then a nasty thought filled my mind: Could my mother think I might be hiding out at some friend's house? Because of our fight? Because I had done it once before? Because Bea would tell her I hadn't wanted to drive home with her and Patrick? I pushed the idea away.

"Let's go," Mrs. Porter said, tugging on my arm. Then, as an afterthought, "Sweetie."

"I think I'm going to throw up again," I said, bending from the waist, crouching down.

"What's taking so long?" Mr. Porter shouted.

"She's about to be sick," Mrs. Porter called back.

"I'm freezing," Chloe said in a whining tone.

"Then wait in the car," her father said.

I crouched, as if about to barf, then used my legs as springs and smashed into Mrs. Porter, knocking her down, making her cry out. I turned and ran as fast as I could into the trees. The smell of pine was fresh and strong, clearing my brain like an antidote to whatever had been in that juice.

There was no real path, but I ran by instinct, like on the field when I played touch football with my sisters and brothers. Patrick always gave the ball to me; in spite of the fact he teased me about being a theater geek, I was super fast. I dodged trees and boulders as if they were the other team. I heard someone behind me and wheeled straight toward the footsteps, a buttonhook move that brought me face-to-face with Mr. Porter. I caught him off guard enough that I could take that second to disappear behind a rock ledge to the left.

He was out of breath. I heard him. Mrs. Porter, too. I had speed and being fifteen-almost-sixteen on my side. The disadvantage was the drug, because even though the chilly air and my racing heart were pushing it out of my system, I still felt I was wrapped in cobwebs. I kept thinking of my phone. Where was Chloe? I strained to listen for her, too. I wanted to have everyone's position in my mind when I made my next dash.

"Lizzie!" Mrs. Porter said.

"She's not going to answer to that," Mr. Porter said. Then he called, "Emily!"

My heart froze to hear my real name. I'd been half thinking they had lost their minds. It seemed beyond belief, but what other explanation could there be for taking me away from Black Hall, calling me the name of their dead daughter? But Mr. Porter had just proved he knew who I really was, and that terrified me.

"How far can she get?" Mr. Porter asked.

"The juice had too small a dose," Mrs. Porter said. "I told you. I calculated body weight, I did everything but measure it out for you . . ."

"I didn't want to kill her!" Mr. Porter said.

Their voices receded. They were walking away. I stayed still behind the boulder. I had to reach my phone. I twisted back and forth, contorting myself, trying to get my hands into my pocket, but it was physically impossible. My only choice was to stay hidden, then make a dash for it.

The sky was very clear, and pinpricks of starlight came through the pine needles. My eyes had gotten used to the dark. I wondered what time it was. My parents and siblings would definitely be worried. Thinking about shouting at my mother before school that morning, I practically lost it.

"I am going to Boston with Dan this weekend, period, end of story," I had announced in the kitchen.

"On a train, fine, but not in a car. He just got his license," my mother had said.

"He's a good driver."

"He might be a great driver, Emily, but he's brand new. I-95 is brutal, and Boston streets are hard to figure out unless you're really familiar with them."

"He *is*! His brother goes to Emerson! He visits him all the time! And that's all we're going to do, a bunch of us, we're going to meet up with his brother Henry and check out the theater department."

"That's fine. Take the train," my mother said.

"We're driving."

"Emily, I know you like him," Mom had said. "He texts you, and you practically launch out of your seat. You cast him in your play, fantastic. I realize you have a crush, and that can turn your mind around. But you're not driving on the highway with him till he's had his license for longer than two weeks."

I could feel she meant it, and I felt sliced by her words. Did I really jump out of my seat when he texted? And the way she said *I know you like him*—as if he didn't like me back. Probably what hurt worst was that I wondered about that very thing.

"You just don't want me in a car because of what you used to do," I'd snapped. "Because you used to drive drunk!"

"I'll never stop being sorry for that, but it was a long time ago," she said calmly, as if I hadn't just verbally slapped her.

"Dan's not going to do that," I said. "He would never drink and drive."

"That may be. But he's not going to drive you at all," she said. "Not to Boston."

I just walked away.

"See you after school," she called.

"See you never," I muttered under my breath.

A tidal wave of panic hit me now—had my mom heard me say those words? Could she possibly think I'd run away? That I hadn't come home because I'd said I'd see her never? She might. There'd been that other time.

She had been sober over a year now. Since the last horrible fight that had sent her to rehab, it was rare to hear raised voices in our house. The fact was, Mom and I had both changed during that time. She had quit drinking. And I'd had to deal with my best friend's death.

In the weeks after Lizzie died, I'd heard the words *depressed* and *withdrawn*, *shocked* and *mourning* coming from my parents. They sent me to a therapist. I saw Dr. Ferry pretty regularly. What helped me most was writing. My most recent work, since losing Lizzie, was about death. That might sound morbid, but it wasn't. It had made me feel better.

I needed my mother—my whole family—so badly in that moment, I wanted to cry. But then I took that emotion and turned it around. We were the Lonergan family, close and tough, all for one and one for all. We had dealt with my mother's alcoholism. We had rallied around her during early sobriety, attended AA meetings with her, even gone to Al-Anon with our dad. My family would work nonstop until they found me. I was sure. They would pull out all the stops. That's how we rolled.

We even had a motto: *Faugh a Ballagh.* Fighting Irish for "Clear the way."

I took three deep breaths of cold air. The Porters' voices had drifted away and the forest became silent. I didn't hear footsteps or voices anymore, and I decided to count to one hundred before moving again. Just like playing hide-and-seek. But instead of *one Mississippi, two Mississippi*, I silently said the full names of my family: my parents and my siblings, in order of oldest to youngest. There were so many names—first, middle, confirmation—for nine people, I figured that was almost the same as counting slowly to a hundred.

> *Dad—Thomas Francis Aquinas Lonergan*
>
> *Mom—Mary Elizabeth Rose Lonergan*
>
> *Tommy—Thomas Francis Aquinas Lonergan, Jr.*
>
> *Mick—Michael Joseph Aloysius Lonergan*
>
> *Anne—Anne Agatha Anastasia Lonergan*
>
> *Iggy—Ignatius Loyola Lonergan*
>
> *Pat—Patrick Benedict Leo Lonergan*
>
> *Bea—Beatrice Felicity Michael Lonergan*
>
> *And me—Emily Magdalene Bartholomea Lonergan*

Just thinking the names filled me with power and strength. When I was done, the only sounds I heard were wind in the trees and the occasional rush of a passing car or truck. Instead of running, I crept away.

I kept wrenching my wrists against the sharp, tight bonds, trying to free my hands. The plastic edges cut into my skin. It hurt, and my wrists were bleeding, but I didn't care. My phone was so close, but the ties refused to loosen, and I couldn't get my fingers into my pocket. When I had more distance between me and the Porters, I would find a sharp rock and saw the ties off, and then I would call.

Pine boughs hung low. I ducked beneath them. Needles tickled my face and the top of my head. I heard blood rushing in my ears, my heart beating so hard. The taste of poison was in my throat. I didn't want to circle back to the highway right away, in case the Porters were close by and still looking for me. They probably were.

Had they driven away yet? Or were they waiting at the minivan, thinking I'd get scared or tired in the woods and give up? I nearly snorted. No member of the Lonergan family gives up. Thinking of my clan again gave me even more courage, so I started to run, sure of my feet and overflowing with confidence and fire.

"Emily." The voice was quiet.

I stopped short, swallowing my breath. It sounded like Lizzie. Had her ghost come to help me? But no. There, sitting on the side of a steep hill, was Chloe.

"You have to come back with me," she said in a low voice. "Back to the van."

"I won't," I said. "I'm going home."

"They won't let you."

"Don't tell them," I whispered. "Just let me go."

"I can't," she said, her voice breaking, as if she felt sorry.

I stared at her—she was just Lizzie's little sister, she wasn't going to stop me—and took off in a blazing sprint, as if I was racing the fifty-yard dash. I heard her shout, "Mom, Dad, over here!"

That didn't matter. I was on my way, up the hill, feinting around boulders and trees. Chloe was the least athletic person I knew. Lizzie and I used to encourage her, work with her to up her game so she wouldn't embarrass herself on the field. I wasn't exactly sporty, but theater can be pretty physical, so I stayed in shape.

I scrambled up the ledge, hoping there wasn't a cliff in my future, and there wasn't—just another stretch of pine trees with a row of house lights beyond the ridge. My salvation: Someone there would call 911 and this nightmare would be history.

"Yes!" I said. I put on the speed, and with all that adrenaline, I missed the narrow crevice.

My foot got caught in the rock. I tried to put out my arms to catch my balance, brace my fall, but my hands were still snagged behind my back. I went down hard, my ankle twisting so violently, I cried in pain. My head smacked the ground.

I would have kept going. I would have crawled to those houses, I swear. But I saw purple sparkles behind my eyelids and everything went black.

* * *

The next thing I knew, I was in someone's arms, being carried like a baby toward the van, shoved into the back seat, buckled up.

"Her head's bleeding," Chloe said. "We have to take her to a hospital!"

"We'll be home in half an hour; we're almost there," Mrs. Porter said. I realized that she was now in the back seat beside me, Chloe up front. My head throbbed, but my ankle hurt even worse.

The Porters, like my family, always had a first-aid kit in their car. Mrs. Porter clicked the plastic box open.

I felt her hands on my left temple, dabbing at a very sore spot with a piece of gauze. Then I smelled alcohol and felt the sting. She was cleaning the wound. I remembered that she was a nurse. When Lizzie and I were little, Mrs. Porter had worked at our school. Then she got another job, working privately for people who were sick at home. She said it was better because she had more time for Lizzie and Chloe.

"Okay, ten minutes to the exit," Mr. Porter said.

"Got it," Mrs. Porter said, carefully taping a bandage to my head.

"Give it to her," Mr. Porter said.

"Not with a head injury," Mrs. Porter said.

"You want to get caught?" he asked sharply.

"No," she said after a few seconds.

"If we hadn't stopped for that bathroom break, we'd have gotten through the toll and been home safe by now," he said. "Just do it, Ginnie!"

I heard her rummaging in the kit. A bottle clinked. I turned my head, saw her lift a small vial in front of her face, insert a syringe into the rubber cap to withdraw liquid, and lightly pump the plunger so a tiny clear stream squirted into the air.

"Please," I said.

"It won't hurt, Lizzie," Mrs. Porter said, her voice soft and soothing.

"I'm Emily," I said.

"You're my sweetie," she said. She reached behind me to roll up my sleeve. She swabbed my upper arm with alcohol. I felt the needle prick, then a slow ache in my bicep. Almost instantly, I felt light-headed. I could taste the bitter drug in my mouth. The pain in my head and ankle dulled.

"Why are you doing this?" I asked. The medication made me feel so trapped and helpless that tears filled my eyes, splashed onto my cheeks.

"Shhh," she said.

"Where are you taking me?" I asked, a sob bubbling up. "Mrs. Porter, I want my family."

"We are your family, sweetie," she said. She reached into a canvas bag, pulled out a black wig. She gently eased it onto my head, tucking my long, reddish-blond hair under the snug cap. I tossed my head, trying to shake it off.

I heard the van's turn signal, and we veered right, leaving the highway. This was the exit Mr. Porter had mentioned. Up ahead I saw a brightly lit small building in the middle of the road. A toll-booth, twenty yards ahead! The sign on top said MAINE TURNPIKE. There was a man in the booth. Mr. Porter slowed down. He lowered his window, held out his arm, the ticket in his hand. Chloe slouched down in the seat, looking out the opposite window.

I fought the drug. I forced myself to stay alert. Mrs. Porter propped me up, an arm behind my back.

"Help," I said. "Help me."

My tongue felt thick. The words came out garbled, so I said them again, louder. "Help me!"

The toll collector was right there, so close, I saw his mustache, his bald head, the Maine Turnpike Authority patch on his shoulder. I heard a radio playing. He was listening to a football game.

"Please," I said. "They're not my family."

He looked inside the van. I swear he smiled right at me. Mr. Porter started to pull away.

"Hold on," the man said.

"Yes, sir?" Mr. Porter said. Then, reading the name tag right on the tollbooth window, "Yes, Dave?"

"Patriots fan?" the toll collector asked.

"Help me help me help me," I said. I was screaming inside, but even to my own ears the words that came out of my mouth sounded like gibberish. But I tried to lock eyes with him, signal with my expression that I was in trouble. I fought to stay conscious.

"Yeah," Mr. Porter said. "How do you know that?"

"Sticker on the window," the toll collector said.

I could picture it, the Patriots helmet right next to the Red Sox World Series Champions oval and the *Proud Parents of a Black Hall High Honors Student* emblem.

"Are we winning?" Mr. Porter asked.

"Up by ten, just got the field goal," the toll collector said.

"Yeah, well, go, Pats," Mr. Porter said, chuckling, driving away.

As the tollbooth disappeared behind us, Mrs. Porter leaned into my face. She looked worried. She removed the wig, dabbed at the bandage. "It's bleeding through," she said. "I'll give you stitches when we get home."

I was crying, talking, calling out for Bea, for my mother, for my family.

"No one can understand what you're saying," Chloe said sharply. "Will you just shut up? Just *stop*?"

"She will," Mrs. Porter said, her arm around my shoulder, giving me a squeeze that was probably meant to be comforting. "She'll be fine."

Then, to me, her lips against my hair, "Sleep now, sweetie. You'll feel better in the morning."

I slept.

CHAPTER THREE

DAY ONE

I woke up in Lizzie's bedroom. This was surreal: Everything was exactly, I mean *exactly*, as she had left it. I lay in her four-poster bed, the maple posts topped with carved pineapples. Up above was the canopy that wasn't supposed to be there—she and I had fashioned it from old lace curtains we'd found in her grandmother's trunk in the attic. The quilt that covered me was purple paisley, and I recognized a faded stain from a sleepover when, laughing so hard at one of our Bad Movie Night selections, she spilled her hot chocolate.

Her desk—actually her grandparents' old enameled kitchen table—was across the room. Lizzie had gotten it when her grandmother had broken her hip and had to move into assisted living. In fact, a lot of the things in Lizzie's room had belonged to Mame. (I'd called her grandma that, too, just like Lizzie, Chloe, and all their cousins.) The milk glass lamps on the desk and bedside table, the Seth Thomas steeple clock on the bureau, a collection of swan figurines, had all belonged to Mame.

The bookshelves—I couldn't believe it. Every single volume was set in the same order Lizzie had used, which was to say, no apparent order at all. Lizzie loved to read, and even though she wasn't the tidiest person, she arranged her books according to logic that only she and I understood. Her categories were dead poets, living poets, awesome modern women writers, hot modern guy writers, non-hot modern guy writers, and British cozies. Lizzie had adopted Mame's love of mysteries set in wartime England.

Somehow her parents, or whoever had created this room, had either figured out Lizzie's system of shelving her books or had transported the bookshelves intact from Black Hall.

Or had we returned to her old bedroom in her old house? That thought made my heart lurch. Had we looped around, back from Maine, gone home to Connecticut? Were we in the Porters' old house back in my hometown?

The steeple clock struck ten, and so—very distantly—did what I recognized as the grandfather clock that used to stand in their front hall. But instead of coming from downstairs, where the foyer had been in relation to Lizzie's old room, the sound of the chiming bell echoed from up above.

Was it ten in the morning? There was a window in the alcove between Lizzie's desk and bureau, but the familiar blue velvet curtains were drawn, and no light came through. Could it be ten at night? Was it the same day I'd been taken or the next? Or even the day after that? How much time had passed?

I noticed a plate of food on the bedside table—a cheese sandwich, an apple, and a bottle of Snapple. I was starving, but my mouth tasted terrible and I had to brush my teeth. If this was Lizzie's room, the bathroom would be to the left, just past the closet. I tried to turn on my side, to get up. Pain shot through my left ankle. My foot felt heavy. I lifted it slightly: I had a support boot on. I kicked with my good leg, to move the covers, and realized my right foot was knotted to a long line tied loosely to the bedpost. My hands were no longer bound.

I climbed out of bed. It was hard to walk, with one foot in the boot and the other hitched to the bed, so I hopped as far as the line would let me go—luckily into the bathroom, about ten feet away. Surrealism continued to reign. Lizzie had been allowed to redecorate her own bathroom back home, and it was reproduced here, exactly: black marble counter and wash basin, black-tiled shower, a ruby-red stained glass window embedded with black-and-white lilies, black towels, Lizzie's favorite Paris Nights soap and body wash, her purple toothbrush and—I couldn't believe it—the pink toothbrush I had always left at her house because I slept over so often.

I started to brush my teeth, then stopped. What if the water was drugged? Or what if they had sprinkled a sedative on the toothbrush? I turned off the faucet and looked in the mirror in total shock.

My hair was black. This wasn't the wig—it was my true, normally reddish-blond hair dyed nearly blue-black, the same color as Lizzie's, with a Lizzie-like tendril curling down my unbruised cheek. And my blue eyes were green. I reached up, gingerly touched my eyeball, and the surface shifted. That made me jump and screech out loud. Someone had inserted contact lenses.

There was a dark purple bruise on my left temple and cheekbone. I ripped off the gauze bandage on my forehead and saw butterfly stitches. A small patch of my hair, around the cut, had been shaved. It looked ugly.

I continued to stare at myself. I was wearing Lizzie's orange-and-black Halloween nightgown—the flannel soft from so many washes, the colors of bats and pumpkins faded and bleeding into each other. Someone had darkened my eyebrows and drawn Lizzie's little mole on my cheek. I wet my thumb and rubbed the color off my cheek and brows.

That got me started. I wanted to undo every change. I turned on the shower, threw the nightgown on the floor, ripped the Velcro straps to remove the boot, and stepped into the hot water. I doused my hair with Lizzie's shampoo, scrubbed my head so hard my scalp felt raw. Lizzie and I had been known to streak our hair pink, green, and purple. The color had always washed out. I watched the drain, waiting for the black streaks to rinse off, but the water ran clear.

When I stepped out and dried myself with her towel, I looked in the mirror and saw that my hair was still black. Total horror—it must have been permanent dye.

In a way, that was weird, because I had always wished I had dark hair. Lizzie had it, and so did most of my brothers and sisters. Our family was "black Irish"—our ancestors came from Kerry and had the same coloring of the Spanish whose Armada had once landed on that west coast. Somehow only Iggy and I wound up with light hair. At least we had the same blue eyes as everyone else. Only now mine were green.

I had never worn contacts before. It made me squeamish to reach my fingertips into my eyes, but I steeled myself and forced myself to do it. I threw the soft green plastic discs into the toilet. I flexed my ankle. Putting pressure on it hurt, but I knew it wasn't broken. The rope was soaked and chafed my skin.

I put on Lizzie's nightgown again and limped back into the bedroom. I looked around for the clothes I'd been wearing—no sign of them. My cell phone had been in the pocket of my army jacket. Would the Porters have realized it was there, thrown it away? If I could just find it, I would call home. I wouldn't know where to tell them I was, but I was pretty sure they could track me using GPS.

I tore through Lizzie's closet. Her style was totally different than mine. She loved clothes that were dark and sleek, always brand-new because her parents had money, while mine were a colorful melting pot of pure quirk: hand-me-downs from my older sisters, Anne and Bea, and the occasional ModCloth splurge. Lizzie loved black anything, I went for polka dots, cotton prints, flowers, and stripes.

"Zany, baby," Lizzie would say, teasing me when I'd show up for a night out in Bea's cast-off red-checked dress, a scarlet cable-knit cardigan knitted by Anne, the hand-tooled brown leather belt Mick had forgotten in his closet when he'd left for college, and my very own teal-blue canvas flats. Meanwhile Lizzie would be sultry and gorgeous in black leggings, a black jacket, and silver-studded motorcycle boots.

I knew every single thing in her closet by heart. The coats and sweaters, the silk blouses, Mame's old black velvet opera cape; they all smelled like Lizzie's lemongrass shampoo and Mame's faded L'Air du Temps perfume. In spite of my situation, I half swooned from missing my best friend, but I forced myself to concentrate. No sign of my jacket. I raced to her bureau, ransacked the drawers.

There was nothing of mine. My cell phone—gone.

I tried the doorknob. I already knew it would be locked. The steeple clock ticked loudly. It was 10:45—still no idea whether a.m or p.m. I pressed my ear to the door, listened for any sound. Nothing but silence. That was good. I had no interest in seeing any Porter ever again.

I had to escape, but I still felt so weak from last night, I was afraid I wouldn't get far. I needed my strength, so I wolfed down the cheese sandwich and apple. Swiss cheese, of course—Lizzie's favorite.

I felt better after eating, almost supercharged, determined to find a way out. There had to be one.

The window. Even if it was bolted shut, I'd break the glass. I walked across the room, pulled back the curtains.

There was no window, no glass. Only a cinder block wall.

That's when absolute panic hit me. I wasn't just locked in—I was walled-in. The Porters had built me a prison. I started pacing the room.

Framed photos stood on Lizzie's bureau. Three had me in them—standing next to Lizzie in the back row of our middle school soccer team, a selfie of the two of us on the beach the week before she'd died, and one of me and Dan at play rehearsal when I hadn't known she was taking our picture.

And then a lightning bolt struck: the box of Mame's photos. That would be my salvation. It was full of a million Porter family pictures, but it also had a hiding spot with three of Mame's secret things, one of which would help me get away.

Lizzie had been Mame's oldest and favorite grandchild. Sometimes when I slept over, Lizzie and I would have dinner at Mame's instead of the Porters', and Mame would talk to us for hours on end, telling stories about when she had been young, hilarious and crazy adventures no one, not even Lizzie's mother, knew about: things you would never imagine an old lady having done.

We especially loved when Mame talked about Hubert, the love of her life. They had met when they were older, after they'd been married to other people. They wanted to be together, but he lived in France and she lived in Connecticut. As much as they adored each other, neither wanted to move across the ocean, far away from their kids and grandchildren. Instead, they talked on the phone every day.

Hubert had given Mame what she called a "dedicated cell phone"—because they were dedicated to each other, because it was set up to make international calls, but also because she only used it to call him.

Lizzie had kept Mame's box on the top shelf of her closet. I dragged the desk chair over and clambered up. There were notebooks, winter hats, scarves, an old laptop, plastic bags full of folded sweaters, and a bunch of other stuff, but no sign of Mame's box.

I kept looking, as if maybe I'd missed it, but there was only so long you could search through a small top shelf without knowing you weren't going to find what you were looking for. Maybe her parents had thrown the box out. Her mother had sometimes seemed a little jealous of how close Lizzie felt to Mame.

But deep down, I didn't believe that was true. Mrs. Porter had loved her mother—I'd seen them together plenty of times, and when Mame had broken her hip, Mrs. Porter had given up her private nursing jobs to take care of Mame until she'd gone into assisted living.

To keep myself from feeling completely crushed over not finding the box, I told myself the phone had probably long since lost its charge. I had no idea if the kind of phone programmed for international calls could make local ones. They probably couldn't. I told myself that even if the Porters hadn't discarded the photos, they'd most likely gone through the box, found the hiding place. Maybe that's why the box wasn't where it was supposed to be.

But in spite of all that, I kept looking. *Trust your instincts*, my brother Patrick would tell me. *When in doubt, trust your gut over your mind. It will never fail you.*

Ha-ha, I'd say to him. *That's why I make honors and you don't. I use my mind.*

Ha-ha, he'd say back. *Wait till something happens—you'll know what it is, and you'll remember what I said.*

Well, something was happening now. And I did remember what he said. Every instinct was telling me that if this was Lizzie's room, exactly as it had been, the box was still here. Just because I had last seen it in her closet didn't mean she hadn't moved it.

But where? That's what I had to figure out.

The energy I'd gotten after eating drained away, and I felt as if I were dissolving. My mind began to buzz, the way it did when I stayed up late studying, when I was exhausted from thinking too hard. Every step I took was more like a stumble. I had to keep looking for the phone, but I was afraid my knees were going to give out. I aimed toward the bed and fell hard onto the mussed-up sheets.

DAY TWO

"Good morning, sleepyhead. You must be hungry," Mrs. Porter said, walking into the room with a tray. It was the first time I'd seen her enter the room. The steeple clock had struck twelve a little while before. My head felt thick, and my sense of time was upside down.

"Is it day or night?" I asked.

"Do you think I'd be feeding you breakfast at night?" she asked with a little laugh. She pursed her lips with amusement.

"I slept till noon?" I asked, shocked. I'd never done that before.

The food smelled good, and my stomach growled. I sat on the edge of the bed and refused to look at her. And there was no way I was going to eat in front of her.

"Your tummy was so upset on the car ride," she said. "I wanted to make one of your favorites, but I think it's better to stay mild for now. Toast, chicken soup, tea. You love my soup, my special touches. Just a squeeze of lime, a snip of cilantro, but today

I didn't use as much as usual. I'm afraid citrus might be too acidic for the moment."

I stared at my knees. I heard her place the tray on the desk, felt the bed press down as she sat beside me.

"For both our sakes, I'm going to talk to you honestly," she said. "As much as it pains me to go backward. To call you by that 'other' name. Emily." She spit my name out as if it tasted bad.

I refused to acknowledge she was there. My stomach rumbled, and I hoped she didn't hear. I didn't want to give her the satisfaction of knowing how much I wanted to eat that soup.

"I miss my daughter," she said. "I know you miss her, too. Those letters you wrote after she . . ." Mrs. Porter paused, seeming to search for the right word. "Was gone. They meant the world to us. To me. She thought of you as a second sister. I thought of you as a third daughter."

I forced myself to say something, to try to appeal to her rational side, if she had one. "It's true, you were my other family," I said. "But I have a mother, Mrs. Porter. And a father, and my own sisters and brothers."

"You said it yourself—we were your other family. And you needed it, considering your mother."

I bristled. "She's better now."

Mrs. Porter sighed. "I know you want to believe that. But she doesn't deserve you, after all the harm she's done. Her drinking. She's an alcoholic! And I need you more than she does. Your parents have six other children. I am not saying you are not special. Anything but. Every child is unique. I'm sure your mother felt about you just as strongly as she did about her first baby."

"She does," I said, choking up.

"But she will go on, I promise you. You live with us now," Mrs. Porter said.

"No, I don't! I can't!"

"Emily—and this is the last time you will hear that name— you will get used to it. You have to. So will they."

"NO! You know that's not true."

A distant look entered her eyes. "When she was born," she said, "I used to check to make sure she was breathing. Every night, standing over her crib. She was such a healthy baby, but that didn't matter. I loved her so much, I had no idea such love was possible. Babies are so tiny, and you think they're fragile. But then . . . they grow, and they keep breathing, and after a while you forget to worry."

I listened to Mrs. Porter's voice. It was thin, as thready as spiderwebs, and she stood up from the bed and began to pace slowly around the room, as if she was sleepwalking.

"When she got sick, I refused to believe it could be bad. It just wasn't possible. She was my child, my beloved girl, and she was strong, and she was good. Every checkup, her entire life, showed how healthy she was. Her illness . . . it came on so fast."

"I remember," I said, tearing up to think of those weeks when Lizzie went from shining bright as a star to dimming away, fading out of the sky.

"Time slowed down," Mrs. Porter said.

"It did," I said. "When things got really bad with her, when we knew she wasn't going to get better, I heard every single second of the day tick by in my head. I wanted to hold on to each one, make it last longer so she would stay." But of course she didn't. Losing Lizzie was an explosion. It had ripped through me, left a hole where my heart used to be. The part of me that had a best friend was gone, destroyed.

"When the doctor told me she had days—not years, not her whole life—I wanted to die before she did. It was the simplest wish I'd ever had," Mrs. Porter said.

I looked up at her. "But you have another daughter. She needs you," I said.

"I love Chloe; there is no doubt about that. And she is so dear—you saw how she colored her hair and how she curls that one section, just like her big sister. To help me, to try to keep Lizzie alive in our lives."

"Lizzie *is* in your life," I said. "Talk to her, the way I do. She'll never leave."

"That's a nice thought, but you don't understand. She was your friend, not your daughter. For so long, since those last days in the hospital, I've thought there is no way I could be on this earth without her."

"I'm sorry," I whispered.

"I thought I would have to die. I wanted to."

"You don't have to," I said.

"And then I thought—I have to bring her back," she said.

"I wish more than anything that was possible," I said.

"But it *is* possible. With you."

I shook my head. "You already found out, Chloe can't be Lizzie. And neither can I," I said, my voice shaking. "No one can.

There's only one Lizzie! You're not being fair to her to think you can just replace her!"

"You were so close, the two of you," Mrs. Porter said. "Hearing your voice right now brings hers back to me. You know, if I close my eyes, your voices merge together, and after a while I hear only hers."

"But it's me talking!"

"'Me,'" she said. "What a funny word. Who is 'me,' who are 'you,' after all? I suppose it depends on who is asking the question. To me, you are Lizzie. Maybe we started too soon, calling you by that name as soon as we got on the road. I honestly thought it would make things easier."

"Easier?" I shouted.

"Please don't raise your voice to me," Mrs. Porter said, rage in her eyes, a look I'd never seen on her before. "I've cooked a nice meal for you. I've taken care of you—stitched that cut in your head, put a bandage on your ankle. And I will continue. I will treat you like my own child because you *are* my own child now. I need you. Haven't I explained that?"

She was crazy, that was the only explanation. She had lost her mind.

"Do you understand?" she asked, insistent.

"No," I said. "I don't." I stared into her face, trying to see the Mrs. Porter I had known. I searched for the gentle mom of my best friend, and I swear I saw a glimmer of her, of the sane and kind person I'd known and trusted for so long. The anger had left her eyes, replaced by sorrow.

"I don't believe you want to do this to me," I said. "You know me. My mom is your friend. You wouldn't want to put her through this. Or my dad, either. Or Tommy, Mick, Anne . . ."

"I don't want to hear their names," she said.

". . . Iggy," I continued.

"You have one sibling now. That's Chloe."

". . . Patrick, Bea . . ." I caught my breath. "I'm closer to Bea than anyone, even Lizzie."

"Stop it."

"They're my family. They're the people I love."

Her eyes narrowed. I felt maybe I was getting through to her. I reached out and grabbed her hand. "You don't want to keep me in this cell; it's like a jail. If you care about me at all, you would know what a horrible thing that is."

"Oh, we're not going to keep you locked up," she said, letting out a small laugh. A genuine smile touched her lips. She squeezed my hand.

"Good," I said. "Thank you! When can I leave?"

"Well, you're not leaving."

"But . . ." I said, confused. "You said you're not going to keep me locked up."

"Of course we're not. This is your bedroom. We took the precaution of putting a solid lock on the door and bricking up the window. That's for your own good. But once you're calmer, when you're ready, you can join us. The rest of the house is yours. Everything is yours. You can run outside, come to the store with me, we'll get you into school, you can write poems for the literary magazine. You will love this part of Maine. It's small-town

America, so quaint, and I can't wait for you to discover why we chose to move here. Lizzie would be over the moon. And so will you. You'll love exploring it."

"When?" I asked. This confirmed it: She was totally crazy to think I'd stick around. The second I got out of this house I'd run for help so fast.

"When I'm sure you understand the *situation.*"

"What situation?" I asked.

She was still holding my hand. She stroked the back of it with her thumb, stared into my eyes with something like compassion. "Your mother drinks," she said. "Everyone knows."

I felt shocked, as if she'd slapped me. "She doesn't. She stopped."

"She'll start again," Mrs. Porter said. "This will make her."

"The fact you took me?"

"She will think you ran away. Kids do, all the time. Especially kids from alcoholic homes. Remember when you ran away last time? Your mother brought it on herself."

"That was different," I said, panicking at the memory. "She's sober now. Nearly fourteen months now!"

"Some of us never drank to begin with. I'll never understand," she said, "how the good mothers lose their children and the bad mothers get to keep theirs."

I was trembling with fury. I wanted to attack her for implying my mother wasn't good. I felt like telling her things Lizzie had said about her, times Lizzie had gotten mad and spilled family secrets. *She* wasn't the perfect mother. But I held the words inside.

"I'd be a better mother to you," Mrs. Porter said.

"No one could be better than mine," I said.

"Is that how you felt in seventh grade? Your parents didn't know where you were for twenty-four hours."

"I don't want to talk about that," I said, looking away. My parents had been so worried, they had called the police. My uncle Derry was on the force then, and he had done his best to keep it quiet once they found me. Lizzie had broken down and come clean, and they had found me in Mame's attic—Mame had left her home to move into assisted living. Her house was for sale—empty but safe, the perfect place to hide out.

"I know how hurt and worried you were about your mother, even before you ran away," Mrs. Porter was saying. "You'd come to our house, all those nights you stayed over. I knew you were suffering, that you were upset about her drinking—oh, when I think back, I would have done anything to help you."

"You did help me," I whispered. "You were . . . my other family. You were there for me."

"So let us be your family now," she said.

"We can go back to the way it was," I said, thinking quickly. "I can be Lizzie's friend—your friend. I know we fell out of touch, but I'll fix that. I'll visit, all the time. I can spend time here during vacations, and on weekends . . ."

"That's not enough," she said. "Because Lizzie was here every day."

"But I'm not Lizzie."

"You can be—you already are, to me. And, oh, I know I can be a good mother to you. Lizzie told me how despairing you were, how your mother hid bottles in her car, under her bed, in the toilet tank. She told me how much pain you were in, your mother slurring her words, embarrassing you in front of your friends."

"She doesn't do that anymore."

Mrs. Porter's eyes looked so sad. "Do you hear yourself? You were mortified. Alcoholism runs in families, you know. You've probably inherited the addiction gene. I can guide you."

"I'll never drink," I said.

"That's right. Because I'll be a good example. You'll see how you can have fun, get through life without alcohol."

"But I can't stay. You have to let me go."

"Please don't make this worse. You say you love them. Your 'family,'" she said, putting the word in air quotes, as if they weren't that at all.

"Of course I do," I said. "More than anything."

"Then you'll realize that the only way to protect them is to accept this as your home. To be my other daughter. To be Lizzie."

"How will that protect them?" I asked.

"Because if you don't do this, if you try to run away, I will hurt your father and every one of your brothers and sisters. And I will kill your mother."

"No!" I said, sliced with horror. I jumped up, and pain shot through my ankle. "Mrs. Porter!"

"I don't want to hear you call me that again," she said.

"Take it back," I begged. "Say you didn't mean it! Please!"

"But I do," she said. "I hope you never find out how deeply I do mean it. Do you want to test me?"

I couldn't speak. How could this be Lizzie's mom, the woman I'd felt so close to for so long? I shook, unable to believe this was happening.

"You would never do this, Mrs. Porter," I said. "I know you—this isn't you!"

"I don't want to do it," she said, her voice cracking. "But you don't know what it's been like—her seat at the table empty. Her bed unslept in. You can't imagine how much I want to hold her, get her back . . . There is nothing worse, Emily!"

There—she'd used my real name. We were back in reality, and my whole body shaking, I gave her a hug. I rested my head on her shoulder, remembering the old kindness and warmth between us.

"That's right, I'm Emily," I said.

She pushed me away, shook her head violently.

"I need you to be Lizzie. I've thought this through. People will think it was an accident. That you disappeared, and your mother started drinking again and fell. Hit her head. It's so easy to do when you're unsteady—you should know, it happened to you, on the hillside. And who would blame your mother for going back to the bottle? Her youngest daughter runs away."

"I would never do that again."

"She doesn't know that. Not for sure, not after last time. She has no clue where you are." She paused. "But it doesn't really matter. Whether you left on your own or some other way, you're gone. At first, that will be painful. And it will be worse if you force me to hurt her. *Murder* her."

"Don't say that!"

"I'll do it without thinking twice." She sounded resolute, and even though I couldn't believe it, I knew she meant it.

I closed my eyes and saw my mother's face. The look in her blue eyes was pure anguish—an imprint of the last time I'd seen her. Why had I fought with her? Why had the last words I'd said to her been *see you never*?

"*Do* you understand the situation now?" Mrs. Porter asked. "How serious I am?"

"Yes," I whispered.

"Then let me see you eat the soup I made you. Made you with love. A sip at least." She dipped the spoon into the soup, lifted it to my mouth. "Eat the soup so I won't hurt your mother," she said.

I opened my mouth and tried not to gag while she fed me like a baby.

"Another," she said.

"I can do it myself," I said, taking the spoon from her. I ate until half the soup was gone.

"There," she said. "Now, one more thing. The most important."

"What?"

"Are you sure you understand that I mean what I say? That if I have to, I will go to Black Hall and do what needs to be done?"

"Yes," I said, terrified.

"Then say it. Let me hear you. Call me by the right name. If only you knew how much I need this."

I knew what she meant, but I couldn't open my mouth.

"What is my name?" she asked, a hard edge in her voice.

All I could think of was putting a shield between her and my family, the people I adored. It was one word. A single syllable. I thought of it as saving them from being hurt, my mother from being killed.

"Mom," I whispered, feeling sick.

Mrs. Porter hugged me.

CHAPTER FOUR

DAY THREE

That night, my mind raced and my eyes felt zapped by a thousand tiny electric wires. Lying awake, staring at the ceiling, I realized that they'd been drugging my food before. That had to explain the deep sleeps.

Now, because I had called Mrs. Porter "Mom," they must have felt they didn't have to control me that way anymore.

I used to lose sleep over three things: homework, the play I was writing, and boys. Namely, Dan Jenkins. I would obsess over him, and when I got to school, I'd tell Lizzie everything I'd been thinking about. But right now I was too scared to even think of Dan, and Lizzie wasn't here to tell anyway.

Now my eyelids were glued open because of what Mrs. Porter said she would do to my mother. I veered back and forth between refusing to believe she really would and remembering the sharp tone in her voice when she'd said the word *murder*. Besides, I had never imagined she could ever do *this*: take me, lock me in a dungeon. So maybe she was capable of other terrible things.

Suddenly I couldn't breathe. The cinder block room felt so claustrophobic I thought I would pass out. I nearly wished for the drugs so I could sleep through this horror, but I didn't really. I needed my head to be clear so I could escape, or at least hear the voices when people came to rescue me.

I wanted my cell phone so badly, I felt crazed. I imagined texting my brothers and sisters. And Jordan and Alicia: I thought of how I had turned my back on them that last day at school. What would have happened if I'd gone with them? My fingers clenched hard, and my whole body ached with the desire for my phone.

I was having a panic attack. I clawed the blankets off me, jumped out of bed. I turned on the light and walked around and around the room, my hands on the walls, feeling for any opening, a way out. Was this how a tiger, newly captured from the wild and thrown into a zoo, felt? I wanted to roar.

I wanted to break through the concrete, smash into the fresh air, and run until my muscles burned and my feet were tattered. Once I got out of this house, there were so many possibilities: I could run to a neighbor's, to the police, or all the way home. I could warn my mother, and be with my family, and we would all save each other.

Mrs. Porter had planted another worry in my mind. She had said my mother would start drinking again.

This is the weird thing: When you have a mother who drinks, you love her more than ever, maybe more than other kids love theirs. Partly because sometimes you also hate her, and the emotions swing back and forth, and you feel so guilty. The Magic Mountain of Mom, Tommy called it.

"It's an amusement park," he said to me one day about two years ago when I was really upset about something she'd done. "And not always fun. You know how you sometimes get too scared on Batman?"

I nodded. Roller coasters in general weren't my favorite, and Batman was one of the wildest.

"But then there's the water park, and you love that. Or Balloon Race—nice and gentle—going on it at night, swinging up high, looking down at all the beautiful lights. I remember how you never wanted to get off that one."

"But she's our mom—not a bunch of dumb rides," I'd said. "Plus you're out of the house now. Did grad school erase your memory of what it's like?"

"Of course it didn't," he said, his arm around me. "Listen, Em. *The Magic Mountain* is also a book. An amazing novel by Thomas Mann. I read it last spring. It's about Europe before World War I. A young guy, Hans, who goes to a sanitarium in the Alps. But it hit me because it reminded me of home, of us. Of her. Hans is sick, he's in this beautiful place, and he just can't get better. There's a blizzard dream, and witches and wizards, this cousin who's nearly as close to Hans as a brother. Closeness and secrets . . ."

"Like all of us," I said.

"Maybe that's one of the worst parts about Mom's drinking," Tommy said. "The way it forces us to keep secrets."

"But you're away," I said again. "You can escape it."

"You can't escape love, Em. And I love her, the way you do. The thing is, as bad as it feels when she's drunk . . ."

"She falls, she sounds weird, she smells," I said.

"Yeah," he said. "All that. And it's embarrassing, because as much as we try to keep the secret and protect her, everyone knows. But there are the other times."

It was true. Our mom gave the best hugs in the world. She was thin but not too thin, and her hugs were warm and soft. Even with seven kids, she made each of us feel she always had time for whatever we needed. She saw what was special in each of us. When she was sober, her blue eyes sparkled. When she wasn't, they had a dull, faraway look, as if her truest wishes in life had passed her by.

On days when she wasn't drinking, she surprised us constantly. She was the champion of spur of the moment. So many Saturday mornings she'd tell us to get in the car, and we'd go off on adventures. Once she took us to Vermont, to search for wildflowers on Sugarbush. She'd brought us each a tiny watercolor kit, and we'd sat in the shade painting lady's slippers, bloodroot, and trillium. Another time we drove to New London, hopped on the high-speed ferry, and spent the day biking around Block Island. We had an ongoing contest, to try all the clam chowder in New England, till we found the best—at the Black Pearl, in Newport, Rhode Island.

My dad loved her. After us kids were in bed, I'd hear my parents put on music, and if I snuck to the top of the stairs and looked down, I'd see them slow-dancing. He knew she loved anything with shamrocks on it, and he'd bring home shamrock earrings, shamrock bracelets, a green hoodie with a white shamrock on the front, a special edition St. Patrick's Day Boston Celtics jersey. I hated when he watched her too closely, as if gauging whether she had taken a drink or not. Sometimes he'd hug her and I'd hear him sniff the air. It made me cringe, partly because I did those things myself.

But then she went to rehab and got sober—I mean, it's supposed to be One Day at a Time, but this time she meant it for good, and ever since she came home, she went to a meeting every day. When she'd made it one year without a drink, she had stood in front of her home group to pick up her coin—we all went to hear her qualify. That means standing up in front of the room and telling your story: *what happened, what it was like, and what it's like now.*

"The afternoon of my daughter's dress rehearsal, I had a vodka and soda," Mom had said. "She had both written and performed in the play, and I was so proud of her. I was going to pick her up, and we were going to celebrate with pizza. I thought, maybe another drink, start the celebration early. I told myself it was no big deal—two drinks never really affected me. Then I had another, but I told myself it was fine, because I was sipping it slowly.

"The next thing I knew, I was passed out in bed. I had missed my daughter's play and left her standing outside school waiting—but that was the gift. Because I know I'd planned to drive. When I woke up, I had the car keys in my hand. I'd been on my way out the door. I could have killed Emily. Or someone else's kids. It had been bad before, but that was the moment for me. It brought me to my knees, and I knew I was done. By the grace of God, I haven't picked up a drink since."

Everyone cheered, our family louder than anyone. I didn't think I could love her more than before, but I did. I do. So she can't drink; she just can't. Mrs. Porter can't be right, that thinking I ran away could drive my mother back to the bottle.

I couldn't let that happen.

But how could I stop it?

The only thing I could prevent was Mrs. Porter going to Black Hall to kill her. And there was only one way to do that: go along with whatever Mrs. Porter wanted.

DAY FOUR

Sleep had been my refuge those first days, but now it was gone.

I spent every free moment—which is to say EVERY moment—looking for Mame's box. Day spilled into night, or maybe it was the other way around. Time lost meaning. It was either moving very slow or very fast. I had gone through a looking glass that even Alice couldn't have dreamt up.

Whenever Mrs. Porter wasn't serving me food or taking away the plates, I scoured the room, looking for Mame's cell phone. I removed each book from the shelves, repeatedly looked through the bureau drawers. I took Lizzie's laptop down from the closet shelf, but it didn't boot up; the screen didn't even flicker. I couldn't find the power cord to charge it. I went through the pockets of her clothes. Scents and memories of her came back to me. They would start to reassure me, and then I would panic again.

I tried to pretend this was a play. I had written it and was acting the lead role. My writing had never strayed into the dystopian before, but this play was about the last girl in the world. Or maybe she just thought she was. The apocalypse had come, and she'd barricaded herself in this bunker. Outside, the sun was blocked by the earth's dust, exploded into a brown cloud when a meteorite the size of Florida crashed into and pulverized the Berkshires. Maybe the girl's family was still alive, and as soon as the particles cleared the air, she had to find a way back to them.

That version of the play gave me a feeling of bravery: I was here by choice. I was just waiting for the air to clear, for the sun to come back, and then I would undertake the journey.

Another version of the play took away all power.

The girl had been kidnapped. She was trapped, being held captive, in an underground cinder block room. The kidnappers were her best friend's family. The clock struck every single hour, but she lost track of time. She spent all day every day scouring the chamber for a box of old photos that probably didn't matter anyway. Her ankle and head hurt, from when she tried to escape, but the worst part was her bleeding fingers: from trying to claw through the concrete, chip away at the mortar.

My fingers really *were* bleeding. My fingernails were bent backward, and I had left shreds of them in the lines of cement between the blocks. It was slightly softer there, and I'd thought if I could dislodge even one section, I could scrunch my shoulders and suck in my gut and crawl through. But I hadn't managed to create even a crack. Instead, I'd just mangled my fingers, which hurt all the time, more than I thought was possible.

When the steeple clock chimed five, I was on my hands and knees, once again pulling out the books on the bottom shelves to see if Mame's photos were hiding there. That's when it hit me: This was just a re-creation of Lizzie's bedroom, not the real thing, and of course the Porters would have found the box, discovered the cell phone, taken it out of my reach.

Mame's phone was gone. The hope was gone.

This wasn't a play: It was my life.

DAY TEN

Once I gave up hope, I stopped caring what day it was. The hours and days just blurred together anyway, and all that mattered was that I was still here. No one had come to rescue me.

Breakfast, lunch, dinner: day five. Breakfast, lunch, dinner: day six, day seven, day eight. Breakfast, lunch, dinner: Who cared? The meals ticked by.

Mrs. Porter was the only person I saw. I had no idea where Chloe and Mr. Porter might be. It seemed that she and I were the only ones in the house. She sat with me while I ate. I was too hungry to refuse. I figured that even if she sedated me again it wouldn't matter. I was still in that room. But there were no more drugs. And even though I thanked her for the food, said *thank you, Mom*, she didn't let me roam free through the house or go outside.

I guess she wasn't yet convinced that I understood the situation.

But I did.

I still couldn't reconcile this Mrs. Porter with the one I used to know, but I'd started to realize she had changed. She had lost Lizzie, and her mad grief had turned her into a monster. Dr. Jekyll and Mrs. Hyde.

I kept wondering: What if she doesn't wait for me to bolt? What if she hurts my family anyway? If there was no one to go home to, wouldn't that stop me from wanting to return to Connecticut? It would destroy me so much I might forget who I was. I might want to wipe out my own memory.

But all I wanted to do was remember. I thought about my family all the time. Their names were my prayers. We were Catholic. We only went to church about one Sunday a month. When we did, we sat in the same pew each time, four rows back from the altar on the left. Now that the older kids were away at college, they only came on Christmas and Easter.

"Do you think they go to Mass on campus?" my dad asked my mom once.

"That's up to them. They do their own thing," my mom said.

We weren't exactly strict when it came to religion. I never told anyone that I wished I could have a vision, like the kids at Fatima, seeing the Virgin Mary and having her speak to them directly. Everyone would have laughed at me.

But our names? Catholic to the max. My mom had gone to St. Joseph's College; my dad had gone to Holy Cross. They'd been taught by Sisters of Mercy and Jesuits, and once, when I asked why all us kids had saints' names, my father had said, "Because life throws so much at us. We want you to remember to be kind, patient, and tolerant. To have empathy for other people, care about them. And to have that extra help, your own saint backing you."

"But we don't always go to church," I'd pointed out.

"Caring about people doesn't just take place there. It's how you act out in the world, when no one is looking, where it really counts."

"I think I get it, Dad."

Our family volunteered at a soup kitchen in New London once a month. Tommy wanted to become a journalist and cover stories about immigration and refugees, families who had to leave their own countries because of war, violence, and poverty. Anne knit scarves and hats for people at the homeless shelter near her college in Hartford.

Twice, before I was born, my parents had taken in foster children. I never knew the kids, both girls, but my older siblings had told me about them. Arlene had a mother addicted to heroin; Janice had been removed from her home because of abuse.

I tried to imagine what it had been like for those girls. Were they afraid? Did they cry and want to return to their real homes, or did they feel safe, relieved to be in our house? They stayed only a short time, until a more permanent placement could be found. My parents eventually stopped having foster kids. No one said why, but I thought I knew. My mom's drinking. When it got worse, it was harder for her to take care of her own kids, never mind someone else's. Had Arlene realized my mother's addiction was as powerful as her own mother's?

I didn't exactly know how I could help others, but I thought someday, when I was older, I might become a therapist kids could

talk to about having addictions in their family. That was something I understood.

So, even though we skipped Mass a lot, we did our best. We
believed in the sacraments and had all made our first commu-
nions and confirmations.

That was one major plus, being a Catholic kid—when you
made your confirmation, basically bonding your faith to the Holy
Spirit in front of the bishop, the priest, your family, and the whole
congregation—you got to choose an extra name. It had to belong
to a saint, but it didn't have to be one of the regular old ones like
Joseph or Mary. You were allowed to get creative, and believe me,
we did. My siblings and I vied for best, most unusual confirmation names, choosing saints who'd done awesome things.

I ran my family's names through my mind, just as I had in the
highway woods, when I was waiting for my chance to escape
the Porters. I said each full name—nickname, first, middle, confirmation, and last—over and over. Doing it was sort of like a prayer.
I was invoking what I loved and believed in most: my family.

My father, Thomas Francis Lonergan, had chosen Aquinas
for his confirmation name. Thomas Aquinas had been a philoso-
pher, and that was perfect because my father was so smart, a
scholar, and down-to-earth as well.

My mom was Mary Elizabeth, and she'd chosen Rose after
St. Rose of Lima, a mystic who cared for the poor.

Tommy, my oldest brother, was named for my dad, whom he
adored, so when the time came, he chose Aquinas, too. Tommy
was half saint, half devil, always so good to us, but known to do
things like get the entire track team to climb onto the catwalk

beneath the Langdon Bridge and cross a hundred feet above the Connecticut River at night.

Mick's confirmation name was Aloysius, after Aloysius Gonzaga, an amazing nobleman who gave up his riches and became a Jesuit to work with people dying of the plague in Rome. He was lead singer in the Rabid Squirrels, a band at college—we teased him that he was taking his nickname too seriously, trying to be the next Mick Jagger.

My oldest sister, Anne, chose Agatha Anastasia; St. Agatha was a martyr and St. Anastasia was a healer and exorcist. Anne didn't have a nickname—she was just Anne. If you knew her, you'd get it. Anne was perfect. Even her choice of saints—she would die for us, heal us, and, if she could, drive the demon of drinking from our mother.

Iggy was, well, Iggy—just the sweetest, funniest, best brother. Always falling in love, getting his heart broken, then being comforted by the next girl with whom he'd fall in love and, in time, would break his heart. His confirmation name was Loyola, after the saint Ignatius Loyola, who patterned his life after the story of Camelot and later founded the Jesuits. Totally Iggy.

Patrick Benedict Leo Lonergan—Patrick. He refused to answer to "Pat" because Tommy and Mick always turned it into "Patty." We called him Pat anyway. I'm closer to him than my other brothers, probably because he's just a year and a half older than I am. We have a pact that, when we're old enough, we're going to Ireland together to climb Croagh Patrick—St. Patrick's mountain.

Beatrice Felicity Michael Lonergan—Bea. I love that she chose a boy's name, "Michael," for her confirmation, because she totally adores—practically worships—our brother Mick, but also because

St. Michael is an archangel—not a saint at all, but an actual angel. That is my Bea. She's less than a year older than I am—and Patrick ten months older than her. That makes us Irish triplets. Look it up, it's a real thing.

Then me. Emily Magdalene Bartholomea Lonergan. I took Bartholomea because she was a teacher, and I want to be one, too. My family calls me Emily, Em, Emms, Emelina, but mostly just Emily. I was named for this awesome saint, St. Emily de Vialar, founder of a French order of nuns, Sisters of St. Joseph of the Apparition. I mean, *apparition*! I'd sometimes talk to Mame about her—because even though Mame wasn't Catholic, she knew a lot about France.

"Your namesake's convent is in the charming town of Gaillac, near Toulouse," Mame said to me once. "It's in an absolutely marvelous wine region, with this incredibly romantic hotel built straight into a cliff, like a luxurious limestone cave. When I was there, I ate snails and wild boar and drank Gamay and walked through misty vineyards under a full moon."

"What kind of apparition did St. Emily see?" Lizzie asked.

"Probably the Virgin Mary," I said. "That's the usual."

"Huh," Lizzie said. She was amazed and impressed. Congregationalists didn't much go in for miracles and mysticism. It was a testament to our bond and best-friendship that Lizzie did her history project on the Reign of Terror because St. Emily was born in 1797, right in the midst of it.

I told myself that Lizzie wouldn't recognize her own mother's behavior right now. She would hate what she was doing to me.

But would she? Would Lizzie take my side or be on her mother's?

Family was family, and blood was thicker than water.

Wasn't it?

But if that was true, why hadn't my family found me yet? Why hadn't they come for me? They were all named for saints who'd sacrificed everything without fear. I had to believe they were doing everything they could. I ran through all the possible clues they could find. The day the Porters took me, Patrick and Bea had driven right past the minivan—how could they not have spotted me? I had left my backpack by the stone wall; hadn't someone seen me talking to Chloe? When I'd tripped crossing the street, the driver of that blue car had blasted his horn. Wouldn't he remember?

The toll collector: If news of my disappearance had made it to Maine, wouldn't he realize that I was the babbling girl in the back seat of that van emblazoned with a Patriots sticker?

And what about the navy-blue minivan itself, the family's original one? Where had the Porters hidden it when they'd driven into Black Hall? Going by the license plates, they must have rented the white decoy somewhere in Massachusetts. Surely that was a clue.

But who would notice a family renting a minivan?

In my worst moments, I'd despair and wonder whether my family was even still looking for me. Asking myself that question proved how psycho I was getting, isolated in this room—of course they were, they would never stop. Would they?

I thought I really would go crazy, that I would never hear another human voice, other than Mrs. Porter's, but that changed.

That day, when she brought me my dinner, Mr. Porter entered the room behind her. He was holding a TV.

Behind them stood Chloe holding her cell phone.

"We're going to plug this in and let you watch whatever you want," Mr. Porter said.

It seemed weird and made me feel suspicious. I hadn't mentioned TV or really even missed it. I'd had too much else on my mind. Besides, all I craved was my cell phone. Before the Porters took me, I'd had it with me always, and I sometimes felt the ghost of it in my left hand, my thumbs itching to text.

"You can watch the news," Mrs. Porter said. "I need you to see what's being said about you."

"Your family has been interviewed," Mr. Porter said. "They show the clips constantly. Anne passing out flyers at college, Bea sitting on your bed with your dog, Seamus. Your brothers searching the neighborhood. Your mother and father at the Westbrook State Police barracks, standing at a microphone in front of the cameras, begging for you to come home."

The idea of seeing everyone, even on a screen, made my heart leap. I wanted to grab the TV out of his hands and find the news channel.

"Just one thing," Mrs. Porter said.

"What?" I asked.

"Chloe," she said, beckoning.

Chloe stepped forward, handed me her smartphone. It was almost too much to believe—my thumbs itched to dial my home number. But the screen was open to Gmail. My screen name was already typed into the login.

"Put in your password," Mr. Porter said.

I nearly did—it would mean I could check my mail, send a message home. But the fact he wanted me to do that made me freeze with suspicion. I scanned their eyes for a sign that this wasn't a trick.

"You're going to write a message," Mrs. Porter said. "You're going to tell them you've run away. Say you'll go back when you figure things out."

"When you do this, you'll be one step closer to being able to join us upstairs. To have more freedom," Mr. Porter said.

I'd always wanted to be a playwright, to act in plays. But at that minute I couldn't have acted to save my life. I threw the phone into the hall. It clattered against the wall. Chloe swore and stalked out, picked it up, and disappeared. Mr. Porter shrugged and followed, carrying the TV. Mrs. Porter stood beside me, looking sad and disappointed more than anything else. She touched my hair, as if with the deepest regret, and she shook her head.

As soon as she closed the door behind her, I grabbed the locked doorknob and shook it.

"Mrs. Porter!" I called. "Wait!"

I wanted to change my mind. I imagined what I'd given up— the chance to see my family on screen, all their faces, and hear their voices, feel their presence. I called and called for Mrs. Porter to come back, but she didn't answer. No one did.

I wondered if they'd give me another chance.

I wondered if Mrs. Porter was climbing into the blue minivan, driving south toward Connecticut, toward my house, toward my mother. The realization that through my stubbornness I might have put my mother in danger made my knees buckle, and I fell down to the ground crying.

CHAPTER FIVE

DAY SEVENTEEN

For one week, Mrs. Porter didn't speak to me. We sat in silence while I ate my food. Even though I was dying to get that TV, I clamped down and told myself that watching the news, even the possibility of seeing my family on the screen, wasn't worth it. There was no way I was ever writing that email.

Mrs. Porter didn't have to tell me she was furious at me for my refusal. I saw the darkness in her furrowed brow, her pursed lips. I flashed, as I so often did these days, on how she used to like me. She'd always greet me with open arms and her unusual smile—not full-on, like most people's, but three-cornered, as if her warmth contained a secret, as if half of her face was in on it and the other half resisting.

"You think she's so great," Lizzie said once. Her mother had taken us to Paradise Ice Cream, the little stand overlooking the Black Hall marshes and the mouth of the Connecticut River. Mrs. Porter stood by the window, drinking iced tea and chatting with Jordan Shear's mother, and Lizzie and I sat at one of the picnic tables, under a yellow-and-white-striped umbrella, eating our ice cream cones.

"She is," I said, raising my black raspberry, clinking Lizzie's toasted coconut cone in a sort of toast.

"She's a street angel/house devil," Lizzie said. "She shows one face to the world, another to our family."

"You're pure angel," Jeff Woodley said, overhearing her say that as he walked over to sit with us. He liked Lizzie; she was trying to decide how much she liked him back. He was tall, with ginger hair and a sparse beard, and he crooked his arm around her shoulders and nuzzled her neck. Then he licked her ice cream cone and she made him miss and dabbed his nose with it.

"Are you sure I'm so angelic?" she asked, laughing.

"Yep," he said. "Positive."

That June, Jeff asked her to the Full Moon Dance at the beach club. I'd been hoping Dan would ask me, but he showed up with Gillian Bowen instead. Jordan and Alicia, each single at that time, drove together. I went solo—well, actually I tagged along with Lizzie and Jeff. By then Lizzie had decided she liked him— in fact, more than that.

At one point, Jeff stood talking to Slater Jones and a bunch of other boys, and Lizzie and I took a spin on the dance floor. She wore a black dress with a tulle skirt twinkling with rhinestones; my dress, an Anne hand-me-down, was strapless taffeta, dark green-and-red tartan. While Lizzie wore a pair of black silk ballet flats, my favorite Doc Martens complemented my ensemble.

"How do you know if you're in love?" Lizzie asked me.

I shrugged. "When you think about him, you see stars."

"Well, that happens when I kiss him."

"Enough said."

"Do you feel that way about Dan? When you think about him?"

"No," I said—even though I did—watching him slow dance with Gillian, never mind the fact the song was fast.

"Way to lie," Lizzie said, twirling me. We'd practiced dancing from watching my brother Mick and his girlfriend, Fiona. And Mick had learned from my parents—a couple who seemed like one single creature when they danced: They moved so well together, in grace and unison.

That night Lizzie and Jeff had wandered down the beach. I watched them disappear into the shadows and wondered if that would ever be me and Dan, or me and someone else. The sad thing, and it really made me mad at myself, was that even seeing Dan with Gillian didn't make the stars go away. I had written that play. The kiss hadn't been real, but it had happened.

"Hey," Dan said, walking over to the refreshment table, where I'd wound up serving lemonade because why not.

"Hey."

"Pretty cool night, huh?" he asked. He was wearing surfer-boy formal—pink hibiscus-emblazoned board shorts with a white shirt and tux jacket.

"Yeah. I like the DJ."

"Why aren't you dancing? Where's Trevor?"

Did he mean Trevor Griffin, from Patrick's class? "No idea," I said. "Why?"

"Uh, because I thought you guys were dating. I've seen you in his car."

"No, he just gives me rides sometimes. He's my brother's friend."

"Hmm. My mistake. Too bad."

I handed him a paper cup of pink lemonade to cover my mad blush. He sipped it, looking into my eyes. At that moment I saw not just stars but a whole galaxy. *Too bad.* Was he saying that if he hadn't thought I was with Trevor, he would have asked me to the dance?

"You going to write any more plays?" Dan asked.

"I'm always writing one," I said.

"Bring back Ada and Timothy," he said, referring to the characters he and I had played onstage, in front of the whole school. The characters who had kissed. I turned even redder.

Then Gillian walked over in her slinky white slip dress, straight blond hair spilling over her tan shoulders. Dan reached out for another cup of lemonade, handed it to her, and slipped his arm around her waist. They walked away, and in a move designed to torture me, Dan glanced back over his shoulder with a small head shake of regret.

A while later, the song "Angel" by Jack Johnson began to play. That brought Lizzie and Jeff back from their walk down the beach, onto the dance floor. He had called her "Angel" ever since that day at Paradise Ice Cream. Dan and Gillian were dancing, too, along with half the school, but I felt that song was for Lizzie and Jeff alone.

And sitting on my bed in the cinder block room, I remembered again the phrase Lizzie had used to describe her mother: *street angel/house devil.*

"Everyone has moods," I'd said to Lizzie that day.

"You don't get it," Lizzie replied. "And I hope you never see her the other way."

Before now, I did, just once, see Mrs. Porter "the other way."

When Lizzie went into the hospital, I skipped school to go see her. Her mother had told mine that I'd better go soon. My mother not only gave me permission, she drove me to Williams Memorial in Boston.

"Take all the time you need, love," my mother said. "Don't worry, I'll be right here when you get out."

"Thanks, Mom," I said, kissing her, lingering in her embrace for an extra moment because I was nervous about seeing Lizzie.

When I stepped off the elevator onto Lizzie's floor, I smelled antiseptic. The linoleum gleamed like ice. Walls were lined with bright drawings, obviously by children. They had been enlarged and framed, and some of the stick figures were grinning and others had big round tears plopping down their cheeks. Speech bubbles said *Hope!* and *We've got this!* and *Cancer makes me mad.* The grass was green, the chimneys were red, nearly every picture had a garden full of flowers. A handsome doctor with a stethoscope around his neck passed by and smiled when he saw me looking at the art.

Lizzie was in the third room down. Jeff stood in the hallway. He saw me coming. His face was wet, and he shook his head. Tears streamed into his red beard. He wiped his face with the sleeve of his plaid shirt.

"Only one person at a time can see her," he said.

"Who's in there now?" I knew her mother was spending most days here as both mom and nurse. Chloe had missed school all week to be with her sister.

"No one," Jeff said. "She got tired. I wanted to let her rest."

"Is she okay?"

"No, Emily. She's not okay."

"But she will be," I said, stubborn and refusing to believe otherwise.

His tears just kept running. His mouth was slack, no words. He looked hopeless. I touched his hand, then stiffened my shoulders and walked past him. I was expecting to see Lizzie bald— people who had chemo lost their hair. My aunt Cathleen had. But when I walked through the door, there was Lizzie, with her long black hair flowing on the white pillow, that one strange curl— natural, she didn't do anything to make it happen—falling across her terrifyingly pale face.

I tiptoed to the chair. I didn't want to make a sound because Lizzie's eyes were closed, and I assumed she was asleep. I leaned close, over the bed rail, to watch her breathing. Her chest went up-down, up-down. Was her respiration really fast, or was that my imagination? I had figured she'd be in an ugly hospital gown, so it was reassuring to see her in one of her familiar nightgowns, this one dark blue silk. But there were bottles hanging on poles over the bed, tubes going into her arms.

"I'm awake," she said without opening her eyes.

"Oh," I said. "I couldn't tell."

"It's kind of creepy that you're watching me."

"I'm totally not watching you. I'm spying on that doctor out in the hall. Pretty cute."

"Yeah, and he went to Harvard."

"How do you know which one I'm talking about?"

"I know your taste," she said. "Both Jeff and I think he looks like Dan Jenkins. Tell me he doesn't."

"Well, he does," I said, even though he didn't really. I always loved talking about Dan. Just hearing his name then sent chills through my bones, and it relieved me to hear Lizzie joking. We always joked about boys.

"Is Jeff jealous?" I asked. "You and Dr. Handsome?"

"We're getting married," she said.

"You and the doctor?"

"Me and Jeff."

I laughed and pretended to jab her arm, brushing it lightly with my knuckles, and she flinched and cried out.

"What's wrong?" I asked, shocked.

"It hurts," she said. Tears were plopping down her face, just like Jeff's, just like the ones in that picture in the hall.

"I'm sorry. I barely touched you," I said.

"It's not your fault," she said. "They're everywhere."

"'They'?" I asked.

"The tumors," she said.

"Where? How many?" I asked, steeling myself, because I couldn't really bear to know.

"I wasn't kidding about me and Jeff," she said. "We're going to get married before . . ."

"Before what?"

"I die."

"Don't say that!"

"I don't want you to be shocked when it happens. You're my best friend, my other sister. I love you."

"I love you," I whispered.

"I want you to do something for me," Lizzie said. "Marry us."

I tried to laugh. "I'm not a minister."

"You can sign up online. There's a website, you sign up and get ordained right then and there. Do this for me, Em. And don't tell my mother."

"Okay," I said, completely confused, wondering if Lizzie even knew what she was talking about. We were fifteen. Jeff was a class ahead of us, sixteen. But in my church only men could become priests, a fact that seemed ridiculous, totally unfair, and completely ticked me off. So yes—I was on board with becoming a minister.

"I'm tired, Em," Lizzie said. "You'd better go now."

That scared me more than anything. Lizzie had never asked me to leave before. We always wanted to stay together longer, prolong our visits, delay making it home in time for dinner. We were always asking our mothers if the other one of us could eat over, sleep over, spend the weekend. What did it mean, how bad was her cancer, that she was kicking me out?

I stood in the doorway, just staring at her for a long time. If she knew I was still there, she didn't say anything. I told myself the tubes were full of strong medicine making her better. The fact her hair hadn't fallen out was a good sign; she was tough, and the tumors would disappear without chemo.

Outside the room, I looked for Jeff, but I didn't see him. I figured I'd wait a while in the hospital and return to Lizzie's room later, maybe in an hour, when she was feeling better.

A family clustered at the end of the hall. I could see sunlight pouring through big windows in the room behind them. It was probably the solarium. Visiting Aunt Cathleen, taking turns with everyone else in my family for the chance to go into her room, I'd gotten very used to the comfy chairs in the hospital sunroom. Bea and I were usually in there together, bored and texting our friends till it was time to leave.

So I aimed toward the solarium to wait for Lizzie. Later, I'd go back and sit by her bed and tease her about wanting to get married. Or, riffing on the fact she'd kicked me out before, I'd sing lyrics from a song my dad constantly butchered on the Fender Stratocaster us kids had chipped in to give him on his fiftieth birthday to fulfill his middle-aged rock-guitarist dream: *Should I stay or should I go now?* I'd make her laugh.

Halfway down the main corridor there was a small alcove, the door ajar. I heard the familiar voice with a hissing buzz in it and stopped short.

"... so talented, so smart," Mrs. Porter was saying. "Everything your sister does turns to gold. While you . . . well, I'm not seeing any gold. I'm seeing laziness, a bad attitude, a selfish girl. That's what you are, selfish. Your sister is lying in that bed, she is dying, yes, dying, and she is my shining one. Will you be that for me? I don't think so. I don't think so."

I melted against the wall.

Chloe walked out of the alcove. Back then, she still looked like herself. Her straight hair was chestnut brown. She met my gaze. We stared at each other long enough for me to register her shame and grief. Her eyes brimmed. I reached out my hand, and she did, too, and we brushed fingers, like members of opposite teams after a game. She drifted away.

I wanted to follow her, to not have to face her mother, but it was too late.

Mrs. Porter emerged from the alcove with an armful of sheets and towels. Her forehead was a knot, her mouth was pinched with rage. I turned into a statue, hoping she would just walk by. Instead she stopped, her face relaxing into warmth and the affection I'd always felt pouring my way.

"Oh, Emily," she said. "You've come to see Lizzie."

"I—I did," I said, slowing, stammering, wondering if she knew I'd heard her. "She told me she needs to rest."

"Yes, she's right. And you're a peach for understanding. She needs that right now."

"Can I do anything? I want to help her. I want to be here for her."

"Just be you," Mrs. Porter said. She hiked the linens under one arm, hugged me close with the other. "Be her other sister and be strong for Chloe. She's having such a hard time. She loves Lizzie so. It's so awful for her. I know she'd trade places if she could."

"So would I," I said.

"I believe that," Mrs. Porter said, hugging me even harder. "What would we do without you? Now, come with me. We'll let Lizzie sleep for a little while, and you, Chloe, and I will go down to the nurses' lounge. I'll sneak you in. We can have some hot chocolate; that's just what we need."

"Okay," I said.

I was in shock that day. I had heard the words *cancer, tumors, soft tissue, rhabdomyosarcoma, metastases,* and *stage four* about Lizzie. But that afternoon was the first time I had heard the word *dying.* I wanted to run, scream, and tear my hair out. But I was a zombie. All I could do was stagger alongside Mrs. Porter and try to block out the vicious way she'd talked to Chloe.

In that moment, Lizzie's voice had filled my mind. *Street angel/house devil.*

Now, sitting in the jail-cell replica of Lizzie's room, with Mrs. Porter silently watching me eat, I glanced up from my chicken sandwich and met her eyes. She smiled, just as she used to, but hadn't since I'd thrown Chloe's phone. Just as if I were her third daughter, happy to see me enjoying the food she'd so lovingly made.

When I was finished, she examined the stitches on the side of my head. Then she undid the support boot and gently prodded my bruised ankle. She was making sure I was healing. Then she took my plate and empty glass. She didn't say good-bye or ask if I wanted anything else or whether I was ready to send that email.

But she turned, gazed at me with pure love, and shut the door behind her.

I sat very still on the bed for a long time after she had gone.

DAY TWENTY-TWO

Five more days of silence. That seemed to be the pattern: If I did something out of line, they'd stop speaking to me. The food came, the empty tray went, and as the days went by, Mrs. Porter would barely look me in the eye. I started to wonder if I was real. Was this a dream? One night she brought me an orange. I sat on the side of the bed, holding it in my hands. I lifted it to my face, smelled the citrus tang.

If the orange was real, then wasn't I? But the scent faded, and I put the orange back on the tray, and the feeling of unreality came back.

Also on the tray was a small white container holding green contact lenses along with a note: *No more blue eyes. Practice putting these in and taking them out, please.*

I couldn't believe it: another way for me to not look like myself. Touching my own eyeball made me blink like crazy and feel like throwing up. The contact lens was squishy. The fact that tears were spilling out didn't help. I was shaking and stopped after two tries.

I took a shower. The water felt warm on my skin. It trickled down my back; I stared at my wet arms, how they glistened. When I washed my hair, some shampoo got in my *blue* eyes, and the sharp sting was a reminder that I was still human, I was still alive, not floating between worlds. My fingernails were growing back, my scabbed, raw fingertips starting to heal. That wasn't all good, because it meant I hadn't tried to claw my way out lately, that I was somehow getting used to the horror of being held prisoner in a basement, and I turned up the water as high as it would go and screamed.

Then, one morning, Chloe brought my breakfast. She entered the room with the tray, but instead of locking the door behind her, she left it a few inches ajar. I noticed the food was different this morning. Instead of the super-healthy farm-fresh eggs, whole grain toast, and bowl of cut fruit that Mrs. Porter had served every day since I'd gotten here, this tray contained a bowl of Frosted Flakes and a glass of orange-mango juice.

"I'm supposed to eat this?" I asked.

"Yeah."

"You probably poisoned it."

"I didn't," Chloe said. "And I thought you'd like something sweet instead of the usual organic whatever. Besides. It was Lizzie's favorite cereal. When Mom wasn't looking."

"I thought I was Lizzie."

Chloe gave me the fishiest look ever. She raised her eyebrow. "You're Emily," she said.

I felt this huge swoon of emotion—a combination of relief and despair that rushed through my skin and bones. "If you know that, how can you keep me here? Why are you helping them?" I asked.

"You don't know what it's been like," Chloe said. "Since she died."

"I do," I said. "I lost her, too."

"It's not the same. She was my sister, your friend. But she was my mom's favorite daughter. Yeah, I know Mom loves me, blah blah blah, but, Lizzie . . . oh my God. Without her, my mother might die herself."

"But she won't. Not literally."

"She's draining away, Emily. My dad sees it, too."

"Your mother was . . . like my second mom. I cared about her, I always did," I said. "I still do, in a way. Because she has to be sick to be doing this. Really sick. She needs help, and you should get it for her."

"You're her help," Chloe said.

"If you think that, you're as insane as she is! Lizzie wouldn't want you to be doing this. I can practically hear Lizzie begging you to stop, to let me go."

"See?" Chloe asked. "That's why they want you here. Because you loved Lizzie so much, you can still get right into her head. They are making you part of Lizzie World. Actually you are pretty much the whole thing."

My skin crawled. Did she mean that ironically? Or was her family literally creating something called Lizzie World? It sounded like a theme park, but the opposite of the Magic Mountain of Mom. There was nothing exhilarating here, only a dull and creepy basement dollhouse filled with furniture, objects, and clothes from Lizzie's past. My eyes were on the half-open door.

"But I have a life," I said. "With my own family."

"You can say that all you want," Chloe said. "But that's over." She paused, as if she knew that sounded harsh. "You feel it, right? You know they're serious?"

"But I'm serious, too," I said. "I'm a Lonergan. I'm stubborn."

Chloe shook her head sadly. "That's the problem, and why you're still in the cellar. They won't let you out until they're sure you've let go of that dream, of ever going back. Don't you get it?"

"What?" I asked, but I wasn't really listening for the answer. I was just making conversation. In a minute I'd distract her and bolt.

She ruffled her hair, and I saw: Her roots had started growing out. There was a half inch of reddish brown showing along her part and forehead.

"Now that they've dyed your hair black, mine can go back to my natural color. I don't have to have the curl anymore. They don't dab the birthmark on my cheek. Just look around this room. They took a million pictures after Lizzie died, before we moved here. They documented every inch. Movers came for the rest of our house, but not this room. My dad moved it himself, with every single box labeled exactly, and the three of us put it all together. Do you know how long that took?"

"A long time," I said.

"They made me stay here once we got it ready."

"You mean they wanted you to be Lizzie?" I asked.

"My mom did. But you see—there was still that empty chair at the kitchen table. She couldn't pretend our family was the same because one of us was still missing. Lizzie wasn't here."

"She still isn't," I said.

I was bigger and stronger than Chloe, and if she tried to stop me, I'd have no problem shoving her aside. While she was still staring at her feet, I walked straight toward the door.

"Don't," she said.

"I think you left it open because you know it's right," I said. "You know I shouldn't be here."

"You have to," she said. "They don't need me to be Lizzie anymore, because now you are."

"No, Chloe. No matter how I look on the outside, they can't change what I think or feel. And I'll always be Emily." I took a breath. "I'm out of here."

She stared at me with obvious pity in her eyes. "My mother said you might say that. See, leaving the door open was a test. She told me to do it."

"Well, thank you," I said, half stepping through. I peered into a shadowy basement. It smelled musty. The walls were fieldstone and concrete. Some of the stones were damp, as if groundwater was seeping in. There was a washer and dryer in the corner. Tall shelves held canned goods. There was the Ping-Pong table that used to be in the Porters' family room in Black Hall. I picked up speed, heading for the stairs.

"She told me you'd want to see this!" Chloe called. She held up her cell phone and I glanced at it. The screen glowed blue. I caught sight of Seamus, our golden retriever, bounding through tall grass. That stopped me dead. I stood still as Chloe walked closer.

At first I thought it was a video. It could have been taken at any time. I saw Seamus run toward my mother. She was taking him through the marsh—my family's favorite place to walk, and the exact same place where I'd seen Mrs. Porter in August. Then, through Chloe's phone, I heard voices.

My mother's and Mrs. Porter's.

"It's FaceTime," Chloe said. "This is live."

The picture wobbled, as if Mrs. Porter was holding the phone casually, not actually pointing it at my mom, just catching glimpses of her khaki pants, her Merrell boots, her blue jacket, the back of her head, hair in a messy ponytail.

"Anything I can do," Mrs. Porter was saying. "Absolutely anything in the world, just tell me. I drove down as soon as I could. When John and I first heard Emily was missing, oh, Mary—our hearts broke."

"Thank you, Ginnie," my mother said. Her voice was gravelly with tears. "They've already searched this area for her body. Hundreds of people, and they found nothing—of course! Because Emily's still alive. I come here every day, just to think, to get through the days, waiting to hear something."

"I can see why. It's very peaceful," Mrs. Porter said. "I needed a lot of quiet after Lizzie died."

"Oh, Ginnie." My mother stopped, half turned to clasp Mrs. Porter's hand. She must have knocked the camera because the image bobbled up and down before Mrs. Porter steadied it again.

"It's not the same as what you are going through, of course, but I know what it's like to lose a daughter," Mrs. Porter said.

"We all loved Lizzie so much. I pray for you every day," my mother said.

"That means a lot," Mrs. Porter said.

"But Em is coming home. I wish more than anything that Lizzie could, too," my mother said.

"I know you do," Mrs. Porter said. "You've always been such a good friend. I want to be here for you now."

They started walking again, and all I could hear was the sound of their feet tromping through the tall, dry grass. The camera showed they were on the remote marsh path. Unless someone else was taking a walk there, no one would see Mrs. Porter and my mother. Mrs. Porter could do anything. "Have you heard from Emily?" she asked my mom.

"No. I always have my phone with me, and Tom has his, and there's always someone at home, waiting," my mother said. "I'm sure whoever has her won't let her call . . ."

"Is it ransom they want?" Mrs. Porter asked.

"We have no idea," my mother said, her voice breaking. "Martin Wade, the head investigator, tells us to be patient, but it's driving us insane. Why would someone take her?"

"Are you sure she was taken?" Mrs. Porter asked.

"What else could it be? Emily would never stay away without calling us."

"Of course not, Mary. I was just remembering that time she ran away . . . but never mind. You must be absolutely devastated to think of what she's going through."

"That's what's killing me," my mother said, a sob tumbling out. "I keep imagining what someone could be doing to her . . . I can't stop thinking about it. It's driving me out of my mind."

They kept walking, my mom in the lead. The camera bounced, revealed a corner of Mrs. Porter's red plaid jacket and then, in her other hand, a knife with a thick, sharp silver blade. She made a jabbing motion. I grabbed the phone from Chloe's hand, pressed my mouth to it, and screamed.

"Mom, run! *Get away from her!*"

"She can't hear. My mother has her phone on mute," Chloe said. She pressed the OFF button, and the screen went black. I slapped her face as hard as I could, fumbled for the phone. Chloe charged at me, clawed the phone out of my hand. We kept fighting for it, but then she shoved me.

"You're wasting time! Your mother has five minutes to live!" she said.

"What?" I froze.

"I was supposed to make sure you saw that," Chloe said. "My mother meant what she told you. I have to call her back within five minutes, or she'll . . . well, you know what she'll do. To your mother. She'll kill her. That's what the knife is for. So come on. We're going upstairs. You'll send that email to your parents. Then I'll call my mom to let her know, and everything will be fine. Your mother will get to live."

I couldn't even think. Chloe led me up the stairs. They were made of unfinished pine. It's strange how I noticed that at a time like this, but my dad did carpentry, and the wood was the kind of thing he would have remarked on. There were little amber beads of pine pitch on the banister. I stared at them; they made me feel connected to my dad, to things he had taught me. How to measure carefully, how to hammer a nail the right way, how to sand a surface. I was in some kind of trance—it was the only way I could survive what was happening.

I half expected upstairs to be an exact replica of the Porters' house in Black Hall, but although I recognized most of the furniture, it wasn't arranged as precisely as Lizzie's room. Chloe led me to the big faded chintz sofa, the one we'd all spent hours on, watching TV and playing Scrabble. The coffee table was a large brass-bound leather trunk that had been Mame's. It had traveled the world with her. It had taken the *Queen Elizabeth II* across the Atlantic Ocean.

There were windows on two sides of the living room. Everything happened very fast. I blinked in the daylight—my first time seeing natural light in twenty-two days. While Chloe clicked the keys of her laptop, I looked outside and saw a house next door. It was big and white, like one of the sea captain's houses in Black Hall, but it looked old and deserted. The paint was peeling, and the roof looked as if it might cave in. There was a line of beehives along a garden choked with weeds. But as I stared, I noticed a boy standing in the shadows on the front porch.

He was tall and skinny, his dirty-blond hair tied back in a ponytail. Torn jeans slipped low on his hips, and he wore a faded red T-shirt. His face, a pale oval, was turned toward me. He looked about seventeen, Patrick's age. My heart began to pound even harder than it already was. Was there a way I could signal to him, get help for me and my mother? I glanced at Chloe; she was intent on the computer screen. Turning back to the boy, I raised my hand, just slightly.

"Come on," Chloe said, and I dropped my arm fast so she wouldn't see. She gestured for me to sit beside her on the sofa. She had her laptop open to Gmail, my username typed in, as if this was pre-destined, as if she'd already known I would be doing this. All I had to do was insert my password. Mrs. Porter had written out what I was supposed to say. There it was in her neat handwriting on a piece of geranium-emblazoned notepaper next to the laptop.

"You have to type it exactly. No code words. Mom's going to check," Chloe said. "And don't get your hopes up."

"About what?" I asked, as if I had any hopes.

"Your family finding you through the IP address. My mom figured out how to have a fake one, a virtual private network." Chloe paused. She glanced away, then back at me. "She thinks of everything."

Tracking me through the IP address hadn't even occurred to me. But now, Chloe telling me it could have been possible—but wasn't—filled me with despair.

My heart was in overdrive. My chest hurt so much I wondered if I might drop dead. I read the message on the notepaper, and I couldn't get my fingers to work.

"Hurry up," Chloe said. "If I don't call my mom right away . . ."

"Okay," I said. I logged in. My password was LiZZiePOrTEr4ever. I had changed it from my old one on the day of Lizzie's funeral.

My inbox was overflowing. Emails from my mother, my father, all my brothers and sisters, school friends, even Dan. I caught the subject line of the most recent from Bea: *I love you so much! Emily, I need you now, come home!!!!!* Did they really think I was able to read my emails? Why wouldn't I have written back? A yearning for my cell phone overtook me, nearly knocked me down.

"Do it," Chloe said, tapping the time in the upper right corner of the screen. "You have sixty seconds or the knife comes out for real."

I heard myself moan, and then I stopped thinking. I addressed the email to both my parents and just typed:

Mom & Dad,

Everything got too hard. I know Mom is back to drinking—
I found the bottles. If she really loved us, she would have
stopped for good. Don't look for me. For now, I don't
want to be part of the family. There's too much wrong.
I'm safe, and I'll come home when I figure things out.

Love, Emily

I hesitated before sending—I couldn't bear to think what this would do to them. But I looked at the time—one minute had already passed. Was I too late? My heart was pumping so hard, in sheer terror for my mom, and I hit SEND. The instant the email went, Chloe turned her phone back on and dialed her mother.

"It's done. I'll take a screenshot and send it to you so you can see," she said into the phone. Then she hung up and nodded at me.

"Why didn't you just forward it to your mother?" I asked Chloe. "That would be her proof."

"My mom says the police have probably already hacked your account. They'd get suspicious if they saw you forwarded it to my mom."

I pictured my mother, over by the marsh in Black Hall. Mrs. Porter getting a call from Chloe would be the most natural thing in the world. My mother would be wishing she'd get a call from me. Her smartphone would buzz, an email notification, and she'd pull it from her pocket. She'd see my screen name. She might cry out. Then she'd open the email. She'd read it. My father, wherever he was, would be reading it at the same time. Their hearts would be broken.

Tears were pouring down my cheeks. I stood up and started stumbling toward the cellar stairs. Chloe caught my arm.

"You don't have to go down there now," she said. "You proved yourself."

"What?"

"By sending the email. You've officially joined our family, *Lizzie*. You're allowed to be anywhere you want in the rest of the house during the day. You can sleep down there. It's a nice room. But you're free to be up here with us."

I stared at her with all the hatred I felt.

"But one more thing," she said. "You'd better put those contacts in. My mother said if your eyes aren't green next time she sees you, the email won't matter—she'll hurt your mom."

And I walked downstairs, my hand sliding down the rough wood banister, bumping over the tiny, hard orange beads of pine sap, and barely feeling the pain of the long splinter that slid into my palm.

In the back of my mind was that boy next door. Maybe he had seen me. Maybe he would know something was wrong and call the police. But the thoughts dissolved. I felt too hopeless to really, seriously consider the possibility that someone could help.

I went into the bathroom and stuck the contacts into my eyes, first try.

CHAPTER SIX

DAY TWENTY-THREE

I kept thinking of the email I had sent, wondering if my parents would think it sounded like me, if they could tell I hadn't written it myself. If they didn't figure out the truth, my mother would feel so hurt I believed she was drinking, and the rest of the family would be filled with suspicion that she was. I didn't have long to wonder, though.

"You've earned this," Mrs. Porter said, beaming as Mr. Porter filed silently in, carrying the TV, setting it on the left side of Lizzie's desk, hooking it up to the cable that was already there.

Mr. Porter handed me the remote and left without a word, but Mrs. Porter took the remote from my hand and switched on a news network. She sat next to me on the bed to check the stitches in my head and the puffy red splinter gouge on my palm.

Then she took out her cell phone.

"You're everywhere," Mrs. Porter said. "Online, on TV."

That felt weird to think about, but I didn't react.

"You know the next step, don't you?" she asked.

I stared at the TV screen. There were my parents. They walked silently from our car up our sidewalk toward the house.

At the same time, Mrs. Porter scrolled through her phone. She pulled up the same video on CNN online, held it in front of my face. She closed that window, opened another news page, and there was my smiling photo from last year's yearbook.

"You see?" Mrs. Porter asked, shoving her phone into her pocket before I could grab it from her. "I don't want you dwelling on it, but I think it's important for you to see what is being said. And you need to think about this: You know what is possible. You saw with your own two eyes how close I came to your mother. When you're ready, you will join us upstairs. The invitation was extended the minute you did the right thing—wrote that email."

"I didn't write it," I said. "I only *sent* it."

"The point is, you will come upstairs and we will all be together. As a family. Now watch."

On TV, I saw that my father's arm was around my mother's shoulders. He was tall and thin and towered over her. I leaned close to the screen. Mom's posture looked hunched, as if she was curving into her own heart. She wore the same blue jacket she'd had on yesterday, when Mrs. Porter had broadcast their walk to me.

Or maybe this news report had been taped yesterday. I heard reporters calling, asking for a reaction to my email, but my parents didn't answer. They walked up our steps, across the front porch. It was late October, so the house was decorated for Halloween. Bea and I had always done it. There were the jack-o'-lanterns our family carved, the haystacks we tied to the posts, the dry ears of yellow-and-purple corn we would get at Sloane's Orchard and hang on our bright blue front door. Someone inside the house opened the door, and my parents disappeared inside.

Marcela Perez, our family's favorite newscaster, who wore tortoiseshell glasses just like my sister Anne's, and who reported on all the big stories in Connecticut—fatal accidents, a home invasion in Guilford, drugs on the streets, and missing kids— stood in front of my house holding a microphone.

But this wasn't about other people. It wasn't even all about me. Marcela was talking about my whole family.

"Breaking news in the Emily Lonergan case. After twenty-two days of silence, Emily made contact. Her email hasn't yet been released, but a source close to the family says that Emily ran away once before and that, according to the email, she is safe and will return home when she is ready. A spokesman for the Black Hall Police Department confirms that Emily was once a runaway. More as this story develops."

Mrs. Porter switched to a different news channel. I glanced at her. I wondered if she was the source close to the family. In this news clip, *she* was standing right on our front porch, hugging Patrick, an expression of concern on her face. She glanced at the camera, as if surprised to see it there.

"Two families, united by loss," this other reporter— a TV-perfect-looking man I didn't recognize—said in a fake TV-modulated voice. "Virginia Porter, mother of Emily's best friend Elizabeth—a tragic victim of childhood cancer—is here in idyllic coastal Black Hall to comfort another family in distress. Emily Lonergan, missing for three weeks, sent this email to her family."

The network showed a screenshot of what I had written. I wanted to die. Everyone in the world could read it: my mother drinking again, me not feeling like part of my family. I twisted my head away, but then I had to look back at the screen.

There was Patrick. I always teased him and said, *You're the best brother in the world except for my other brothers.* Patrick had the classic Lonergan black Irish coloring I'd always wanted—for real, not fake and dyed like the way I was now. His blue eyes blazed. His mouth was set in a hard line. Was he mad, sad, confused? I tried to read his face. Then he bowed his head, and I saw his shoulders shaking. He was crying—my big brother. On TV. Mrs. Porter embraced him.

The reporter continued, speaking in a grave voice. "Alcoholism is a tragic illness that all too often plagues not only the drinker but entire families. Tune in at eleven for our special report. 'Problem Drinking: Destroyer of Families.'"

"He likes the word 'tragic,'" Mrs. Porter said, sitting beside me. "He said it twice."

"It is tragic for my family," I said. "Because of what you made me do."

"Well, the *death* of a daughter is a *true* tragedy. Your parents have the hope that their child will return. Even though you won't, because you're ours now." She put her arm around me, just as she had around Patrick, and the physical sensation made me want to throw up. "Lizzie, you've come home."

She muted the sound and handed me the remote. I clicked around, searching for more views of everyone I loved. There was Anne at Trinity College, bundled up in the red wool cape she'd sewn herself. Even though the black satin lining didn't show on

TV, I knew it was there because I had helped her pin the pattern to the fabric, kneeling on the floor of our living room.

The next channel showed Tommy, Mick, and Iggy. It must have been an older clip, before my email, because they were shoulder-to-shoulder, taller than anyone else, searching the marsh where my mother and Mrs. Porter had been walking. There were other people, too, in horizontal lines like you see on newscasts where there is a missing person, when neighbors join the police to scour in fields and stretches of water for the dead body. My brothers had returned home from their faraway colleges to look for my corpse.

The shot that hurt most was one of Bea. She stood alone on the front steps of our church, staring into the distance. She looked desolate—in the close-up I could see circles under her eyes, her skin so pale you couldn't even see her freckles. I remembered when once she'd told me about her boyfriend, James, how they had figured out how to get into the church steeple, how they went up there to look all the way down the Connecticut River and across Long Island Sound to Orient Point, and to kiss.

But I could tell she wasn't at church for the view or to meet James. Standing right there, oblivious to the camera, her lips were moving. Was she talking to me, the way I talked to Lizzie, or was she praying? Was she angry at me for leaving? All three. I was sure of it.

"My three colleens," my father would say about Anne, Bea, and me. In Ireland, *colleen* was another word for "girl." I looked at Bea, my colleen, at her bright azure eyes and long, straight brown hair, at the thick Aran Isles sweater I realized—with a tiny, surprising burst of outrage—she had taken from my closet. We were always borrowing each other's things, getting mad at each other for stealing clothes, especially sweaters. This one had been knit for me by Anne. She'd given it to me for my last birthday.

"Brat," I would have said to Bea, if I were there.

The last clip showed my parents walking on the beach. My dad's hands were jammed into his pockets. My mother's arms were tight across her chest, as if holding herself together. The screen caption said, *A family torn apart by alcohol.*

They weren't speaking. They were fighting. They usually walked the beach holding hands, but now there was ten feet of space between them. I was sure my father felt betrayed because he believed what I had written: that Mom had relapsed and was drinking again.

"You're a drunk!" he had shouted at her once, the worst thing I'd ever heard. My gentle father, my always-loving mother. But she'd missed seeing the dress rehearsal of my play that afternoon. It was called *Ghost Girl,* and not only had I written it, I had played Ada, the spirit girl. I had felt so nervous and thrilled about kissing Dan—well, his character, Timothy—that I didn't even notice my mother wasn't in the audience.

But later, after we finished rehearsing and I stood on the school steps with cold rain pelting down, I had a sinking feeling. I hitched a ride with Tilly McCabe's mom, and when I got home, I found my mother passed out in bed. The fumes left no doubt that there'd been vodka involved.

I looked for the bottle. My mom had hidden it behind cleaning supplies under the kitchen sink, so I carried it to the recycling bin in the garage. I shoved it down beneath the milk cartons and cardboard boxes and yogurt containers. We had all taken turns doing that over the years. No one had been better at it than my dad. Patrick called it "bottle music"—the sound of my father cleaning up after my mother, when Dad would wait till we'd all gone to bed to get rid of her empties.

It was our way of protecting her, protecting each other. When you love someone as much as we love Mom, you don't want anyone, even in the family, judging her. You tell yourself she doesn't mean it, she'll never do it again. Or you tell yourself she's sick, she can't help it. My dad and my brothers and sisters and I all took turns feeling furious at her, despair for her, hope that she'd stop. We never felt the same way at the same time.

That day my dad reached his breaking point. He had planned to surprise my mother and me—meeting us at Beach Road Pizza, where she'd normally have taken me after a play, but we weren't there. Because she'd blacked out.

"Mary, you're throwing everything away," Dad had said. "I've given you a hundred chances—we all have. The only thing I'm grateful for is that you didn't drive—that you missed the play, left your daughter in the rain. That's good. Better than the alternative. You could have driven her into a telephone pole. So congratulations. You're a drunk, but at least you didn't kill Emily."

"Don't even say those words," my mother had said, starting to cry.

"You want her to run away again?" my father asked. "Just stay on this path and she will. And I swear, Mary, when she does, I'll never forgive you."

The next day my mother was on her way to rehab. The good news: She got sober. I know my dad was glad—we all were. But I'm not sure he ever really trusted her after that day. Not the way he had before she'd gotten so bad.

Staring at the TV screen now, watching my parents recede down the empty beach, my mother's back hunched and my father's posture poker-straight, I remembered that day, my dad's voice ringing in my head. This wasn't my mother's fault at all. This was because of me.

"When you're ready," Mrs. Porter said now, "you will come upstairs. I want you to. I can't wait."

Her eyes held my gaze. For just that minute I remembered how I'd practically lived at the Porters' house after school, and during the years of my mother's drinking, I'd relied on Mrs. Porter in ways she'd probably never know.

"I'm sorry about the threat," she said. "I don't want it to be this way."

Her tone of voice made me realize she meant what she said. "Then don't let it," I said.

She was silent for a long moment. Her chin started to wobble, and tears pooled in her eyes.

"I don't have a choice," she said. "It's like being possessed, like having a demon inside. Not a real one, I don't mean that, but a compulsion to keep you here no matter what. That's how much

I need you. You're sleeping in her bed; you'll come upstairs and sit in her chair. I can never let you go, never."

I'd seen parents cry before—well, my mother—and it was always shocking, and I always tried to make it stop. In spite of everything, I felt Mrs. Porter's desperation. Part of me cared. One thing a daughter of an alcoholic knows is how to take care of people: to keep the peace, to try to figure out how to make things better, to have compassion, to twist yourself into a pretzel in the hope you can keep them from drinking again. Because something is going on that you can't possibly fathom, a hurt so deep it makes the sick person do terrible things—get drunk, kidnap your dead daughter's best friend.

"I'm sorry," Mrs. Porter said again, wiping her eyes. "Your parents will be fine, you know. You're just another runaway."

My throat ached, holding back a scream.

"Good night," she whispered, kissing my forehead.

I didn't answer. She left the room, and I heard her footsteps on the wood stairs. I lay awake, my heart pounding. In some way her apology convinced me even more than the knife that this was real. She had said she would never let me go, and suddenly I knew with absolute certainty that she meant it with everything she had.

I pressed my face into my pillow and finally let out the scream. My chest heaved, aching as if I were having a heart attack. I sobbed until the pillowcase was soaked, and I hugged the pillow as hard as I could, wishing it were my mother, needing her comfort and needing so badly to protect her.

I thought of how weird it was, that I'd written *Ghost Girl* before Lizzie had died. It had been about Ada, of course. But lying there in bed with my pillow soaked, it felt as if the play had been predictive, and about me—or a girl like me, anyway. To have a best friend die, to have her parents kidnap you, to have her mother threaten to murder your mom: It leaves you so alone, so off balance and unreal-feeling, that *you* become the ghost, the changeling, and *you're* the one haunting school and the town you grew up in together. You used to be solid and strong. Now you're mist.

DAY THIRTY

I waited as long as I could. I wouldn't give them the satisfaction.

She had said "ready," and I swore I never would be. But she had told me about her need to keep me, and I had seen how close she'd gotten to my mother. Nearly every night now I dreamed of a knife slashing through skin and bone. I fought hard, my muscles burning as I grabbed, slapped, and punched to defend my mother. I turned the weapon on the attacker.

The news stations stopped running my story. I flipped through the channels obsessively, hoping for a glimpse of my family, some indication they were still looking for me, that they still believed in me. After a while, the reporters moved on to other dark news: a six-year-old boy accidentally shot by his thirteen-year-old brother, the discovery of a human trafficking ring in a small Maine town, a search for two teenage hikers missing on Mount Katahdin.

The steeple clock chimed six. Was it morning or night? She hadn't come down with breakfast yet, so it had to be morning. My head felt foggy. In my dreams, I felt so alive. I was doing something, fighting back. When I woke up, I felt deadened. Numb, going through the motions. I felt the way my family had looked on TV: in shock, helpless, with no hope left.

I washed my face and changed out of Lizzie's nightgown into some of Lizzie's clothes—jeans and a T-shirt. I tried the doorknob. Somehow I knew it would open, and it did. My legs felt heavy. I heard my feet clomping up the wooden stairs.

There was a moment, just a few seconds, when I could have changed my mind. I stood on the top step, my hand on the brass doorknob that opened onto the kitchen. I knew that by walking through that door, I would be agreeing to the Porters' way, entering their world. I would be leaving a big part of myself behind—I just didn't know how big.

I opened the door.

Mrs. Porter was cooking eggs. Chloe was making toast. Without a word, I sat in the empty chair at the round kitchen table with bright yellow place mats. I noticed there were four place mats, as if the family had been expecting me. Mrs. Porter beamed at me.

"Good morning, Lizzie," Mrs. Porter said.

"Good morning," I said.

"Orange juice?" Mr. Porter asked. But he just sat where he was. His face looked blank—or was that a tinge of annoyance behind his eyes? I got the sudden feeling he didn't want me there.

"She knows where it is," Mrs. Porter said. "Help yourself, sweetie."

I went to the refrigerator. I was moving in slow motion, sleep-walking. I took out the carton. I stood in front of the cabinets and automatically opened the one that held the glasses. I poured the juice. A tiny bit slopped onto the shiny green stone countertop, and I wiped it with a sponge.

We ate. The scrambled eggs were fluffy and perfect. I buttered my rye toast and smeared it with pear preserves. I knew they were homemade. All through the year Mrs. Porter made fresh preserves with fruit that Lizzie, Chloe, and I would pick at local orchards. I concentrated on every movement I made. Now I am taking a bite of toast; now I am having a sip of juice.

"This is a special day," Mrs. Porter said.

"I thought we decided we would not treat it as remarkable," Mr. Porter said. "What is so unusual about our 'older daughter' joining us for breakfast?"

Definitely air quotes around *older daughter.*

"You are so right," Mrs. Porter said. "But I am in a celebratory mood. Look out the window! Bright sunshine, blue sky, and that maple tree! The leaves were flame red just two weeks ago, Lizzie! They've mostly fallen now, if only you had come up a few days ago, but there are still a few on the branches. Remember when you were little and you used to gather autumn leaves, and we'd iron them between sheets of wax paper?"

"With melted crayons," Chloe said.

"Stained glass," I said. That's what Lizzie had called it. We would hang the colorful squares in our windows, and the sun would shine through and splash red and orange light on the floor.

"Let's go leaf peeping," Mrs. Porter said. "It's the weekend!"

"Mom," Chloe said. "I have Saturday study with Mel and Junie."

"Besides, the foliage is gone," Mr. Porter said. "This is Maine, not Connecticut. You can see for yourself, Ginnie—the damn trees are practically bare."

"I feel like a ride," Mrs. Porter said, smiling but with that now-familiar sharp edge in her voice. "Don't you, Lizzie?"

"Yes," I said.

"It won't kill you to miss one Saturday," Mrs. Porter said to Chloe. "You're smart, you can figure it out without Mel and Junie. We'll go to the cider mill."

They gave me one of Lizzie's jackets to wear, and together we left the house. Walking outside, I gulped fresh air. It tasted so good. My first non-basement, non-house air in nearly a month. I drank it in, blinking at the bright light. My eyes hurt to look at the sky. I was like a cave creature, dragged out of the darkness.

This was my first time seeing the house from the outside: a small saltbox with silvery shingles, white shutters, and a dark green door. There was a brick chimney, and tidy curtains hung at every window. It looked nice. No one would ever guess it was a house of horrors. Now that I was out, I vowed I would never go back inside.

I wouldn't. No matter what, I would never return to that basement. The old Lonergan spirit rippled through me, made my blood race and my muscles come to life. My legs felt like springs.

Before the end of the day, I would escape. Whatever it takes, I told myself. That was my mantra and battle cry. Whatever it takes, whatever it takes, *Faugh a Ballagh*, Emily. Emily, not Lizzie.

As I got into the Porters' minivan, I glanced next door. The large house was as ramshackle as it had seemed at my first impression, with a fading grandeur—it belonged, or had once belonged, to someone important. It loomed over the hedge between its yard and the Porters'. The Porters' house was tiny in comparison. White paint had weathered down to the bare wood, and there were slate tiles missing from the mansard roof. A second-floor shutter creaked in the wind. Even the beehives looked forlorn. I looked for the boy, but he wasn't there.

I wanted to scream for help, but this wasn't the right place anyway. I needed to get farther away from this spot, where I would somehow gain the advantage, where I could run to the police so they could warn my mother before Mrs. Porter could reach her.

Chloe and I sat in the back seat. This was the minivan they'd driven when they'd kidnapped me. Now I was riding in it as if it were normal. My hands were not tied, I wasn't drugged. My heart jumped so hard, I was worried they'd hear it banging in my chest, my breath coming fast, as if I'd just run the fifty-yard dash.

Mr. Porter was right: Many of the branches were bare, and most of the remaining leaves were brown. But every so often we'd spy a tendril of woodbine holding on to the last of its scarlet leaves, and Mrs. Porter would cry out with joy, and we'd pull over to gather a few. These roads were twisty and deserted, lined with stone walls and the occasional farmhouse. I held my breath, wanting to open the door and tumble out, run away, but I knew I had to bide my time.

A few miles later, we pulled into the parking lot of Jeb's Olde Cider Mill, a big red barn surrounded by hundreds of pumpkins and baskets of gourds. As soon as I stepped out of the car, I smelled apples. I heard the grinding of the press, extracting juice from cartloads of Macoun and McIntosh apples.

The Porters barely kept their eyes on me. They must have been confident no one would recognize Emily Lonergan with her hair dyed black, blue eyes hidden behind green contacts, a mole drawn on her cheek. Mr. Porter wandered over to a display of apple wine and maple syrup. Chloe stuck close to me. She grabbed a box of fudge and another of maple sugar molded into the shape of jack-o'-lanterns. Employees wore khaki jackets with Jeb's patches on the chest.

I tried to catch the eye of a woman handing out cups of hot cider, but she was talking to a couple. I overheard them say they were from Kentucky, meandering through New England on vacation. This would be the place to yell. I wouldn't even have to run—people would surround me to find out what was wrong.

And there he was—the boy who had been on the porch next door. Today his dark blond hair was tied back with a leather cord, a few strands falling into his face, and he wore a brown canvas jacket. He was with three other kids, all of them wandering past the crates of apples, drinking cups of hot cider.

One of them was a girl in a long dress, with wavy strawberry blond hair flowing almost to her waist. She laughed, a trill as pure as birdsong. Just behind them was a stocky boy with a beard and sunglasses and a dark-haired boy wearing a cap that said MARTIN GUITAR.

"Oh, look, it's Casey," Chloe said.

The boy with the dark blond hair must have heard his name because he turned and waved. He left his friends and walked toward us.

"Hi, Chloe," he said.

"How's it going?" she asked.

"Saturday at the cider mill," he said. "Life is good, right?"

"Pretty much," she said.

He smiled. His eyes were turquoise and cloudy. His lashes were so long they brushed his cheeks when he blinked. But it was the color and opacity of his eyes that mesmerized me.

"Hi," he said.

"Hi," I said.

"I bet I know who you are," he said.

"You do?" I practically died then and there. Had he seen the news stories? Unconsciously I touched my dyed hair—could he look right through the disguise and see who I really was?

"Please, you've got to . . ." I began, instantly grabbing for what felt like my best and last opportunity, my heart smashing through my ribs, when I felt sharp fingers grip my shoulder.

"I see you've found our neighbor," Mrs. Porter said, smiling warmly. "Casey Donoghue, meet my daughter Lizzie."

"I knew it had to be you," Casey said. "Home from Europe. How was it?"

"Europe?" I asked.

"I told Casey and his dad all about your semester as an exchange student," Mrs. Porter said. "How badly we missed you but how we absolutely could not deny you that once-in-a-lifetime chance."

"Must have been cool," Casey said.

Mrs. Porter prodded me.

"Was it cool, Lizzie?" she asked.

"Uh, yes," I said.

"It was really great," Casey said. "Your family moving in last year—we don't exactly get a lot of new people around here. It's a little rural."

"It's just so scenic and beautiful," Mrs. Porter said. "A great place to raise a family."

"That's what my parents said when we moved here," he said, looking straight at me. "But I was a lot younger than you and Chloe."

His eyes seemed to bore into me, but at the same time, they looked through and past me. Did the cloudiness mean his vision was impaired? But he'd walked over so easily, sure of himself, no cane. Still, there was something.

"Everyone's waiting to meet you," Casey said. "Let me get my friends."

He started to walk away, and I was shaking. I couldn't help myself—as if my hand had a life of its own, as if it knew this was my best chance for help, I reached out toward him. My fingers brushed his.

"What is it?" he asked.

Mrs. Porter clutched my upper arm so hard, I felt her fingernails through my thick jacket.

I twisted, trying to wrench out of her grasp. But she wouldn't let me. She held on tighter.

"Are you okay?" he asked.

Her grip dug into my bicep.

"I'm fine. I'm just . . . happy to meet you."

"Yeah, me too. Let me get the others," he said.

"Another time," Mrs. Porter said. "We have to get going. See you soon, Casey."

"Okay," he said. "Well, see you at school, Lizzie."

"Yes," I said.

Walking away, I glanced back at Casey. He hadn't kept walking. He was looking in my direction with that spooky long gaze that seemed to see beyond what was actually visible.

"Poor boy," Mrs. Porter said. "Legally blind. His mother was very foolish and didn't care for him properly."

"What did she do?" I asked.

"Just another case of a bad mother," she said. "Like yours. Not like me, that's for sure. I would kill for my children."

A chill shuddered down my spine, and I stared into her sparkling emerald eyes.

"Now, you weren't going to say anything to him, were you?" Mrs. Porter asked.

"No, of course not."

"Why did you grab for his hand?"

"I didn't," I said.

"You little liar, I saw you! And I'll tell you—he can see, but not well enough to get a license. He's considered legally blind. He can't drive you anywhere, if that's what you're hoping."

I shrugged, trying to convince her she was wrong, that I had no idea what she was talking about.

She was wearing the red plaid wool jacket with big square

pockets. Her smile went away, replaced by that hollow sorrow I'd seen the night she'd told me about her demons. And then as if it was the last thing she wanted to do, as if it gave her actual pain, she reached into one of the pockets and surreptitiously showed me the bone handle, the glint of silver blade.

Suddenly the red of her jacket was the color of blood, my mother's. The knife was the one I'd seen on FaceTime, the same as the one in my dreams: long, sharp, and jagged. There, in the midst of Jeb's Olde Cider Mill, I stood frozen. My mind went stupid and numb again. I didn't scream, I didn't run. The picture in my mind made sure of that.

Mrs. Porter and I climbed back into the car. Chloe and Mr. Porter were sipping cups of hot cider. Chloe opened a box of fudge and passed around the creamy walnut-studded squares. I didn't take one.

When we got back to the house, Mrs. Porter ripped off pieces of wax paper, and while she hovered over us, Chloe and I took turns arranging the meager leaves we'd picked up, shaving crimson, orange, and yellow crayons in swirling patterns, and pressing a second square of paper with a hot iron, creating the waxy stained glass windows Lizzie had always loved.

Later, we peeled apples for a pie. Going through the motions, I sliced the apple skin into long red curls. I pasted them onto the pie, and when it baked, they turned golden brown. I wondered about the phrase *legally blind*. How, if a person could see, could they be considered any kind of blind?

"This was a good day," Mrs. Porter said, pulling Chloe and me close in a hug. "I'm so happy we're all together."

"Yeah, it's great," Chloe said, giving me a look as if it was anything but.

"One thing," Mrs. Porter said to me, peering at my face.

"What?"

"You really need to shape your eyebrows. Lizzie's were always perfect. In fact, I'll do it for you. Let's get the tweezers."

"No, I can," I said quickly.

"Okay," she said. "Get the arch right. Do it before I see you tomorrow."

That night we sat in the living room watching TV. The news came on. No mention of me, no clips of my family. I thought: If I'd made a fuss at Jeb's, begged Casey or someone else for help, Mrs. Porter would have sped away.

She could have gotten to Black Hall in a few hours. If that had happened, this newscast could be very different. There would be a story of Mary Lonergan found murdered in the marsh, her throat slit and the cold, weedy tidewaters rising around her body.

Mrs. Porter hadn't had to say a word to me. She'd only had to show me the barest glimpse of that knife.

I was becoming like a dog so used to being beaten its owner had only to raise a hand, a rolled-up newspaper, to send it cowering into the corner.

This was mine. This middle seat on the comfortable chintz-covered couch where I sat between Mrs. Porter and Chloe, the TV droning on, Mr. Porter across the room in his lounge chair, eating a second piece of pie.

This was my corner.

CHAPTER SEVEN

DAY THIRTY-ONE

It's terrible when your eyebrows get messed up. It's not as bad as getting kidnapped, of course, I reminded myself, with a twisted smile.

My approach to makeup and grooming was always *less is more*. I was more natural than Lizzie. She studied YouTube for the technique, and she had these expensive Tweezerman bling slant tweezers that felt bizarre in my hand. That night, I stood at the bathroom mirror and went at it. I made one mistake, and compounded it by keeping on. I wound up leaving myself with these scrawny little crooked lines of eyebrows.

I fell asleep in despair. Being kidnapped and kept in a dungeon was surreal, and being forced to have my friend's eyebrows tripled the nightmare. The next morning, I checked the mirror—they were worse than I'd thought.

I stepped into the shower and turned the water as hot as I could stand, feeling it almost burn my scalp. I kept touching my eyebrows. Horrible. The smell of Lizzie's shampoo had started to make me sick. I shouldn't be using it—she should. She should still be alive, filling her spot in the family. Fury had replaced my grief.

"You did this, Lizzie," I shrieked into the water. "Why did you leave? Why didn't you fight harder? Why can't you be alive? I hate you. I hate your eyebrows."

I wanted to hear her answer me back, to be outraged, then to tease me, to tell me I was being a loser and a jerk and the worst eyebrow plucker in the world. I wished so hard to hear her voice, that laughing lilt as she agreed with me about her mother.

"Your father, though," I said. "What's up with him? He can't stand having me here, I can tell."

Idiot, what do you expect? Lizzie would have asked. *You're not me.*

I dried myself off with her towel. As disgusted as I'd felt at her shampoo, the touch of the terrycloth comforted me. The weird thing was, it had been so easy to feel Lizzie with me back home in Black Hall, when I'd walk along talking to her. Since being forced into her family, I'd barely sensed her presence.

But right now, I pretended my best friend was here—she was out in the bedroom while I was drying my hair. We'd pick out the clothes we wanted to wear and head to our favorite spot on Main Street for chai lattes. She'd get pumpkin because she loved pumpkin everything in the fall, and I'd get cinnamon.

We'd go to school, study in our favorite out-of-the-way nook. It was on the second floor, called the Apiary because many years ago a science teacher had built a beehive directly into the wall. It was covered with glass so students could study at tables and watch the bees fly in and out of the brood chambers through a passage to the outdoors, where they'd build their honeycombs.

Looking in the mirror I had that jolt—it wasn't me staring back. It wasn't even Lizzie. It was some freak. I felt like one of those bees trapped behind glass in our school apiary. The bathroom door was closed, the air steamy. I thought I heard someone in the bedroom; I froze, listening to footsteps. The closet opened and closed. Same with drawers. Someone was taking inventory, maybe searching for signs I was planning to escape, to fight back.

Finally, silence.

I stepped into the room, looked around. At first everything looked normal. I hadn't yet made my bed, so the covers were rumpled. There was something dark red on the white sheet. I approached slowly, my heart pounding.

It was a shoe.

I'd know it anywhere: maroon suede, old laces that were slightly frayed, a leather sole that had recently been replaced. My love of quirky clothes had been inspired by my sisters, and before them, my mother. My mom usually wore this shoe and its mate with a tartan skirt and a brown leather bomber jacket. She loved to put together comfortable shoes and clothes in her own style, a combination of preppy and tough Irish girl, and this shoe was part of one of her favorite outfits.

Inside the shoe was a note:

I came into your room last night and saw what you did to your eyebrows. You have ruined yourself, you look nothing like Lizzie, and until they grow back, you are not leaving this room. Did I really need to remind you of what can happen? It was so easy to get this memento of your mother. So easy.

My hands were shaking. My mother kept her shoes in her bedroom closet, on the second floor of our house. How had Mrs. Porter possibly gotten it? Had she attacked my mother, pulled it off her foot? Or had she somehow . . .

My house key. It had been in the pocket of my army jacket the day they took me. Had Mrs. Porter found it? Would she have dared let herself into my house while my parents slept? I hated myself for letting her get to my key, but I prayed that she had done just that.

The alternative was too much of a nightmare to even consider.

DAY THIRTY-TWO

Do you know how long it takes eyebrows to grow out?

Basically forever.

On the other hand, my roots *had* started to grow out. Chloe delivered a batch of black dye and told me her mother wanted me to touch them up. The dye was sticky and gross, smelled like chemicals, and made my scalp sting.

Wasn't I supposed to start school? Weren't Casey and his friends expecting me? The teachers? What was Mrs. Porter telling them?

DAY THIRTY-FIVE

She checked me every night. I'd hear her enter my room like a sleepwalker, drift over to my bed, stand there staring down at me.

I pretended to be asleep.

She didn't speak. Sometimes I felt the spider's touch of her fingernails on my eyebrows.

She'd stay long enough to give me a pit in my stomach, and then she'd leave, closing the door softly behind her.

I never closed my eyes after her visits.

I would lie awake and imagine who I would text if I had my cell phone. What I would say, how I would describe my location, how I could get my whole family to charge in and rescue me.

DAY THIRTY-EIGHT

She still didn't speak to me during the days, but she continued to enter my room at night. She did the same thing as before—hovering, touching my eyebrows, tracing them with her fingernail, peering at them to see if they had grown out—but with one change: She began whispering.

"Lizzie, my baby."

"Lizzie, my little girl."

"I carried you in this body, you were part of me, I was part of you. Oh, the days before you were born. I tried to imagine what it would be like, this little creature living inside me, who would you be, how would we feel about each other?"

"How could I have known that you would turn me into a different person entirely? I was one Virginia Porter before you, another after you were born. How can I ever go back? I only exist as your mother."

"Sweetie, you are forever my child, forever my baby girl."

Her words made me sick. Once, after she left, I tore into the bathroom and barely made it in time to retch into the toilet.

CHAPTER EIGHT

DAY FORTY-TWO

It was Lizzie's birthday.

We had always celebrated together, because mine was two days later. But Lizzie had died on the day in between, so last year I hadn't wanted to even think about it. My mother and Bea made me a cake on my day, but I refused to eat it.

I figured it would be the same here. Lizzie's family would want these days to pass quietly, especially considering I was in eyebrow exile. But I was wrong.

A note was slipped under my door. *Happy birthday! This is your special day! Come upstairs for breakfast so we can celebrate!*

I'd almost gotten used to the creepiness of having Mrs. Porter come into my room every night. I barely slept, waiting to hear the door latch click. I'd tense up, sensing her move around the room, coming to stand over my bed. I'd feel her looking down at me, studying me. I'd wait for her spider-silk touch. I'd hold my breath for that, pretending to be asleep.

Now I looked in the mirror. My eyebrows still hadn't grown out much. They were scrawny, with sparse reddish-blond hairs poking through the skin. But it was "my" birthday, and I suppose that outweighed Mrs. Porter's need to wait until my eyebrows were Lizzie-ready once again.

"Here she is, the birthday girl!" Mrs. Porter said when I emerged from the basement a few minutes later.

"Happy birthday," Chloe said, sitting at the table and barely looking up from her notebook. She was writing furiously— probably an essay due that day. She was notorious for doing her homework at the last minute.

Mr. Porter seemed as numb as ever. He pointed at my spot at the table, which was piled high with wrapped presents.

"Happy birthday, sweetie," Mrs. Porter said, throwing her arms around me. "I'm making your favorite chocolate pancakes."

"Thanks," I said.

"Yummy, yummy," she said, bustling back to the stove. She served me a plate of pancakes with smiley faces made from M&M's—just as she'd always made for Lizzie. She drizzled them with fresh maple syrup. But before I could take a bite, she handed me a small, unwrapped purple velvet box.

"It's a tradition, as you know," she said. "One present before first bite. Go ahead, open it."

I did. There inside was a necklace. A finely wrought gold anchor hung from a delicate chain. The sight of it made my hands shake.

"A family heirloom," Chloe said. "Lucky you."

"Stop the sarcasm!" Mr. Porter said.

"Let me help you, sweetie," Mrs. Porter said. Very gently she pushed my long hair off the back of my neck, clicked the tiny

clasp. I felt the anchor dangle against my skin, against my collarbone. "How lovely, how beautiful. May it always anchor you in
the safe harbor of our family. Do you love it?"

"Yes," I said, my mouth dry.

"Okay, eat that breakfast before it gets cold!" she said. "And
look at these cards—some of your friends wrote to us, remembering your special day."

I forced myself to take one bite, then another. The pancakes
tasted like sawdust. The syrup tasted so sweet I thought I might
get sick. I glanced at the cards. One was a sympathy card from
Jeff—not written to Lizzie, of course, but to her parents. *I still
think of her every day,* he'd written. *And I always will, for the rest
of my life.*

I believed that was true.

After the pancakes were gone, Chloe pushed her chair back,
and I took that as a signal.

"May I be excused, too?" I asked.

"Yes, sweetie. We'll save the rest of your presents for tonight."

"Great," I said.

Chloe headed out to wait for the school bus, and I went downstairs to my room. I stared at myself in the mirror again. I held the
gold anchor lightly in my fingers, fought the urge to rip the chain
off my neck.

The last time I had seen this necklace was on Lizzie, the day
before she died. It had glimmered gold against her ashen skin. She
had worn it for as long as I'd known her, a gift from Mame,
brought back from one of her romantic travels. Other than the
silver ring Jeff had given her, it had been Lizzie's favorite thing—a

reminder of her grandmother, of the fact that the world was so big, that there were other places than right here.

I had figured the Porters had buried her wearing it. She would have wanted that. She had once told me she'd never take it off. It was bad enough she couldn't wear Jeff's ring. She had made him take it from her finger and place it on a chain around his neck, right after the ceremony by her hospital bed, the day before she died. She'd known her parents would have freaked out to see a wedding ring.

And now, staring at myself—a girl with black hair and green eyes, wearing the gold anchor that had once belonged to a beloved grandmother, bought in some faraway port—I saw not Emily Lonergan but Lizzie Porter. I looked at that girl standing there and knew she-I-she was becoming someone else.

After school, Chloe came downstairs to find me.

I was lying on the bed with my notebook open. I wanted to write, but I felt stuck. My insides were churning. I couldn't find the inspiration that had always found me—I'd never had to go looking before. Without writing, without being able to create characters who expressed their feelings (that were really mine), I felt like a cove jammed with debris—fallen trees, sunken boats.

"Come on," Chloe said. "Let's go out."

"'Out'?" I asked. It sounded like a foreign word.

She nodded and held out her hand. I wouldn't take it, but I followed her up the stairs. The parents were nowhere to be seen. We walked out the back door, onto a narrow trail that led into thick woods, the trees bare of leaves. The afternoon was warm with ripples of a chilly breeze slicing through the sunlight. I heard a brook rushing, then saw the thread of silver water spilling over rocks.

"Where are we going?" I asked.

"You'll see," she said.

"Do your parents know about this?"

"I told them we were going for a walk. I didn't say where. As long as we stay hidden, it's okay. Mom's tired of keeping you in the basement."

"How can you go along with them, Chloe?"

We walked along in silence for a while, dead brown leaves crunching under our feet. Then she stopped short and wheeled around. Her face was bright red. Her green eyes sparkled with tears.

"I don't have a choice," she said. "You must see that."

I couldn't say a word in response. I used to think all people had choices, but over the last forty-two days, that belief had been wiped out. We kept walking, crossed the brook. My foot slipped on a wet, moss-slick stone, but I caught my balance.

In the distance, beneath the sound of wind whistling through branches, I heard music. At first I thought it was Irish—it reminded me of the Celtic bands my family loved so much. But there was also a country twang. The sound was so sweet, it actually made my heart soar.

The path climbed a hill, then rounded a bend. There in the clearing was a dilapidated hut—basically just a roof held up by stone pillars, no walls. A band of remarkably cool and raggedy-artistic-looking kids perched on milk cartons and bales of hay, playing instruments. And I knew them—or had seen them before: Casey Donoghue and the friends he'd been with at the cider mill.

There was that ethereal-looking girl on a fiddle, her wavy strawberry blond hair cascading down her back, wearing a sheepskin vest over a long yellow-print dress; the dark-haired boy playing guitar, his head bent low in concentration as his fingers flew over the strings; the stocky boy with shaggy red hair and beard, wearing a T-shirt that said MERLEFEST and playing an odd-looking guitar with a large silver disc where the sound hole should have been; and Casey in his torn jeans and barn jacket, his turquoise eyes seeming to scan the sky, coaxing heart-piercing sounds from his mandolin.

Drawn by the magical strains of music, I started walking out of the trees toward the hut. Chloe gripped my wrist.

"We can listen, but we can't talk to them," she said.

"Do you know them?" I asked.

"Casey, of course. The others, no. They go to the high school; they're older than me," she said. "They're a bluegrass band, and they practice here almost every day."

"What's the name of the band?" I asked.

"Sapphire Moon. I don't know that much about them. They're Lizzie's age. Your age. I just like coming out here."

We sat on the ground, in tall, dry grass. I watched as Casey's fingers danced over the mandolin strings, tickling and chopping them into a cool, thumping melody. The girl's fiddle tugged at every emotion I'd ever known. One guitarist played a rhythmic bass line and the other made this haunting, sliding sound. All four voices harmonized, rising and combining, high and low, singing the song:

> *Last night I dreamed of the mountain*
> *And our cottage in the dell,*
> *And I dreamed a love story,*
> *Of the girl I knew so well.*

I tapped my knee in time to the beat, feeling a combination of unbelievable bliss and sorrow. I heard true love in the lyrics, and the feeling resonated deep inside my chest. I wondered who I felt it for. I wished it was for a boy. I tried matching it to Dan Jenkins, but that didn't feel right.

Maybe it was for my family.

For my sisters.

For Lizzie.

For myself—the girl I used to be.

I had no clue. Instead I just listened to the band. Had one of them written the song, or was it a folk tune from long ago? I watched Casey play the mandolin. I stared at his beautiful, cloudy eyes and wondered exactly what he could see.

"We'd better go home now," Chloe whispered.

"What happened to him?" I asked, reluctant to leave.

"To who?"

"Casey. His eyes?"

"His mother had some kind of disease when she was pregnant. She was raised overseas and didn't get the right vaccines as a kid, and he wound up with birth defects—vision problems.

I don't know, that's what my mother says. Come on, let's go. She'll be waiting."

She: Mrs. Porter.

As we headed back through the woods, I walked as slowly as possible, to hear the song to the end. Someone in the band began to play a harmonica, its crooked, keening sound adding an extra note of poignancy. Then Chloe and I rounded the bend, and the music was lost.

We entered the house to the disgustingly sweet scent of a baking cake. I wished I was back in the woods, surrounded by the smell of fallen leaves and a clear-running brook, by a song that echoed the yearning in my heart.

That night the Porters sang "Happy Birthday" to me. The name on the cake was *Lizzie*. I blew out sixteen candles, even though I wouldn't actually be that age for two more days.

DAY FORTY-THREE

On the anniversary of Lizzie's death, the day between the birthdays, Mrs. Porter came to my room while I was still asleep. Instead of creeping silently around, she shook me awake. When I sat up in bed, she drew my eyebrows on.

She frowned, stroking the black pencil along the ridge of my brow, just beneath the scrawny over-plucked line.

"It's important you look like yourself," she said. "Every day, but especially today."

"I miss her, too," I finally said.

"The point is to not miss her—but to *be* her. By next year, I hope you'll understand that much better than you have so far. I need you to succeed. For now, you're a disappointment. Get dressed."

"Where are we going?"

"You'll see."

It was barely dawn, a thin line of orange shimmering through the trees. Back into the minivan, where Chloe and Mr. Porter waited for us, down the Porters' thickly wooded driveway, onto the main road. Next thing I knew, we were on the highway, and by the time the sun came up, we were crossing the Connecticut state line.

We were on the way to Black Hall to visit my grave. Well, Lizzie's grave. I felt like two girls, half one, half the other. The Emily part of me had been fading away, but right now I was totally awake, on high alert. What if we'd come here so Mrs. Porter could do something terrible to my mother?

This was my hometown. Whichever girl I was, I had lived here all my life. Each sight was equally familiar to Lizzie and to Emily. The graceful white church painted by so many famous artists—the American Impressionists who had come here over a hundred years ago, pulled by the beauty of the beaches and woodlands. I stared at the sea captains' houses, the golden salt marsh.

The salt marsh stabbed the Emily part of me in the heart—
this was where Mrs. Porter had walked with my mother and
Seamus and first shown me the knife. I stared out the car window, wondering if I'd see a woman who'd lost her daughter,
walking her dog. But today the path was empty.

We stopped at the Black Hall Garden Center. I waited in the
minivan while the Porters shopped. Why didn't I bolt? I was held
in the back seat by invisible chains. I was frozen in place; if I
didn't move, my mother would be okay. We'd get through this.
Summer flowers were long gone, replaced with rows of potted
chrysanthemums. The shades were autumnal—maroon, burnt
orange, vibrant yellow—and when Mr. Porter placed two large
plants in the back of the minivan, they smelled dusty.

The cemetery was set along the banks of Blackbird River, one
of five rivers in our town. Sunlight glinted on the water. Wind in
the branches sounded like the whispers of ghosts. It was late fall,
and I remembered past All Hallows' Eves, when my friends and I
would visit the oldest graves, some from the 1600s. We would
light candles and ask the dead to come forth.

We hadn't called these sessions séances, but that's what they
were. Lizzie and I had memorized the names on the most ancient
headstones: Ada Lord, Matthias and Penitence Morgan, Charles
and Letitia Griswold. We would sit cross-legged on the ground,
ask them how they had died, whom they had loved, what they
missed most about life.

We had asked them to tell us about the afterlife.

We had never really gotten answers. That's when I had written
my play *Ghost Girl*. It was inspired by Ada Lord. The dates on

her headstone, worn down by time and weather to spidery script, were 1698–1714. She had been sixteen when she'd died. Across the cemetery, in a grove of pine trees, was the grave of Timothy Lathrop, also dead at sixteen, but a hundred years later: 1814.

My English teacher Mrs. Milne had loved the play, and had encouraged me to work with the theater club to produce it. And we did. I played Ada, and Dan Jenkins played Timothy. We met as ghosts. On nights of the full moon, we rose from our graves and were given our lives back until the moment of sunrise. In the last scene, we stood on the banks of the Blackbird River. The sky was lightening in the west. Lizzie worked the stage lights, to create a rose-gold glow. Timothy kissed Ada, and then he walked into the river and Ada returned to her grave.

"When your first kiss is a stage kiss," Lizzie had said afterward, teasing me.

Now I wondered if it would be my only kiss.

As we drove down the hilly dirt road through the cemetery, I closed my eyes and remembered the beautiful song I'd heard yesterday. I wasn't sure how, but suddenly I knew Casey had written it. I imagined the feeling of his lips on mine. Was that weird, dreaming of a kiss, surrounded by death and mourning? But I couldn't help it.

Mr. Porter slammed on the brakes. The minivan screeched to a halt. I craned my neck to see what was happening. There was a crowd gathered around Lizzie's grave. Kids from our class held candles. My heart stopped: They must have gotten time off from school, to remember Lizzie. Jeff stood by the headstone, his head bowed. I thought I caught a glimpse of Lizzie's ring on the chain around his neck. I saw Tilly McCabe pushing her sister Roo in her wheelchair alongside Newton, Roo's boyfriend. Dan was there, too, right next to Lauren Kingston. He had his arm around her waist. Gillian was in the past, and obviously so was I.

Tilly spotted the van. She pointed at us, said something to the others, and they waved, started hurrying in our direction. When the group began to break toward us, I saw that it wasn't only classmates: There were parents and teachers, too. There was my mother. There were Bea and Patrick. I nearly flew out of my skin.

"Fix this situation, Ginnie. It will look strange if we drive away," Mr. Porter said.

"Back up, John," Mrs. Porter said. "Chloe, run over and meet them, stop them from coming closer."

Chloe was out of the van like a shot, slamming the door behind her. I lurched across the seat, grabbed the door handle. My family was right there—this was my chance. I opened my mouth to yell for help, and Mrs. Porter wriggled between the two front seats and pulled my hair so hard my head smashed the headrest. She slapped my face.

"Duck down," Mr. Porter snapped at me. Mrs. Porter had now wriggled her way into the back seat beside me. Fingers still tangled in my hair, she tightened her grip, shaking my head, making every nerve in my scalp scream with pain. I didn't care—I was going to get away from her.

"You idiot," she hissed. "You stupid girl. You really don't get it? You don't believe I'll kill your mother here and now? I don't care if everyone sees. It will take me ten seconds to get to her, and her life is over. You want that?"

My body froze. Mrs. Porter violently tugged a fleece blanket from the pocket behind the driver's seat and thrust it at me.

"Cover yourself with this," she said. She started tucking it over my head, but before it fell over my eyes, I saw her touch her jacket pocket, weighted down with the knife. That's all it took. She didn't have to say another word.

I heard Tilly's voice: ". . . a vigil for Emily and a memorial for Lizzie . . ." Then Bea—her voice breaking, making my heart crack in half: "I can't take it—I just want Emily to come home . . ." Then my mother, her voice low and gravelly: "Ginnie, John, I'm so glad you're here. Our two girls . . . here, take my candle. I'll get another."

I screamed. Not out loud, but in my head. In my mind I tore out of the van, ran faster than I ever had in my life, grabbed my mother, and got her to safety. But Mrs. Porter was right there with her now, she'd stab my mother in the heart before I could take two steps.

My body was so tense, a sheet of ice, I thought I'd shatter. *Be okay, be okay, Mom.* At least I knew the red shoe had come from her closet, not off her body.

She's going to kill you; she's going to murder you.

Was I talking to myself or my mother? I prayed to the cemetery ghosts to surround my family and protect them.

My mother's voice sounded strong, steady, not drunk. Now my fantasy changed, and I imagined my father yanking open the car door, rescuing me. I felt Patrick and Bea holding me tight, creating a shield between me and the Porters. Then I heard the sound of Mrs. Porter's blade crunching through muscle and bones, saw my mother lying on the ground.

Being in Black Hall felt unreal, a nightmare, full of nothing but threats and dangers. I checked out. I didn't exist anymore, not in life as I used to know it. I was a lump on the minivan floor, and I merged with the blanket, and the gold anchor necklace of my dead best friend lay against my skin. A song filled my mind, a mantra, until I dissolved into the lyrics, the melody, the bright strum of a mandolin:

> Last night I dreamed of the mountain
> And our cottage in the dell,
> And I dreamed a love story,
> Of the girl I knew so well . . .

The music entwined with my breath and my heartbeat, an invisible thread connecting me to someone, pulling me north. If I wasn't here, if I did what the Porters wanted, my family would be safe. I listened to Casey's music and stopped feeling the hot tears burning my cheeks.

DAY FORTY-FOUR

Emily's birthday. My birthday. There was no cake, there were no presents.

We were back in Maine. For the first time, I knew the name of the town where we lived. I'd seen the sign as we'd driven over the covered bridge spanning a stream: ROYSTON, POPULATION 656, WASHINGTON COUNTY.

"It seems obvious they've accepted the story about you running away," Mrs. Porter said to me that morning, as we sat side by side on the living room sofa. "That is very good. You'll send another email soon, but not yet. It's important you stay lost."

Emily Lonergan, lost girl. That could be a new play: *Lost Girl*. But who would write it? Lizzie wrote poetry. Emily had been the playwright. And whoever I was, or was becoming, I was still too stuck to let creativity, in whatever form, flow.

"I've changed my mind about you," Mrs. Porter said. "The trip to Black Hall proved that we can trust you."

I choked down shame and rage. I hated her for threatening my mother, and I hated myself for not screaming while my parents had been so close. All those brave saints whose names my siblings and I had chosen—I was nothing like any of them. I was a coward.

"It's time we enroll you in school," she said.

I couldn't believe my ears. My heart began to thump. "Seriously?"

"I've already talked to the high school, given them Lizzie's records. In fact, if you hadn't butchered your eyebrows, you would have started two weeks ago."

"But what about the last year?" I asked. "Lizzie wasn't in school." Because she was dead.

"I've already told you, that day at the cider mill, don't you listen? Pay attention. You've been in Europe, staying with your grandmother, attending school as an exchange student. We've laid the groundwork. There are rules, of course. We don't talk about the past, and we don't try to return to Black Hall."

"I know that." I spoke quickly. I didn't want to hear the words again; I didn't want her to touch the knife pocket.

"Then we're clear, sweetie," she said, hugging me to her. She wore floral perfume, but beneath the scent, I smelled something dead and swampy, as if she was rotting inside.

"When can I start?" I asked.

"A week from Monday," she said. "After Thanksgiving break. That will give you a little more time to reflect on what you must do, how you must behave when out of the house. On your own."

I stared at her.

"What do you say?" she asked.

"Thank you," I said. I'd gotten a birthday present after all. In nine more days, I'd be going to school again. I'd be out of the prison.

"Go outside now," she said. "Casey is on his porch. He'll be in your class, and you have to be convincing as Lizzie. You're going to have to explain why you haven't started school since first meeting him."

"What will I tell him?"

"That you picked up a virus while traveling. That it was contagious and very serious." She paused. "He'll accept that. His vision problem was caused by a virus his mother caught and could very well have prevented. Of course, the reason you got sick was that you were far away from me. I couldn't do anything from here."

I nodded.

"Remember: Be convincing. That is the only way this will work. In time, I won't have to give you these little tests."

"Okay."

She patted my head.

I walked slowly downstairs to change from my nightgown into Lizzie's skinny jeans, black T-shirt, and fawn suede jacket. I pulled on her black ankle boots. They had silver chains, motorcycle-style, across the front. Checking the mirror, I still, as always, felt shocked to see myself. I felt weird in her clothes. I picked up the kohl pencil, darkened my reddish eyebrows to look Lizzie-black, made sure the beauty mark was drawn clearly in the exact right spot. I adjusted the anchor necklace around my throat. I made my way back upstairs. Mrs. Porter was loading the dishwasher. She pointed at the kitchen door, and I walked through.

Casey sat on the top step of his house, playing his mandolin. The notes were from the song I'd heard in the clearing. I slowed my approach, to listen a little longer, but he turned toward my footsteps.

"Hey," he said.

"Hi," I said. "It's . . ." I wanted so badly to say "Emily."

"Lizzie," he said. "I know."

"I don't want to interrupt you playing."

"It's okay," he said. "C'mon, have a seat."

I sat beside him. He was so tall and lanky, his legs went on for a mile. In spite of the cold air, the sleeves of his faded blue corduroy shirt were rolled up, his forearms taut with lean muscles. His face was narrow, with sharp cheekbones and a long nose. He watched me with those turquoise eyes.

"Are you feeling better?" he asked. "Your mom said you were sick; that's why you haven't been to school yet."

"Yes, I'm fine," I said. "It was . . . nothing really serious. What's that song?"

"It's called 'Take Me Back,'" he said.

"It's beautiful," I said. My mouth was dry. I couldn't tell him I'd been singing it to myself since I'd heard it, that it had helped me survive the trip to Black Hall. "Who wrote it?"

"I did," he said. "You've heard it before, right? When my band played it?"

"How did you know I was there?" Chloe and I had been hiding, and even if we hadn't been, how could he see us? Then I felt embarrassed—it seemed impolite to assume anything about his vision, even though Mrs. Porter never failed to mention it.

"I heard you," he said. "You and Chloe, behind the trees."

"What were we saying?" I asked, trying to remember, sliding a glance toward the Porters' house, half hoping he'd heard the truth.

"I couldn't make out the words," he said. "You were too far away. But I recognized the tone of your voice. From talking to you at the cider mill."

I held my real thoughts inside, knowing Mrs. Porter was watching.

"Well, your music is beautiful. You write amazing songs," I said at last, meaning it.

"Thanks," he said.

"I wish I could write." I held back the part about how there was nothing like being kidnapped to give you writer's block.

"My mom said everyone has a talent. It's just a matter of finding yours."

"I agree with her," I said. "She must be proud of your music."

"She's not here anymore," he said. His face turned red, the blush starting in his neck, spreading into his cheeks and forehead. His mouth tightened into a straight line. "She passed away," he said.

"Oh, I'm so sorry," I said, feeling disingenuous because I already knew. Loss shimmered between us. I wanted to spill everything to him, missing my family, my best friend—Lizzie—dying. But I stopped myself: I was Lizzie now. "What was your mother's name?" I asked.

"Sinead," he said.

My heart leapt. "Irish?"

"Oh, yeah," he said. "As Irish as they come. Grew up in a house ten miles from any town in County Kerry. My dad comes from Dublin. Urban boy and country girl. He played rock on Grafton Street; she worked on her family's farm and played traditional music in the west. They met at a music festival in Dingle—his band was headlining, and she was selling honey at the fairground. They got married a month later. He loved her so much, he never went back to Dublin. He gave up the city, and they had me."

"How did they wind up in Maine?" I asked.

"Long story," he said, "but she inherited this house from a distant aunt. My dad figured the States were a good place to hit the big time with his music, and she thought . . ." He paused. "There'd be better medical care for me here than the rural place they lived. She knew she could keep bees anywhere."

"Medical care?" I asked.

"Yeah," he said.

"What's your full name?" I asked, feeling so soothed by the Irish family connection, and before I thought about it, the rest of my reckless question spilled out. "Confirmation name and all?"

He laughed. "Patrick O'Casey Anthony Donoghue. O'Casey was my mother's maiden name, so Casey's what they always called me."

"My brother is named Patrick," I blurted out, then clapped my hand over my mouth.

"A brother?" he asked. "I thought it was just you and Chloe."

"I'm kidding," I said, blushing with panic. "Anthony's your confirmation name?"

"Yeah. For the saint who restores sight to the blind. I took it to make my mother happy; she never stopped hoping I'd be able to see better someday. She made sure I had the best doctors, but her real faith was in St. Anthony. When things got rough here—financially, I mean—she wanted us to move back to her hometown."

"You said Kerry?" I asked.

"Yes, she lived near Slea Head, this really remote and rugged area. Cliffs over the sea. Her grandmother tended the clocháns— these small ancient stone huts built in the shape of beehives."

"Like those?" I asked, pointing across his yard.

"Yes," he said. "Only big enough for the hermit monks who lived there, probably starting in the twelfth century. And shaped differently. The traditional way in Ireland was to use skeps, curved like parabolas. But that style," he said, pointing, "is more modern, makes honey collection easier."

We stood up and walked over, looked at the ten-inch square boxes.

"That's where the frames go? Where the bees build their honeycombs?" I asked.

"You know about how that works?" he asked, a touch of curiosity in his voice.

"From my old school," I said. "We had an apiary there."

"Cool," he said. "Bees were a big part of our family's life, both in Kerry and here. My mom's family made a living tending the hives, selling the honey. My mother learned when she was a girl. My dad's band had one big hit, but after that, well, music is a very competitive business, and the money stopped coming in. My mom supported us with the honey."

I thought of how much that sounded like love to me. Mrs. Porter had said Casey had had a bad mother; then again, she'd said the same thing about my mother, too.

"Did she have a stand here at the house?" I asked.

"Yes," Casey said. "I'd help her collect the honey after school, take turns running the shop with her."

"You have one of those beekeeping suits?" I asked. Mr. Vibbert was our school beekeeper, and I pictured him in the white jumpsuit that reminded me of an astronaut, with elbow-length leather gloves and a broad-brimmed hat with a veil.

"I did," Casey said. "But I haven't worn it in a long time. The bees went away. She died in September of last year, and they left just before winter."

Those words hung in the air. I pictured the bees flying out of the hive in a swarm, a thousand workers leaving with their queen.

Perhaps scouts had flown ahead, to find a new location, perhaps a hollow tree, to start their new settlement.

"St. Anthony must have heard her prayers after all," I said, hearing the sadness in his voice. "To allow you to see well enough to work in the hives, not get stung."

"I guess he did." Casey paused. "I have some vision," he added. "From what I understand from friends, it's kind of like seeing shadows. No colors. Some shapes—enough so I don't walk into a tree." He paused again, and smiled. His teeth were crooked, a fact that tugged my heart a little more. "I don't think I can miss what I have never seen," he went on. "I see fine. Missing my mother, that's different. She was real. She was the best."

I thought about that. I'd tamped down my feelings so hard, but hearing his words made me feel like a geyser, about to boil over with missing everyone I loved.

"So, you sound like you're Catholic, too. What's your confirmation name?" Casey asked me.

"Emily," I heard myself say—a lie, because it was really Bartholomea. But I found myself wanting him to know at least a vestige of the truth, of who I really was.

"That's pretty," he said. "I'll have to write a song about an Emily."

I nodded, my palms sweating and my heart skittering.

"Well, I'd better get back," I said, hoping he didn't hear my voice quavering.

"I'll see you soon," Casey said.

I turned to leave, then stopped and faced him. "Where did the bees go that winter?" I asked.

"I don't know," Casey said. "Somewhere warm, I hope. A wildflower field. Hives kept by someone who loves them."

He picked up the mandolin, and as I ran through the yards between his house and the Porters', I heard him strumming and plucking a happy, skipping tune, singing these words:

Hey, Emily,
You talked to me,
And now you've walked away.
Hey, Emily,
Come back to me
And sit again someday.

I stopped under a sycamore tree, its trunk scrappy with bark that looked like torn paper. I listened to him play, amazed that he could write those words so quickly, waiting to hear the next verse. But there was only an instrumental; he must have been working the lyrics out in his mind.

Mrs. Porter stood in the kitchen door, watching me. I forced myself to wave and I started to run again, as if I actually wanted to get back "home."

Home. I realized that Thanksgiving was coming, and the following Monday I would go to school. It would be my first Thanksgiving without my family.

I wondered how I could possibly find anything to feel thankful about.

Before I entered the Porters' house, I glanced back toward the beehives. They had reminded Casey's mother of home; she had brought a little Kerry here to Maine. She'd taught Casey the skill she'd learned as a young girl, and Casey didn't have to tell me that the reason the bees went away was that she had died. I knew, from the way he talked, how close he and his mom had been.

That's how family was supposed to be: closeness and caring no matter what.

My throat ached, and I tried to swallow past the huge, choking lump of tears. I had never felt so far away—from my family, my home, myself. I could barely catch my breath.

I wondered what had happened to Casey's mom, how she had died.

Then I pictured the bees wafting through warm air, in a sunlit wildflower field filled with daisies and asters, brambles heavy with raspberries, clumps of wild sage and mint, with a beekeeper in a big white hat and veil, a soft Irish voice with a Kerry accent, and I could breathe again.

In an odd way, thinking about the bees, about Casey and his mother, gave me something to feel thankful about.

CHAPTER NINE

DAY FIFTY-THREE

Going to school used to be the most normal thing in the world. Just like writing your name, tying your shoe, riding your bike: After a while, you don't even think about it. But preparing to start at Royston High reminded me of my first day of freshman year. Then I had worried: Would I fit in? Would I make a mistake? Would people like me? Only now my worries were slightly different. What if someone figured out I was an impostor? What if I let something slip and Mrs. Porter killed my mother?

Looking through Lizzie's closet, trying to figure out what I should wear, panicked me. I was overwhelmed by the dark and chic wardrobe. I wanted to look like myself, my actual colorful and dorky self.

"Quirky," Lizzie would have corrected me. "Don't put yourself down by saying 'dorky.'"

"I mean it as a compliment!" I'd say.

"Trust me, it's not," she'd say.

And while I'd feel grateful that she saw me as cooler than I really was, I also felt a little offended. Most of my clothes were hand-me-downs from my sisters and in some cases brothers, but

I had my own style. I assembled my outfits with care and pride. I loved to wear my cherry-print shirtwaist dress with a white patent leather belt, dark green tights, red Chucks, a baggy hand-knit Irish sweater, and a Red Sox cap.

Today, as Lizzie, I wore cropped black wool pants, a gray turtleneck, and a midnight-blue jacket with a big brass diagonal zipper. Everything was too body-hugging. Lizzie's wardrobe didn't include items that were not form-fitting, that were baggy enough for my comfort level.

Staring at myself in the mirror—the black hair, green contacts, and the little birthmark and perfect eyebrows—I knew I was wearing a costume. And not one that I would have ever in a million years chosen myself.

"You look lovely, sweetie," Mrs. Porter said when I sat down at the kitchen table.

"Thanks," I said, staring at my plate of scrambled eggs.

"Eat up," Chloe said. "It's a big day!"

I nearly laughed. I heard the sarcasm in her voice, but I was sure her parents didn't. It was a sibling thing, being able to detect undercurrents. As much as I wanted my own sisters and brothers, I had to admit it was comforting at least to have Chloe.

"I'm actually not hungry," I said at last.

"Everyone's nervous the first day at a new school," Mrs. Porter said. "But you need a good breakfast to keep you centered."

To not lose it, she meant. *To not forget who you're supposed to be.*

"She's right," Mr. Porter said. "You've got to be ready to rock and roll, to be as excellent as you always are."

He so rarely said anything to me. From the very beginning, I'd figured having me here wasn't something he even wanted. It was pretty obvious he was just going along with his wife. When I glanced over at him now, I saw a glimmer of encouragement in his eyes. Was he talking to Lizzie or Emily? Referring to her excellence or mine? Since those first few days, he never called me by name. Either way, I reluctantly welcomed his encouragement.

I forced myself to eat a few bites of eggs before Chloe jumped up and grabbed her backpack. She threw me a glance, then handed me the black leather satchel Lizzie had always carried to school.

"Come on, we've got to catch the bus," she said.

"Now listen," Mrs. Porter said, standing in front of me, holding my face between her hands. "I thought about driving you but decided it's important you blend in right away. We're in a rural area, and everyone takes the bus. Don't disappoint me, promise?"

"I promise." Did I have another choice?

"I might take a ride past school throughout the day, just to make sure you're settling in. I wouldn't want to see . . . well, anything out of the ordinary. Police cars, for example."

"You won't," I said quickly.

She kissed my forehead. "I know. I trust you. I shouldn't have even mentioned it. Now, have a great day, sweetie! I'll be waiting right here at 3:30."

Chloe and I walked out the front door, across the front yard, and down the narrow, twisting country road. I looked for Casey, but he wasn't at the bus stop. He wasn't aboard when we climbed on, but I noticed the bearded boy from his band sitting behind the driver. Chloe squeezed my hand, then hurried to the back of the bus to sit with some kids I hadn't seen before. I sat alone, about midway back, feeling everyone's eyes on me. No one said hi, but their faces looked friendly.

The bus ride twisted along roads I'd never seen before. I pressed my face to the glass, looking at farms and barns, rocky hills, glimpses of blue saltwater bays, just like a tourist. At the next stop, a girl my age got on and plunked herself down in the seat beside me.

I glanced over. She had dark brown skin and big brown eyes. She was studying me.

"You're new!" she said.

"Yes," I said.

"We never get anyone new. This is great. I'm Carole."

My voice caught in my throat. Besides Casey, I hadn't spoken to anyone but the Porters in over a month. She was a total stranger, and I wanted to grab her by the lapels and start pouring my heart out. My whole body was shaking.

"I'm . . ." My teeth were chattering as I forced myself to say the name. "Lizzie."

"Oh, yeah, now I've got it. You're the world traveler. Been all through Europe."

I couldn't speak. Mrs. Porter had mapped out a whole, lovely lie for me to tell, and she'd spread it around, and all I had to do was carry it forth.

"Yes, I just got back." The words sounded so phony, I nearly gagged.

"Are you feeling better?" Carole asked.

"Better?" I asked, my mouth dry.

"It must have been awful to be so sick, far from home."

"Oh, you knew about that?"

"There are no secrets in this town. Everybody knows everything," Carole said.

"Really?" I asked, thinking if only she knew.

Carole's glistening black hair was twisted up into a knot. She wore a maroon down jacket, navy leggings, and pale blue Uggs with little grosgrain bows lacing up the back. "Sophomore, right?" she asked me.

"Yes," I said. "But starting two months late."

"I'm in your class. I'll help you out if you need it." She pulled out her iPhone. "Let me text you so you'll have my number."

"I forgot my phone," I said quickly. This could be a major problem. How could I tell people I didn't have a cell phone? Everyone had phones. It was killing me that I didn't have mine.

"Here you go," Carole said, writing her info down in her notebook, tearing out the page, and handing it to me. *Carole Dean*. She was so open, so friendly, and I was such a liar. I was a complete fake, not a real person at all. I couldn't even look her in the eye as I accepted the paper with her phone number on it.

The bus pulled into a circular driveway in front of an old stone Gothic-looking mansion-type building. The doors opened and we all got off. Carole walked ahead of me, toward the wide, curving granite steps of the school. I followed her, but Chloe caught up and grabbed my arm.

"You okay?" she asked.

"I think so," I said.

"Carole's nice," Chloe said. "And her mom's our doctor. Mom had to make an excuse about why they didn't take you to her when you had your 'virus.'"

"What's the excuse, in case she asks?"

"That Uncle Jim treated you."

"Who's Uncle Jim?"

"Mom's imaginary brother who's an imaginary doctor. He cleared you to start school."

I shook my head. Nothing surprised me anymore.

"I'll be right next door. That's the middle school," Chloe said, pointing at a low modern brick building across the parking lot. "We share the cafeteria, so depending on which period you get lunch, I might see you then."

"Don't worry, Chloe. I've got her back," Carole said. I jumped hearing her voice. Had she been listening? No, she'd just circled back to walk me inside.

Chloe surprised me by giving me a quick, hard hug. Then she ran away, and I walked with Carole into Royston High.

I missed first period to fill out papers in the office, see the nurse, and make sure the Porters had sent in my medical records and immunization forms—filled out by James Renard, MD. Uncle Jim. I met the principal, Mrs. Amanda Morton, a small woman with wavy brown hair and friendly gray-blue eyes that reminded me of my mother's. She wore a green tweed dress and one of those gold necklaces with birthstone charms, each representing a child. Mrs. Morton's had three; my mother's necklace had seven.

"I've seen your school transcripts," Mrs. Morton said, "and I know you'll have no problem catching up. If you need help, just ask. We'll get you a tutor."

"Thank you," I said, wondering what records she had seen, how the Porters had managed to fill the gap and concoct report cards from the year after Lizzie had died.

"How are you feeling?" she asked. "We expected you at the start of school back in September, but your mother has been filling us in all along. I'm sorry to hear you've been so sick."

September? Wait—if the Porters were already telling the school about me back then, it meant they had been planning to kidnap me for months. Was that why Mrs. Porter had been in the marsh in August? No wonder it had felt so strange to see her. Had she been waiting for me? Planned to take me if I'd walked closer? Had the kidnap plot already begun? A gigantic chill came over me, and I couldn't even speak.

"Lizzie?" Mrs. Morton asked. "Are you okay?"

"I'm fine," I managed to say.

"I hope you'll tell us about your travels," she said. "They sound amazing! My family went to Paris last year. Did you go there?"

"Um, yes," I said.

"Your mother tells me you're quite a poet. Living abroad must have inspired you. It would be fantastic if you could share some of your experiences with the school." She smiled and explained, "Each month we have a program where students present topics and speak about their experiences. Perhaps you would be willing to do one of the next presentations. It would be a unique way for us to get to know you. A poetry reading, coupled with some thoughts about what it was like to attend school in Europe?"

Filled with panic, I could barely nod.

She walked me to my second-period class. Our heels clicked on the polished floors.

The walls were paneled in rich brown mahogany, carved with family crests and Latin mottos. There were no windows in the hall. The only light came from amber lamps on ornate brass sconces. All the classroom doors had intricately tooled doorknobs and stained glass windows, some set with crystal orbs. Beside each door was a painting of a cat—the same one in different poses. The plaster ceiling, at odd intervals, was inset with tiles of thistles and bundles of wheat. It felt spooky, more like a witches' academy than a regular high school.

I wanted so badly to be back home, in my own school, the bright, cheerful, familiar corridors of Black Hall High, with the Apiary, where I'd study and get mesmerized by the dance of the bees. I wanted to look up and see Bea and Patrick and all my friends nearby, to hope that Dan would appear.

We walked past the library. Beside it, instead of a cat painting, was a gold-framed painting of a severe-looking, long-faced woman in a high-necked dress, her black hair held back in a tight bun and a cameo at her throat.

"That's Sarah Royston, for whom the town and this school were named," Mrs. Morton said. "She owned a large paper mill in the 1800s. It was very unusual at that time for a woman to be so independent—wealthy and powerful in her own right. She has a very interesting story. I hope you'll want to learn more about her."

"I do," I said. I felt desperate to say something else, to beg for help, but what if Mrs. Morton didn't believe me? She could call Mrs. Porter, and it would be all over. My chest nearly exploded, holding the words inside.

"Here we go, this is your English class," Mrs. Morton said, stopping beside a door whose painting had the cat sleeping.

Just before we entered the room, I noticed Casey at the end of the hall, talking animatedly to the beautiful girl from his band. I held back, tempted to watch, but I had to follow Mrs. Morton inside.

"Ms. LeBlanc, students, meet Lizzie Porter," Mrs. Morton said in a loud voice. "She is new to Royston, and I know you will make her welcome."

Almost everyone smiled and applauded. I walked to a seat in back, shoulders hunched and my face bright red. Our principal in Black Hall would never have done that. He would have let the new students make their own way, take their time, not embarrassed them.

The worst part was wearing Lizzie's sleek black clothes. They made me look as if I cared too much about fashion, as if I held myself above everyone else. Is that how I'd felt about Lizzie, deep down, put off by her obsession with style that veered into vanity? With a shock I realized it was, at least partly.

While Ms. LeBlanc talked about allegory in Edmund Spenser's *The Faerie Queene*, my mind took me back in time. I pictured Mrs. Porter sitting on the driftwood log. I saw the light glinting on her hair, the easy motion when she'd lifted her hand to wave to me. I smelled the marsh—that unmistakable low tide odor of mud and dead crabs and sea creatures exposed to the air. I felt the summer sun on my shoulders. Why had I pretended I hadn't seen her? That was so unlike me. I'd thought it was because of her sorrow—of mine, too—over Lizzie. But maybe some ancient part of my brain had sensed danger. She'd been watching for me—now I was sure of it.

Why else would she have told Mrs. Morton, all the way back in September, that her older daughter was traveling, would start school later in the year? And why did it make me feel even worse, even more scared, to know that taking me had been premeditated that far in advance?

The world have seemed safe back then, but I'd been wrong. I'd thought I had control, choosing that path through the woods, but that had been an illusion. Even though I had dodged being kidnapped that summer day, Mrs. Porter's plans were in motion.

I started shaking. I forced myself to stop thinking of August. Instead my mind wandered to Casey, and I wondered what he and the girl had been talking about. His hand had been against the wall, his arm braced. She had been standing close to him, in the crook of his shoulder. It seemed obvious they were boyfriend and girlfriend.

But something in their intensity had made me think they were arguing. Casey's tall body looked tense, as if with anger or frustration. The girl had lightly tossed her long, magical red-gold hair. She wore a mid-calf white muslin dress. Although the scowl on her face hadn't quite matched its radiant glow, it occurred to me Spenser's title *The Faerie Queene* could very well apply to her.

I tried to remember the lyrics Casey had sung to me. But my mind couldn't find them, and eventually I began to concentrate on class. I heard Mrs. LeBlanc and the kids I didn't know discussing the character Lady Una, the wizards Archimago and Busirane, the kidnapping of Amoretta, how Duessa had betrayed the Redcrosse Knight to the giant Orgoglio.

Faerie Land was a strange world full of danger. But not as strange, I thought, not as dangerous, as the one I was living in. I sat in my chair shimmering. I felt like air, as if Emily had evaporated. I kept glancing out the tall leaded-glass windows, and twice I saw the minivan drive by slowly; Mrs. Porter's head was swiveled toward the school, on alert for trouble.

When Chloe and I walked through the door after school, Mrs. Porter was waiting for us with hot cider and freshly baked gingerbread cookies. Chloe grabbed the snacks and went straight to her room. Mrs. Porter set a place at the kitchen table and gestured for me to sit.

"Tell me about your first day," she said. She looked eager, expectant, a little afraid of what I might say.

"It was fine." After English class, the day had gone by in a blur. I'd had history and French with Carole, the nice girl from the bus, but that was all I'd really managed to pay attention to.

"Really?" Mrs. Porter asked. "Did you like it?" I could tell the question was genuine. She seemed to honestly care.

"It's . . . not that easy."

She nodded. "New schools never are." She reached across the table and took my hand. We sat there for a minute before I pulled away.

"What about questions? Was anyone too nosy?"

"Mrs. Morton asked about Europe. She wants me to do a presentation about my time there, and I don't even know where I'm supposed to have gone."

"I'll give you the list," Mrs. Porter said. "And you can memorize it."

"But I've never been there! I've never even left the country," I said.

"I have travel books in my room; I should have given them to you before. What else happened? Were there any other problems?"

"Carole Dean wanted to give me her number. But I didn't have a phone of my own. People will think that's weird."

"Thought of that," Mrs. Porter said, smiling. She went to the kitchen counter, opened a drawer, and pulled out Lizzie's old iPhone. "This is for you." She handed it to me. My mouth dropped open.

"Thank you!" I said, shocked.

"I've removed the battery and the SIM card," she said. "You'll have the phone itself, but you'll have to pretend to enter numbers. When people call, you can say you've forgotten to charge it."

"Please," I said. It was as if she'd given me the biggest hope, then smashed it to bits. My heart broke open, the words poured out. "Let me go home."

"You are home."

"Did this start in August?" I asked. "You saw me walking and called my name—is that when you first decided to take me?"

"You thwarted me that day," she said. "You should have come with me then. You could have started school in September, with the rest of your class, and avoided all this awkwardness. It would have been so much better."

"It would have been just as bad!" I said. "This is *wrong*. I can't stay here, pretending to be Lizzie, Mrs. Porter. It's a lie. And I miss my family so much."

With a deep sigh, full of what sounded like genuine regret, Mrs. Porter pushed her own phone across the table toward me and pressed PLAY. It was a video of the scene I'd viewed before: Mrs. Porter and my mother in the marsh—the same path I'd been walking in August—Seamus bounding along the path. I heard my mother's voice. I saw the quick, surreptitious glint of the knife.

"Do I have to continue to remind you?" Mrs. Porter asked. "I need you to be my daughter. I've told you. My heart is broken. Don't break it again, please. I don't know what I'd do if that happened. Well, yes—I am quite sure of what I'd do. And you know, too, don't you?"

I nodded.

"There's something else," she said. "It's very important. I don't care if I get caught. It matters nothing to me—if I wind up in jail it will be worth it. That's how serious I am. That is how determined I am to make this work. If you tell anyone, if I learn about your betrayal—and I will because I'm never far from you, even when you can't see me . . . If you talk about this, I will go to

Black Hall. Remember how we switched vans, the day you came with us?"

Came with us. As if it had been voluntary.

"Yes," I said.

"I'm resourceful. I won't drive my own car. Look in the mirror—you know I'm good at crafting disguises. No one's going to recognize me. You saw the shoe. This time I will get to Black Hall in a way you'll never guess. Even if the police are looking for me, I will find your mother. It will be easy. She's drinking again now."

"She's not," I whispered.

"Don't fool yourself. She doesn't have the strength to stay sober after all this, I can guarantee you."

"You don't know her," I said.

"No, you don't know her," she said. "She's weak. And it will be easy to get her alone. Going into your house that night? Easiest thing I ever did. They slept right through it. Me? If my daughter were missing? I would never close my eyes again. Never."

I thought of the way she haunted the house, came into my room. Maybe she never slept. Maybe that was true.

"Your mother won't have the strength to fight back, and in spite of my disguise, I'll make sure she knows it's me. I'll tell her you came to live with us because you couldn't stand being in that house. If the police learn it's me, no matter. I would rather be in prison than lose you."

I believed her. Sheer terror burned through me, singeing my veins. I felt as if my skin had been turned inside out, as if the air and her words were raking every one of my nerve endings.

"Say it out loud," she said. "Call me by the right name."

The word choked my throat. "Mom," I said.

"That's my girl. That's my Lizzie." She hugged me, handed me a gingerbread cookie. "Enjoy your snack," she said. "Then we'll start right in on your European tour. We'll have fun with it. It will be like a mother-daughter travelogue!"

I couldn't take a bite of the cookie. I just stared at it, watching my tears plop down and melt the crystalized sugar on top.

Mrs. Porter inserted the SIM card and battery into Lizzie's phone long enough for me to text Carole at the number she'd written down for me. My thumbs were so happy to be texting for the first time in forever.

Hey, it's Lizzie. This is my number.

Thirty seconds later Carole wrote back.

Carole: Yay! I was starting to think u didn't want to be friends.

Me: Haha of course I did I just have the world's worst cell reception here.

Carole: Because Maine.

Me: Maine?

Carole: Boonies.

Me: Got it.

Carole: U know it.

"That's enough," Mrs. Porter said. "She has your number; that was the point. Now *get off.*"

"We're having a conversation; she'll think it's rude if I stop now," I said, aching with how much I loved texting, how much I'd missed it, even if Mrs. Porter was standing right over my shoulder reading every word.

"Tell her your mother is calling you," she said.

I hated writing that, using that word *mother* about Mrs. Porter. So I didn't.

Me: Sorry, got to go.
Carole: Pssssssshhhh whaaaattttt? Noooooo!
Me: Lol talk later?
Carole: Pce lve ltr

Mrs. Porter held out her hand. She removed the SIM card and battery and handed the empty phone back to me.

CHAPTER TEN

DAY SIXTY-ONE

By early December the ground was covered with snow. Mrs. Porter had pulled Lizzie's winter clothes from the attic, and every day I went to school wearing her long black cashmere coat and knee-high black leather boots. They weren't warm enough for Maine, and there wasn't enough room in them for thick socks. My toes were always frozen.

On the two-month anniversary of the day since I'd been taken, I was sitting at the breakfast table, preparing for a history quiz and tuning out the TV droning with its cheerful morning shows.

"Oh my God," Mr. Porter said. "Ginnie . . ."

We all looked up, and there I was on the screen. The show was doing a recap of how Emily Lonergan had gone missing eight weeks ago, how after that first email to her family there had been no more communication. Mr. Porter grabbed the remote and changed the channel. But another show was doing a feature on how a parent's addiction could turn a child into a runaway, how alcoholism could tear families apart. Other stations questioned whether Emily's email had been genuine. Could it have been coerced or even fake?

One of the shows ended with a video clip of me I hadn't seen before, but I remembered the day exactly: Iggy had taken Patrick, me, and Bea to Gillette Castle, high on a cliff over the Connecticut River. William Gillette, an actor known for playing Sherlock Holmes, had built it in 1919, and named it Seventh Sister.

"You're the seventh kid in our family, and you're our sister," Iggy's voice said as the camera captured me standing on the parapet, the ice-choked river winding behind me.

"So it must be my castle!" I said. Bea entered the frame and jostled me. We walked through the heavy wood door into the hall, decorated with evergreens and red bows for Christmas.

"What do you want for Christmas?" Iggy's voice asked.

"A white pony and for us all to be together," I said. "As usual. Duh!"

"Duh," he said, and the clip shut off and went back to the sad-eyed, perfectly made-up newscaster.

"With the holidays approaching," the newscaster said into the microphone, "will there be another message from Emily? Or is the mystery of her disappearance something much more sinister?"

"It's time for you to send another email," Mrs. Porter said as I started gathering my books for the school day.

"An email is not enough!" Mr. Porter said. "Ginnie, this is falling apart. We can't keep pretending . . ."

"'Pretending'? Don't let me hear that word!" Mrs. Porter said, sounding truly anguished.

"Okay, okay. But don't you see?" he asked, walking over and trying to hug her. She shook him off. "I told you, if they start looking for her again, they could easily come here and question us. We have to think about that possibility, what we'll have to do. Having her out in the world is disaster waiting to happen."

My shoulders were tense, brittle as glass. I was "her." He spoke about me as if I wasn't there, as if I was just a figment of their imaginations. What was the alternative to "out in the world"? Back in the dungeon? Or would they kill me, as Mrs. Porter said she'd do to my mother?

"You've never been with me on this," Mrs. Porter said to him. "I'm all alone; I feel no support at all. I need her, John."

"I know that, Gin," he said, trying to hug her again, and this time she let him. "But come on. I've done nothing *but* support you. I'm doing this for you."

"Then do it all the way," she whispered. "Believe."

That I was Lizzie. Mr. Porter looked over the top of her head, and our eyes met. I saw terrible sadness there, almost as bad as the day of Lizzie's funeral.

"I do. I believe," he said. His voice sounded genuine, but the lie showed in his face.

"Okay, then," Mrs. Porter said. "We need a plan."

"Let's keep her home from school today. Just till the missing girl stories die down," he said.

"She's brand-new at school—that would make her stand out. No, we have to continue as if nothing is wrong, nothing at all. Lizzie, you can do it, right?"

"Yes," I said.

"We'll schedule an email to Mary and Tom," she told me. My parents, but she couldn't call them that. "We don't want it to seem like you've written them in response to these news reports, so we'll do it later this week. I'll come up with something."

I was sure she would.

"Take extra care at school," she said. "Just as your father says, Emily's face will be fresh in people's minds, if they've been watching the news. Be on guard, sweetie." She primped my black hair, twisted the curl around her index finger, stared into my contact-lens-green eyes. My eyebrows were finally growing back, but she fetched the kohl and filled them in some more. She darkened the beauty mark, too. Then she drew her finger along the part in my hair, examining my roots. Seeming satisfied, she nodded.

Chloe had been standing there, in the corner, the whole time. Her face was pure white, and when I looked straight at her, she turned away. We grabbed our coats and left the kitchen. She walked a few steps ahead of me out to the bus. I tried to catch up, but she picked up speed.

"I wish you weren't here," she said under her breath. "They fight over you, all the time."

"I wish I wasn't here, too," I said.

"Before, they were just sad. Now they're angry. Lots of people get divorced after the death of a child," she said. "I never thought my parents would, but since you came, it seems they're heading that way."

"What did your father mean?" I asked. "When he said if people start looking for me again he and your mother have to 'think about it.' What would they do to me?"

"Shut up," she said. "Shut up, shut up."

It was snowing lightly, but as we stood at the bus stop, the wind picked up, and the flakes started to come down hard. I shivered, but not from the weather; I'd seen fear in Chloe's eyes, and I thought it might be because she knew what they'd do.

I tried to calm myself. The falling snow was beautiful and made me think of Lizzie. Her favorite poets all wrote about New England—Mary Oliver, Maxine Kumin, and Robert Frost. She especially loved Frost's poem "Stopping by Woods on a Snowy Evening."

> *Whose woods these are I think I know.*
> *His house is in the village though;*
> *He will not see me stopping here*
> *To watch his woods fill up with snow.*

I wanted the lovely lines and the thought of Lizzie to soothe me, but they didn't. My shoulders still felt like glass. The bus arrived, and from the minute I climbed aboard, I watched for recognition in every face. I couldn't even breathe. I thought I might shatter. Sitting beside Carole, I waited for her to say something about seeing me on TV. Instead, she pulled out her phone and showed me a selfie she'd taken with Mark Benjamin—the redhaired bearded boy from Casey's band.

"How come you didn't text back when I sent you this?" she asked.

"Huh," I said, peering at the photo. "We have terrible cell reception, remember?"

"Because life in the woods, right," she said.

"The picture's really cool."

"It's on," she said.

"What is?" I felt calmer, talking about something as normal as a selfie. It made my heart slow down, and I started to breathe.

"Me and Mark. We've been circling each other since seventh grade, but he finally made his move. Well, actually, I did. I took this yesterday. Which you'd have known if you got my text. Which you would have if we weren't living in the sticks."

"I know. But seriously, you guys look good together."

Carole grinned. "He asked me to come work at his family Christmas tree farm this weekend. Which means staying warm by the fire, oh yeah." She winked, and I made myself laugh. "And that's one step closer to taking me to the Snow Globe Ball, and if he doesn't figure that out, I'm going to have to tell him the way of the world. We're going."

"The Snow Globe Ball?" I asked.

"Yes, the high point of the long, miserable winters we get up here. Man, do I miss Boston. Why, oh, why, did my mom think she had to be a rural doctor and drag me along with her?"

I wasn't the only one to have been relocated here against her will. I felt like saying that moving someplace was a little different from being kidnapped, but I held back.

"The dance planning committee meets after school today," Carole said. "You should come—it's fun."

"I'll miss the bus," I said, imagining what would happen if I got home late.

"We can catch a ride with Casey's dad. He doesn't go to an office, so he usually drives when he's home and there's an assembly or some activity—he'll beat the bus. See you at the meeting, okay?"

"Will Casey be there?" I asked.

"Of course," she said. "His band will be playing at the dance. Mark's in it, too. They're great, and they'll probably do a song or two this afternoon. You've got to hear them."

"Sounds really cool," I said, wondering why I didn't mention I'd already heard them before. Keeping secrets had become second nature, even ones that didn't actually seem to matter.

In English class, I was chosen to read my paper. I had done it on Book Four of *The Faerie Queene,* how Wizard Busirane had kidnapped Amoretta on her wedding day so she couldn't be with her new husband, Scudamour. It was my subversive cry for help: What would everyone think to know that I myself had been kidnapped?

The wedding theme also reminded me of Lizzie. She and Jeff were not officially married. I hadn't had time to sign up online to become a certified ordained minister. But we had performed a ceremony, and the memory filled my mind the entire time I stood in front of the class.

We had chosen the day and time according to when Lizzie's parents would be busy. I knew they had a conference with her team of doctors that afternoon, so Jeff had driven me up to the hospital in Boston, and we entered Lizzie's room. He brought bouquets of white roses—a big one for Lizzie, a small one for me, her maid of honor.

"Hurry," he said as soon as we saw her. She looked shockingly worse than she had the day before.

"I will," I said. I hoped my voice would work. My face was already soaked with tears.

Lizzie in her white cotton nightgown, its collar and cuffs made of delicate lace, her arms, so pale and translucent they looked almost blue, pierced by needles, tubes twirling down from the pole above her hospital bed. Jeff in his father's tuxedo jacket, the one Jeff had worn to the Full Moon Dance. He clasped her hand. She was too weak to squeeze his. They gazed at each other, their eyes liquid.

"Do you, Elizabeth Porter, take this man, Jeffrey Woodley, to be your husband, to have and to hold, through sickness and health, until . . ." I couldn't say the next part. *Until death do you part.*

"I do." Lizzie's lips moved, but no sound came out.

"And do you, Jeff Woodley, take this woman, Elizabeth Porter . . ."

"I do," he said. He didn't even let me finish. Lizzie was coughing. They had put her on morphine the night before, and she kept drifting in and out of consciousness.

"Then by the power vested in me by best-friendship, I now pronounce you husband and wife."

Jeff leaned down, tenderly kissed Lizzie on the lips. He slid the silver ring he had bought onto her finger. She had lost so much weight, she was skin and bones, so the ring was loose on her finger. He crouched beside the bed, holding Lizzie in his arms for a long time. I stood back, turned toward the window, giving them privacy.

When we'd been there half an hour, I checked the time. Lizzie's parents would be finishing up with the doctors, so it was time for us to go. Jeff lingered, unable to let go of her hand. He stroked her ring with his thumb.

"You have to take it," Lizzie said.

"The ring?" he asked, sounding shocked. "But it's yours; it's our wedding band."

"My mother will see it."

"I don't care. I want everyone to know," Jeff said.

Her eyes welled with tears. "You don't understand. It will make things worse for me, for everyone. Please, just do what I ask."

"But I need you to wear it," Jeff whispered. "So you know I'm with you. Forever."

"I do know that," she said. "I love you, my husband."

Then she looked to me, reached out her hand. I took it, and we stared at each other for a long time. "Give it to him," she said.

Then, because Jeff was unable to do it, I gently removed the ring from her finger and pressed it into Jeff's hand.

His face was in a knot, his shoulders tense. As big as the ring was on Lizzie, it was too small for him. He slipped it into his pocket. Then he knelt by her bed again, holding her. They stayed that way a long time, until Lizzie closed her eyes and went to sleep.

We left the white roses. Lizzie's room was full of flowers already anyway. Who would notice two more bouquets?

That was the last time I saw Lizzie. Every time I thought about it I had to bow my head, fight away the grief and disbelief. I shuddered, remembering how I'd thought there would be another time, at least one more chance to tell her I loved her, to hug her and hug her, to hold on to her for a little longer.

Carole had said she was from Boston, and her mother was a doctor. Could her mom have worked at Williams Memorial? Could she have treated Lizzie, maybe even seen me visiting?

Ms. LeBlanc obviously couldn't tell my mind wasn't on my paper, because she gave me an A for the day. Roberta Alfonso and Laurel Jones told me I'd done a good job. There I'd been, standing right in front of the class the same day my face had been all over TV, but no one thought I was anyone but Lizzie Porter.

And I'd spent the whole class remembering her, my best friend.

I nearly didn't go to the after-school meeting, but at the last minute, I saw Casey walk into the assembly room. He was carrying his mandolin case. I could hear the others warming up, so I followed him in.

The intricately carved wood-paneled walls reminded me of Gillette Castle. Apparently this room had been a chapel in Sarah Royston's day. Photos of past Snow Globe Balls hung around the room. About ten kids sat at a long banquet-like table. Roberta waved and gave me a warm smile. Carole had saved me a seat.

"Thanks," I said.

At the sound of my voice, Casey turned. "Emily?" he said.

My heart nearly stopped. "Lizzie," I said.

"I know," he said. "It's just, I wrote that song, and it reminds me of you." But he had a quizzical expression on his face, as if it was more than that.

"Oh, this lady is your inspiration for your new tune?" the bearded guy—Mark—said, walking over. The dark-haired guy who played guitar walked alongside him.

"I've been wanting to meet you," the ethereal-looking girl said to me, her copper hair tumbling down the back of her long, dark red brocade dress.

"Well, you're an exalted senior," Mark said to the beautiful girl. "Lizzie's a sophomore with the rest of us. Lizzie, meet Angelique Millet. You already know Casey, and here's our guitar player, Hideki Sano."

"Hi," I said to the three of them. "I'm looking forward to hearing you play."

"Casey says you already have," Angelique said. Her gaze seemed indolent, but behind her green eyes—Lizzie-green, the color of my contacts—I thought I saw something sharp.

"Well, yes, I mean, hear you again," I said, stammering. "You guys are great."

"I feel massively spoiled I get to play with such dope musicians, my fam-band," she said.

"Spoken by the legendary fiddle goddess," Mark said.

Angelique smiled. "Well, nice to meet you, Lizzie. We're going to whip up some magic just for you. Get ready."

She, Mark, and Hideki headed toward the front of the room and picked up their instruments.

"Your voice," Casey said, hanging back with me, fixing me with those turquoise eyes.

"What about it?" I asked.

"You sound different."

"I'm the same as ever," I said.

"I don't know. It's like all of a sudden you're someone else."

I felt a jolt. Was it possible he'd had the TV on that morning, heard me speaking on the Gillette Castle video with Iggy and Bea? I wanted it to be true, but even more, I felt terrified that it could be. Mrs. Porter saying *I don't care if I get caught* echoed in my mind.

"I'm not someone else," I said.

"Okay," he said, sounding unconvinced.

I instantly changed the subject.

"Mark's guitar looks so different from Hideki's," I said, once again noticing the big silver disc that filled the sound hole.

"It's a Dobro," Casey said. "You'll hear when we play—it makes the sound resonate, kind of sizzle."

Then he joined the rest of the band, and they played, and I did hear the Dobro's crisp tones as Mark played—a metal tube on his little finger sliding up and down the strings. I listened to Angelique's heart-tugging fiddle, Hideki's rich bluegrass tone, and Casey's blazing brilliance on mandolin. The way he sang and coaxed joy from the strings filled me with yearning.

Hey, Emily,
You talked to me,

And now you've walked away.
Hey, Emily,
Come back to me
And sit again someday.

People applauded when they finished. I beamed with secret pride and tingled at the fact Casey was staring straight at me as he sang.

"It's not exactly a holiday song, though," Roberta said. "Shouldn't we be thinking Christmasy for the ball?"

"It's a love song," Carole said, gazing at Mark. "And that's the whole point of the holidays."

"I wouldn't say 'love,'" Angelique said, laughing. "After all, in the song, Little Miss Emily walks away. Right, Casey?"

He didn't answer. She leaned into him, and their shoulders bumped. I saw her brush his cheek with hers, and then give him a light kiss on the lips. "But I will say this," she added, leaning her forehead against his. "You do know how to put a serious soul spin on a person's heart."

"Man, come on," Mark said. "Roberta, you want Christmas songs, you got 'em. Hit it, Donoghue."

"One, two, three," Casey said, and then they broke into "Santa Claus Is Coming to Town." Part of me was glad the Emily section of their program was over. And the rest of me longed, with everything I had, to have it never stop.

When the music was done and everyone was putting their instruments away, I stepped into the hall and bumped straight into Mrs. Porter.

"Well, hello, Lizzie," she said.

"Mrs.—Mom," I said, turning bright red. "What are you doing here?"

"Volunteering at the nurse's office," she said, brightly. "I signed up for two afternoons a week."

"Did you hear the music?" I asked, my voice shaking, praying she hadn't heard the lyrics about Emily.

"No, how disappointing. But I'll look forward to another time. Now, how about a ride home?"

"Carole said Casey's dad could give us a ride."

"Weren't you going to ask me for permission?"

"Can I?"

She laughed. "I'm here now, sweetie. Let's go."

CHAPTER ELEVEN

DAY SIXTY-TWO

I went to the second meeting of the Snow Globe Ball committee, too. That first day, when Mrs. Porter had driven me back, she'd been furious that I'd have driven with Casey's dad without asking her first. But then she said that the more she thought of it, she realized it would be more normal for Lizzie to do regular high-school-type things, like helping to plan a school event, like getting rides home with friends' parents.

So after the second committee meeting, as Carole had promised, Casey's father was waiting outside. He had a rusty black SUV with three rows of seats. The middle seat was patched together with silver duct tape. His smile was kind and welcoming, and he spoke with an Irish accent. He was tall, but about an inch shorter than Casey, and his style reminded me of Casey's, too: His straight brown hair fell below his shoulders, and he wore leather bracelets on his wrists and a big silver wolf ring on his middle finger.

A bunch of us piled into the SUV. I sat right behind Mr. Donoghue, next to Casey. Our thighs brushed. It made me shiver, and I glanced at him to see if it had been on purpose. Angelique was in the seat behind, and she kept sighing as we drove along, every time Mr. Donoghue took a turn.

"The motion bothers me," she said. "I really need to be next to a window."

"Uh-oh, Ange is gonna barf," Mark said. It reminded me of throwing up in the car the day I was kidnapped, and I almost gagged so hard I had to clap a hand over my mouth.

"Are you okay?" Mr. Donoghue asked, glancing in the rearview mirror. For a second, I thought he was talking to me, but his eyes were on Angelique.

"Not really," Angelique said. "I get motion sick and do better with a window."

"Switch with me," Hideki said. He was sitting beside her.

"Being this far back in the SUV makes it really bad for me," she said. "I feel it swaying."

"You can have my seat," I said, trying to be noble.

That was what she'd wanted all along. She didn't even demur. Mr. Donoghue pulled over, and Angelique, without a word or even a thank-you, passed me to sit beside Casey. As soon as she got there, she put her head on his shoulder. I climbed into the last row, sitting beside Hideki. In the cargo space were three Gibson guitar cases and a slightly battered amp.

"Are these yours?" I asked Hideki. The rumble of the tires on the rutted country road drowned out the conversation from the front.

"No way," Hideki said. "I only wish I could own guitars like these. They're Casey's dad's."

"That's right; he plays music," I said, thinking of what Casey had told me.

"That's one way to put it. Haven't you ever heard of Dylan Thomas Revisited? Their song 'Do Not Go Gentle'?"

The tune came into my head. Both Mick and our dad loved the band DTR, and "Do Not Go Gentle" was one of the first songs Mick had taught Dad to play on his fiftieth-birthday Stratocaster. Mick always said the band's front man was a genius guitar player and he was our dad's favorite songwriter. Dad said it was a sin that musical tastes had changed and the band had fallen off the charts. That songwriter was obviously Mr. Donoghue. And Casey had mentioned how the family finances had changed when his success had faded. I wished so badly that I could tell my family about meeting Mr. Donoghue. They would have thought it was amazing.

One by one, we dropped everyone off. Mark got out first, walking down a long drive lined with snow-frosted spruce trees and marked with a banner: BENJAMIN FAMILY CHRISTMAS TREE FARM.

Hideki and Carole both lived about a mile away, on a street lined with Victorian houses. When they got out, I noticed a small sign in front of one beautiful blue house with a steep roof and ornate gingerbread cutouts around the eaves: PAMELA R. DEAN, MD, FAMILY PRACTICE. So, Carole's mother had her office in their home. It felt weird to know she was the Porters' doctor—and therefore mine. I had never loved my pediatrician before—I had mainly thought of him as the man who gave me shots—but in that moment, I felt a pang. Everything from my old life was gone, even Dr. Croft.

When the car stopped next, Angelique didn't get out. She stayed cuddled against Casey, whispering in his ear, letting out that trilling little laugh of hers. Her gaze slid my way, and I reddened, positive her whispers were about me. Or maybe she just wanted me to see that she was close to Casey. Finally, she got up to leave.

Once she did, Casey half turned toward me.

"C'mon up here," he said. "You don't have to sit all the way in back."

"I like keeping the guitars company," I said.

"My kind of person," Mr. Donoghue said, driving off again. "She doesn't want the equipment to be lonely." His brogue reminded me of Glen Hansard's—Bea and I were obsessed with the movie *Once*, about street musicians in Dublin, and it comforted me to hear Mr. Donoghue talk. But it was killing me not to be able to tell my family about him, not to be able to imitate his voice to Bea.

He tuned the radio to a bluegrass station, and we listened the rest of the way home. Outside the car, snow began to come down heavily again. His headlights were on; I saw their bright reflection in the driving flakes. We turned onto Passamaquoddy Road, where our houses were. Before he could stop and drop me off at the Porters' driveway, I spoke up quickly.

"I'll get off at yours," I said. "That way you won't have to pull in twice, and it's right next door."

Mr. Donoghue did what I asked, driving through deep, not-yet-plowed snow, ice chunks crunching beneath the tires. We stopped at the side of the Donoghues's house. When he and Casey started to unload his suitcase, the guitars, amps, and bags of gear, I helped.

Up close, I saw how run-down the house really was. The porch roof sagged, the concrete step was cracked, the paint had almost completely peeled off the shingles. Casey's mother's empty beehives ran in a row along a garden mounded with snow. Again, I felt a jolt to see them—they reminded me of the apiary at school. Mr. Donoghue unlocked the front door, and when we stepped inside, it felt almost as cold as outside. I saw my breath in the air.

Casey walked over to a thermostat; he turned it up, and I heard the furnace click on.

"Good job saving on heat," his dad said. "But keep it up a few extra degrees when it's this cold. Remember the pipes last year?"

"Okay, Dad," Casey said. He went to a cast-iron stove standing in front of a big stone fireplace. He opened the door, stacked a pile of sticks and logs, and lit the pile with a match. The kindling caught and crackled.

I looked around. The room was full of furniture, paintings, books, thick wool rugs, and a long rustic pine bar. There was a stand-up piano in the corner, surrounded by a trumpet, a mandolin, two acoustic guitars, and one electric guitar, all set up on stands and ready to be played. Things were a little shabby, but in a cozy, well-loved way.

"Thanks," Mr. Donoghue said, gesturing for me to put the guitar cases near the other instruments. "Not a bad week in New York, but it's great to be home."

"How'd it go, Dad?" Casey asked.

"Pretty good. We sold out the pub half the nights. Not the biggest take we've ever had, but better luck next time. We sure could have used a good mando player, though. Jamie is retiring, and I swear, in his heart he's halfway left the band. You know what that means," he said to Casey. "There'll be a spot for you."

"After I graduate," Casey said. "I'm joining for sure."

"Well, two and a half years till then. Four years of college after that. But I'll wait, buddy. That's the reason I do these gigs."

"I know, to pay for my college. I'd rather have you home," Casey said.

"Well, then think of the electric bill, and the heat, and . . ."

"I get it, Dad," Casey said. "Sorry."

"It's okay," Mr. Donoghue said, and I thought I saw strain in his face. Were they really hard up for money? He turned to me then, and smiled. "How about you? Are you a musician?"

"No," I said. "Far from it. I have no musical talent. But I love to listen."

"Everyone has music inside them," Mr. Donoghue said. "It's just a matter of letting it out, young lady . . . what is your name?"

"Sorry, Dad," Casey said. "This is Lizzie Porter."

"Nice to meet you, Lizzie."

"You too," I said. "My dad loves your music. He thinks your band name is amazing—Bob Dylan meets Dylan Thomas."

"Oh ho!" he said. "Cool. He never mentioned it, and I never pegged John for a bluegrass guy."

My stomach dropped. I meant my real dad. What if Mr. Donoghue said something to Mr. Porter now? I tried to think fast, to come up with a way to cover my mistake. "Um, I thought Dylan Thomas was Welsh, not Irish," I said.

"It's true, but Wales is just a ferry ride from Ireland—it always felt like home when I played there. And Casey's mom started reading him *A Child's Christmas in Wales* when he was one. So, the band name was in her honor." He paused, bowed his head for an instant, then looked up, smiling at me. "C'mon. We'll get you playing something. Just a few notes before you go home."

"I really should go."

"Call your parents. They'll say it's fine."

"I forgot to charge my phone."

He handed me a landline. Reluctantly I dialed. Mrs. Porter answered.

"Hi, Mom," I forced myself to say. "Um, I'm at Casey's."

"I know you are," she said. "I saw Sean pick you up at school, and I watched you go into the house. I'm sure you're behaving."

"I am," I said. "Is it okay if I stay for a little while? To listen to music?"

"A little while," she said.

"Thanks," I said.

"Which instrument do you like?" Casey asked as soon as I hung up.

"All of them," I said, looking at the shining brass, the burnished wood. But one stood out for me—it made me think of Mick and my dad. "Guitar," I said.

"Use this one," Mr. Donoghue said, taking a rich golden Gibson acoustic from its stand, thrusting it into my hand. "It's the first guitar I bought with my own money."

"Thanks, Mr. Donoghue," I said.

"Ha," he said. "That makes me feel old. Call me Sean. Everyone does."

Right; that's what Mrs. Porter had called him. "Sean," I said, trying it out.

Casey had lit the stove. Flames rippled from the rolled-up newspaper to bundles of oak twigs, catching the split logs, throwing a wall of heat into the room. He walked over to get his mandolin. He moved gracefully, sidestepping a sofa and low coffee table.

"How do you do it, get around so well?" I asked. I felt embarrassed to ask the question, but the way Casey had called me Emily, not even knowing it was my real name, had broken the normal barrier I'd feel asking something so personal.

"Shadowlands," he said. "That's what my vision is like. I can see shapes, anything big. It's the small things I miss. Like, I can see you, the actual you—shoulders, arms, the fact you have long hair." When he said that, he reached over and lightly brushed the ends, his fingers tracing my shoulder. "But I can't see the color, or your face. Or what you're wearing."

I think I levitated. If he couldn't see Lizzie's clothes, her black hair, her green eyes, that meant I didn't have to be in disguise with him. He was talking to me, Emily. If he could have seen my face in that instant, he would have witnessed the biggest grin— the only real smile—I'd had since being taken.

"Let's see how you hold the guitar," he said.

"But you play mandolin."

"My mother taught me guitar first."

"That's right," I said. "You said she played in Kerry."

"Definitely. Her grandmother told her music would inspire the bees to make more honey. So she'd sit on a rock near their hives and play songs."

"Did it work?" I asked.

"It did, yes. They worked faster than we could collect it. So, come on, let's see what you've got."

I wanted to hear more about his mother, about the bees. I had my left hand on the neck of the guitar, my right hand ready to strum. Casey reached over, helped me place the fingers on my left hand on the strings.

"First, the strings," he said. "From the fattest to the thinnest, from low to high: E-A-D-G-B-E. Just think, 'Eat A Darn Good Breakfast Every Day.' 'Day' is an extra word, but you get the idea and the saying will help you remember."

I plucked each string individually, hearing the clear note. It made me feel proud—my first thought was I couldn't wait to show Mick. He had once promised to teach me, but we were so far apart in age, he was always busy with older-brother things. Then I remembered I couldn't show him now. Or maybe ever.

"The vertical spaces between the fine metal lines on the neck are called frets," Casey explained. "Chords are triangles. You put your fingers on three different strings at the correct frets, strum, and you have a chord. Go ahead."

The metal strings dug into the soft pads of my left fingers, surprisingly sharp, and I let go.

Casey smiled. "You need calluses. You'll get them, the more you practice. Just take it easy now, let me hear you."

I nodded and strummed harder than I'd intended.

"That's an E chord," he said encouragingly. He readjusted my finger pattern on the neck, and I strummed again with slightly more control.

"There—an A."

He showed me D, which was a little harder, an E minor, which was really easy, and a C and G, but by then I got mixed up, trying to remember everything, and by the movement of his hands over mine, his warm breath on my cheek, and the way he closed his eyes when I strummed each chord.

"You're getting it," he said.

"I have a long way to go," I said.

"Not really," he said. "Our songs are really simple, with a typical chord progression, A-E-D."

"But the melodies are so much more complicated!"

"Well, we riff on them, and Hideki completely slays on guitar solos. And Angelique's fiddle always takes the song somewhere else completely."

I hesitated, going back and forth on whether or not I should ask, but I had to know. "Are you two going out?" I asked, trying to sound casual.

He was very quiet for a minute. "No," he said after a while. "We used to."

"I thought, by the way she wanted to sit with you . . . that you were, or that she wanted to."

"She broke up with me," he said. "So I don't really think that's the case."

She wants you back, I wanted to say, but I had the feeling he didn't want to talk about it anymore.

"I'm sorry if I said the wrong thing," I said. "If I reminded you of being hurt."

"It's been since the summer," he said. "It was bad back then, but I'm over it." The way he said it so fast made me wonder if he really was. "How about you? Are you with anyone? From before you came here?"

"No," I said, thinking of my unrequited crush on Dan. "Not at all."

"It's funny," he said. "Earlier today, when I said your voice sounded familiar in a different way?"

"Yeah?"

"I was almost going to ask, are you on the run?"

"The what?" I asked, my spine freezing.

"There was something on the morning news," he said. "A girl who went missing, maybe ran away. It caught my attention, because her name is Emily, and I thought of the song. That's probably why, when they played a clip of her talking, she sounded like you. Crazy, right?"

"Crazy," I said. My voice came out in a croak.

"My mistake," he said. "I tend to listen extra hard—I guess because I love music so much and, I don't know, to make up for other things. You and that girl really do sound alike."

"What a coincidence," I whispered, almost afraid to have him hear and register my voice.

"Yeah," he said.

All I had to do was let the truth spill out. We could tell his dad, the police cars could arrive silently so Mrs. Porter wouldn't hear.

But she saw everything. Shadowlands, Casey had said. I knew what he meant. Mrs. Porter lived in my mind, and she existed in reality, too—constantly in the shadows just out of sight. I was positive she was watching out the kitchen window—or maybe she was hovering just outside the Donoghues's house, behind the sycamore tree, eyes trained on me now.

Wind whistled, coming through cracks in the door, making a loose shutter clunk against the house—boom, boom, boom, over and over again. The stove had started to heat up, and the furnace was humming in the basement, and Casey was sitting so close beside me.

I had the feeling that if he looked at me right then I would tell him everything. And he did—he glanced over. I opened my mouth, but no words came out.

"Are you okay?" he asked.

I couldn't nod, I couldn't shake my head, I couldn't move.

"Are you that girl?" he asked, frowning. The question hung in the air between us. Seconds of silence ticked on. I tried to shake my head no, but I was frozen. Finally, as if he thought he must have sounded foolish, he gave me a hesitant grin. "I'm so sorry. Of course you're not," he said. "You wouldn't be living with the Porters if you were."

Casey went back to music. I practiced the chords. A-E-D, A-E-D, over and over. He hummed along at first, then picked up his mandolin and began to play, so it actually started to sound like a song.

I concentrated on the triangles, my fingers on the strings until my breathing calmed down and I was pretty sure my heart wouldn't fly out of my chest.

I made up lyrics in my head—is this how it was for Lizzie, writing a poem? I didn't know. For that moment, I was myself again: Emily Lonergan. I had no idea what Lizzie would hear in the melody, but running through my mind, in time to the chords, were the words:

> *You heard my voice, you know my name,*
> *Lizzie and I are not the same,*
> *I wish you could look at me and see*
> *I'm Emily, I'm Emily.*

"I want to show you something," Casey said after we had played for a while. He replaced our instruments in the stands. Then he led me down the hallway to the kitchen. Everything was old-fashioned: a yellowing enamel stove, a refrigerator with a motor that hummed as if it were about to give out, a big farm-house sink.

A framed photo of a young woman and a little blond boy hung over the long oak table. The woman's hair was dark, cut very short. They were holding hands standing in front of the beehives, beaming at the camera. I recognized Casey right away. He looked about six years old, and his hair was curly and much lighter, but he had the same mesmerizing turquoise eyes. I knew that the woman was Casey's mother, and I could tell by the way they smiled that they loved the person taking the picture, and I knew that was Casey's father.

Casey opened a door at the kitchen's far end, and we walked into a small room. It was dark. I couldn't see. He reached overhead, pulled a cord that turned on a light, and I nearly gasped.

We stood in a room of gold. The walls were lined with shelves, floor to ceiling, and each contained jar after jar of honey. The colors ranged from deep amber to pale lemon, with every shade of yellow in between. A corner of one shelf held a frame still loaded with honeycombs. I stared at the waxy hexagonal cells, knowing that Casey and his mother had extracted the nectar from them. One cell contained the remains of a dead bee, its black-and-yellow body preserved in wax.

"This guy didn't make it," I said.

"There's always loss," he said.

Did he mean in the world of honey, or in life? Either way, I agreed, and I nodded. The room was small. The jars were sealed, but the air smelled sweet. Was it from the sugar? I was standing so close to Casey, I caught the scent of his soap. He was tall. The top of my head came to his collarbone. I wanted to stand on tiptoes and bury my face in his neck. I tilted my head back to look up at him.

He leaned down slightly, his warm lips brushing my forehead.

"This is my favorite place," he whispered.

"It's a magical room," I said. "I can feel your mother here."

"So can I, but I didn't mean the room. I mean standing next to you."

My heart flipped. He reached for my hand, linked fingers with me. I stood taller, our faces nearly meeting. Distant, from within the house, I heard voices. I froze. Footsteps, and people talking, Mr. Donoghue and a woman. Casey and I stepped apart.

When I saw their faces peek around the door, I wasn't surprised. It was as if I was expecting it.

"Hello, Casey," Mrs. Porter said. "Hi, Lizzie."

"Hello," Casey said.

"Lizzie, I need you home," she said. "Sorry to break up the party."

"Here," Casey said as I walked out of the room, pressing a jar of the darkest honey into my hand. I glanced at the handwritten label: *Wild Thyme.*

"Your mother's writing?" I asked.

He nodded.

"Yes, that's Sinead's," Mr. Donoghue said.

"Oh, I wish I could have known her," Mrs. Porter said, taking the jar from my hand. "You must miss her so."

And then we were in our winter jackets, saying good-bye, walking out the back door into the driveway. She waited until we were away from the house lights; then she marched a few steps ahead of me, not saying a word. I felt the anger pouring off her back. When we rounded the bend into the drive, she smashed the jar down onto the ice-covered craggy rock ledge. I watched the precious nectar ooze into a shallow granite gully, then coagulate in the freezing cold.

"I don't want that in our house," she said. "She was a bad mother, a horrible mother. That stuff would only remind me of how unfair it is, how terrible people think they can get away with everything, how life is just handed to them."

"She died," I said. "Life was taken from her. And I don't think she was a bad mother. She loved Casey."

"Not as much as I loved my daughter," Mrs. Porter said, her voice rising, then breaking. She crouched down as if she'd been kicked in the stomach. Her shoulders heaved with sobs.

"I'm sorry," I said, kneeling beside her, putting my arm around her shoulder because, in spite of everything, I couldn't bear to see her agony.

"I just wanted you home," she said through thick tears. "That's why I went to get you. I'm sorry about the honey. The strongest feeling just . . . came over me. I began to think I can't trust you. That's such a horrible feeling, Lizzie. You can't even imagine."

My whole body tensed because I knew how dangerous her strongest feelings could be. I saw the broken glass from the jar glinting in lamplight filtering through the trees from Casey's house. The edges were knife-sharp clear blades. The honey looked as if it had frozen solid, just like the blood in my veins.

CHAPTER TWELVE

DAY SIXTY-FIVE

Hello. It's me, and I'm fine. You might think I have problems, or whatever, but I don't. Mom, you're the one with the problem. I hope you get help. I love you all but I am doing great without you, so don't worry. Emily.

That was the note Mrs. Porter wrote for me, four days after the two-month-anniversary news stories. I typed it, and I sent it. My whole body was fluttery, like my goose bumps were on the inside, because suddenly I had hope. Unwittingly, Mrs. Porter had handed me a secret clue: I would never say *or whatever.* The phrase was one of my pet peeves.

When Bea was fourteen and Lizzie and I were thirteen, my mother dropped the three of us off at the mall to go Christmas shopping. The parking lot was so full she couldn't find a spot. Or maybe she just wanted to keep us in the car a little longer. We kept driving up and down the rows.

"Look at all these cars," she said. "All the out-of-state plates."

"Mom, we're not on a road trip," Bea said. Whenever our family drove long distances, we'd play a game to see if we could spot all fifty states.

"No. But a major interstate highway goes right by here, and there's the Sub Base in Groton, with Navy people from all over the country," Mom said. "Someone could take you, whisk you away, and we might never find you."

"You're really not being fair to the Navy, but we'll be careful," Bea said.

All I wanted was to get out of there so Lizzie and I could run to the food court and see who was there.

"We'll watch out for strangers and creepy types," I said.

"We promise," Bea said, hand on the door handle, ready to bolt to meet James.

"Listen to me," my mother said. "It's not the suspicious-looking ones I'm afraid of. It's the friendly Santa Claus. Or the lady with pretty blond hair, in a blue coat, with a cute puppy on a leash. Maybe even someone you know. Someone familiar, who looks nice. *She's* the one who you have to watch for."

I was pretty sure my mother had been drinking that day because when she said *she's* it came out "sheez."

Bea, Lizzie, and I finally escaped and tore into the mall.

"The lady in the blue coat!" Bea said.

"Ha-ha, that's so random I'm crying," Lizzie said.

"Raise your hand if buffalo wings have had a positive impact on your life," I said.

Lizzie and I both raised our hands, and finally got to the food court, where bunches of Black Hall, Niantic, and Waterford kids had taken over tables. We sat with our friend Jordan and her boyfriend, Eric Milne, plus Tilly, Alicia, Monica Noyes, and Miguel Santos. James wasn't there yet, so Bea sat with us.

Lizzie and I fortified ourselves with buffalo wings and cheese fries, and Bea swiped a wing. Jordan nibbled around the perimeter of a black bean veggie burger.

"When you're a vegan and haven't mentioned it in the last hour," Eric said.

"You're so ignorant it should be illegal, or whatever," Jordan said, leaning over to kiss him.

Bea made a gag face. Jordan said *or whatever* constantly, and it annoyed us; it made her sound as if she was negating the thing she had just said.

Holiday music surrounded us, putting us in the mood to spend all our money on stuff. Bea's and my lists were longer than anyone's—no one else had six siblings.

Just as I was taking a perfect bite combination of wing and blue cheese, Bea leaned forward.

"This is not happening," she said.

"What?" Lizzie asked.

"Do not turn around," Bea said.

But of course we did, and carrying their trays to the table right next to us was a guy with a buzz cut and a blond woman in a blue coat.

"Is this even real life, I feel like I'm on the set of a horror movie," Lizzie said.

"Or whatever," Bea said, and I laughed so hard blue cheese went up my nose.

Sitting in the basement bedroom, running the email I had just sent over and over in my head, I came up with two gigantic hopes and sent the strongest, most powerful vibes I could to Bea and my mother:

1) That Bea would tell my parents how much I hated and would never under any circumstances but coercion say the phrase *or whatever.*

2) That Bea or my mother would remember the story about the nice, familiar blond lady in the blue coat, and even though Mrs. Porter didn't have blond hair, we had always thought she was nice. And she was definitely familiar.

And there was a third hope, too.

It had to do with Casey. I went upstairs, pretending I wanted a snack. I took an apple and ate it while standing at the kitchen window, looking toward his house. It was much easier to see, now that the leaves were off the trees. The moon had risen, casting a ghostly glow on the big old place. Smoke wisped from the chimney, dissolving in the clear air.

The living room curtains were open, and I could see him sitting in the same spot where he had started teaching me guitar. He held the mandolin, head bowed as he picked the strings.

Was he playing the "Emily" song? Was he still trying to figure out whether he'd heard my voice on the TV? I knew I could never imagine what that was like for him. He'd said something about his other senses being sharpened. I closed my eyes and tried to pay more attention to my own. When I did, the apple tasted more intense. I felt heat rising from the radiator and warming my arms. I smelled gross beef stew cooking for dinner.

And I heard music.

Across the yards, through the window glass and distilled by the cold winter air, the strains of mandolin notes filled me. Yes, he was playing "Emily." Yes, he was thinking of me. With my eyes still shut, I pretended that he knew exactly who I was and would save me. I hoped and wished he would help me get away without Mrs. Porter knowing.

He would help me get home.

DAY SIXTY-SIX

Sunday was a double day.

That's what Patrick called any day with the same numbers— like June 11, September 22, the 33rd day of summer, our grandparents' 55th anniversary. He believed double days were lucky, but I didn't feel that way. Today was the sixty-sixth day since I'd been taken.

Sending the email had given me hope, but that hope was lost this morning. My family would never notice the *or whatever*, and the rest of what I had written would just make them feel worse. I imagined the Porters whispering about what they would have to do to me. Mr. Porter had barely looked at me since that day of the news stories, since he'd asked his wife that question. I felt as if he wanted to stop thinking of me as a person; I was just a problem.

Late that morning, the landline rang.

"Oh, hello, Carole," Mrs. Porter said. "Yes, just a minute." She handed me the phone.

"Hello?" I said as Mrs. Porter stood right there listening.

"I've totally given up texting you since you never get my messages, so I got your family's landline number from my mom," Carole said. "Want to meet up?"

"Meet up?" I asked, watching Mrs. Porter's reaction. She nodded with a head tilt as if waiting to hear more. "And do what?"

"Go to Boston and escape the woods, ha-ha, but forget that. Want to come over?"

"Uh," I said. Then, to Mrs. Porter, "Can I go to Carole's?"

"Have her come here," she said.

An hour later, Carole's mom dropped her off. Mrs. Porter hurried out to the car to talk. She hadn't worn a jacket, so she stood in the driveway, arms wrapped around herself against the bitter cold. I heard laughter, and it struck me—it sounded as if she and Dr. Dean were friends.

I hadn't quite imagined Mrs. Porter having any friends up here. How was actual friendship possible when you were living a lie?

Carole and I made grilled cheese sandwiches—the best kind, fried in a skillet with butter, the bread soft and the crusts crispy brown—and ate them in the living room in front of the TV, watching the first *Mockingjay* on demand. I couldn't pay attention. Carole was a bigger fan than I was, plus I felt weirded-out sitting with her on the same couch where Lizzie and I had watched the exact same movie together.

The furnace rumbled on and off; the house got claustrophobic, so we decided to go outside. Mrs. Porter stood at the window pretending to do the dishes but actually watching us. The snow was deep. Out by the road, the plows had left piles that were taller than we were.

"Snow fort!" I said.

"Never built one," she said.

"You're kidding."

"City girl, baby. I grew up on Beacon Hill. We probably would have stayed in Boston forever if my parents hadn't gotten divorced. Then my mom had to do the independent-woman thing and relocate here."

"That's a pretty cool thing to do," I said. "But it must have been hard, leaving your friends."

"Massively," she said.

"Me too, from when I lived in Black Hall before." I could say that because it was a true part of the Lizzie story.

I ran to the garage, grabbed two shovels, and handed one to Carole. I had excellent snow-fort technique, taught to me over my entire lifetime by older brothers and sisters. Tommy had shown us how to cut hard-packed snow into cubes, pile them up in a square. Mick had instructed us how to tunnel through short-enough sections so we wouldn't get buried if the fort collapsed. Anne used chunks of ice and stray icicles to build castle-like crenellations and window ornaments, and Iggy was great at using the shovel handle to carve out precisely arched windows at eye level. Patrick, Bea, and I built snow chairs and tables inside and stockpiled snowballs in case of attack.

"This is beautiful," Carole said, admiring our work when we were done. "Like a sandcastle, but in the snow."

"If there was a neighboring fort, we could have a snowball fight," I said.

"Well, the only neighbor is Casey Donoghue," she said. "I'm sure he'd love it, but he wouldn't see well enough to hit us."

"Do you know what happened to his eyes?" I asked, looking toward his house.

"An infection when he was a baby," she said. "It was rare, came on really fast, and even though his parents took him to the hospital right away, some damage was done."

"I thought it had something to do with his mother not getting good medical care, not getting vaccinations or taking care of herself, when she was pregnant with him," I said, remembering all the things Mrs. Porter had said.

"That's ridiculous," Carole said. "She was an awesome mom. She did everything possible."

Once again, Mrs. Porter's craziness shone through, her skewed vision of what a mother should be, of how she was the only one who truly measured up.

"You and Casey seem close. I can't help noticing," Carole said.

I smiled and couldn't help blushing, lightly tossing a snowball at her. She threw a big, fluffy clump up in the air, and powder sprayed down on us.

"Look at his house," she said. "It's so sad, the way it's gotten."

I stared at the elegant old place: the tall windows, the porch columns. One black shutter on the second floor hung loose on a broken hinge, creaking and slamming in the wind.

"After his mom died, their honey business did, too," I said.

"Yeah, she was an incredible person. She was super talented, nice to everyone, ran the whole show. His dad being a musician, and all." She sighed. "Artists don't always notice mundane things like falling-apart houses. See, I get that, and I feel sorry for Casey. Did I mention my dad is a sculptor?"

"No," I said.

"He has pieces in the Guggenheim, the Whitney, the Tate Modern, but he didn't know how to change a lightbulb. Or maybe he just didn't notice the hall was dark. He's famous, and mostly sweet, but my mom got tired of doing everything." Carole paused. "I mean, she's a doctor, it's not like she has all this free time. So they broke up. Now that we live a million miles away, they're friends—he visits every few weeks, they go out to dinner. It's so *contrary.*"

"That sounds really hard. I'm sorry."

"Yeah, I look at families like yours, so tight and together, and it kind of kills me—not that I'm not happy for you."

Like mine. "Thanks," I said, my stomach twisting.

"Casey has it harder than I do. I thought divorce was the worst, but having your mom die—I can't even imagine."

"He said she died in September, a year ago," I said.

"I know, it's so sad. He's missing her so badly, and just think of all the things he'll do in life that she'll never know about," Carole said. Lizzie came to mind, and I felt a rush of sorrow.

I wanted to ask Carole how Casey's mother had died, but she went on. "Did he ever tell you why they moved to town?" she asked.

"He said they inherited the house."

"Okay, you know about Sarah Royston?"

I remembered the woman from the portrait at the school. "The one the town's named after?"

Carole nodded. "Well, she was originally from Ireland, too, and it turns out she was Mrs. Donoghue's great-great-aunt. Sarah had one daughter, Nora, who didn't have any children, so when Nora died—she was ninety-nine—she left this house to Casey's mom. That's why the Donoghues came to America."

"But I thought Sarah Royston lived in the school building," I said, staring at Casey's house.

"She did until she had this conversion, later in life. She turned that big mansion into a home for wayward girls—that's what they actually called it: the Royston Home for Wayward Girls. Girls who got pregnant, or were abused, who ran away, whose parents couldn't afford to take care of them, who had to leave home for whatever mysterious reason—she gave them a place to live. And she built this house for herself and Nora."

"Girls who had to leave home," I said, the words making me feel hollow.

"That was Sarah's story," Carole said. "That's why she had a soft spot for girls who couldn't live with their families. She was forced to leave her home in Ireland."

"Who forced her?" I asked, my skin prickling.

"You've asked the right person," Carole said with a smile. "I did my term project on her last spring."

"Tell me," I said.

"Her parents were dirt-poor, starving in the Famine, and needed money, so they sent her to America to work in the mills. They had a deal with Edward Sheffield—the mill owner—that she would work for him until she was twenty-five, and he'd send most of her wages back to her family in Ireland. Supposedly for her future."

"She had no choice?" I asked.

"No. And it was really hard—standing in a sawmill with gigantic logs barreling down the river, below zero temperatures, no safety standards at all. People got cut by the saws, trapped between logs, even killed." Carole paused for breath. "He was evil—he paid the lowest wages around, and he punished the workers. He beat them, withheld their pay. But Sarah was so smart, she figured out a way to make the production line run faster. Because she was making him so much money, he moved her into the office."

"Big of him," I said.

"Yeah, but wait! She took care of the books, convinced the state to run train tracks all the way to the mill so they could ship lumber all over the country. But one day Eddie-boy was down by the river, overseeing a wagon filled with logs from Canada, and he just disappeared."

"He died?"

"Everyone assumed so. He was never seen again. And since no one else knew how to run the mill, Sarah took over and wound up owning the place the year she turned twenty-five. Cosmic, right?"

"Completely. I wonder what happened to him."

"The official word is that he slipped into the river, and the current washed him out to sea. But I've always thought maybe . . ."

"What?" I asked, my spine tingling.

"Well, that Sarah . . ."

"Fought back," I said.

"Exactly."

"Do you think he attacked her or something?" I asked.

Carole was silent for a moment. "My mother says there are different ways of attacking. If you take away a person's freedom and choices, that's a type of violence. When that happens to you, you're not going to stay docile forever. There's always an uprising."

"But Sarah was just one woman."

"You think a woman can't rise up?" Carole asked.

Those words, that one question, filled me with fire.

I thought of Sarah Royston—had Edward Sheffield driven her to a point where she couldn't take it anymore? Had she waited for her chance and pushed him into the river? What would it take for a person to turn violent? I tried to imagine myself reaching that point. What would I do to protect myself, to win back my own freedom? I could never hurt someone; I was sure of it.

But there were other ways of fighting back.

As I contemplated that question, I saw Carole pack a snowball and whip it toward a row of winterberry bushes. A second later, one came whizzing back. I craned my neck, hoping it was Casey.

But Chloe's head poked up over the hedge, pelting us as we returned fire.

"No fair, two against one!" Chloe said.

"You started it," Carole called.

"If you have a fort, you have to expect invaders. You're soooo easy to spy on!" Chloe shouted, lobbing another snowball.

I jumped the fort's wall and ran toward her. We met halfway, tackling each other, into the snow, laughing so hard it reminded me, just for a minute, of how it felt to have a sister.

All three of us were freezing cold. The sky turned deep lavender, the color just before dark when the first planets appear in the west and Orion rises above the eastern horizon. We trudged back to the house, feeling good-exhausted. It was such a relief to forget about everything for a minute.

When Carole texted her mom, she raised her eyebrow at me because she had fine cell reception right here in the spot where I never did, and thirty minutes later, her mom arrived to drive her home.

After dinner, I went down into the dungeon, and that's when something remarkable happened. I almost wondered if I'd imagined or dreamt it, if the spirit of Sarah Royston had somehow cast a spell over me, had entered my life just when I needed her most.

I lay down on my bed, arms folded behind my head, looking up at the ceiling. There was the fan with big white blades, the same one that had hung over Lizzie's bed in her room in Black

Hall. The steeple clock chimed seven. I noticed the bell sounded deadened, as if the striker had caught on something.

Standing up, I went over to investigate. The clock was about fifteen inches tall with two sharp spires on either side of a pointed roof. A glass door with a small brass knob covered the clock's face; clear on top, the glass was etched with a colorful wreath of holly on the bottom. The door could only be opened with a key.

As if I knew exactly where to find it, I turned the clock around and there, taped to the back, was a tiny skeleton key. It fit into the lock perfectly. I had never thought to look in here before, but this was the first time I'd heard the clock ring in such a dull, muffled way.

When I turned the key, the glass door opened.

I heard myself gasp.

Here were Mame's photos and letters, jammed into the small space. The corner of one envelope had slipped between the chime block and rod. My hands shook as I pulled the letters and photos out. I scattered them onto the floor, looking for the cell phone, but it wasn't there. Still, I felt I'd been given a gift, treasures from Mame—a woman I'd loved, who'd cared about me as if I were her own granddaughter.

I spread the photos and mail out on the bed. There were pictures of Mame with Hubert in France, in Gaillac in Languedoc, the hometown of my patron saint Emily de Vialar. There were photos of Lizzie and me when we were little, on day trips with Mame to the carousel in Watch Hill, the ferry to Orient Point, Newport's Cliff Walk.

The letters from Hubert: the love letters that had sustained Mame during his illness and death, when she'd missed him so terribly. Each was written on fine white onion skin stationery, the envelopes emblazoned with his monogram and the French tricolor flag.

But there was one envelope that had Lizzie's handwriting. It shocked me to see my best friend's writing, so clear and plain, as if she had written to her grandmother just days ago, as if she was still alive. I turned it over in my hand, raised it to my face hoping for her scent. It smelled only like paper.

I had a sudden lightning-bolt feeling these letters and photos had not been here before today, that Lizzie had left them for me.

Very carefully, I pulled the letter from the envelope. *Dearest Mame*, I read Lizzie's sharp, perfect script. *I researched, just as you told me, and found out everything there is to know about Sarah Royston . . .*

"What are you doing?"

I looked up quickly, straight into the eyes of Mrs. Porter. I fumbled the letter, and it would have fallen to the floor if she hadn't snatched it from my hand.

"Where did you find those?" she asked.

"In the clock," I said.

Without a word, she gathered the letters and photos up and left the room. She closed the door behind her. I could still feel the letter from Lizzie in my hand. I knew it was real; I'd seen the name Sarah Royston. And I was certain, absolutely positive, that Mrs. Porter hadn't known the papers had been in the clock. That realization gave me a triumphant thrill, a feeling of surprise and totally unexpected victory over her.

But who had put the letters there? And when?

And how had Lizzie known about Sarah Royston at least a year before her family had moved to this town?

Maybe it was a lucky double day after all.

CHAPTER THIRTEEN

DAY SIXTY-SEVEN

Standing at the bus stop Monday morning, I pulled my jacket collar up over my face, and the zipper metal was so cold it stuck to my lips. I had to take off my mitten and warm the spot with my palm to thaw the zipper off. I had thought Decembers in Connecticut were frigid, but they were nothing compared to Maine. I figured the temperature out here was close to zero, and it hadn't been much warmer at the breakfast table, Mrs. Porter's ice-cold eyes silently accusing me of finding the letters.

Chloe and I stood in the shelter of the snow fort Carole and I had built. Chloe was fiddling with one of the icicle ornaments that had frozen straight down the smallest cutout window. We stamped our feet to keep the blood from freezing. I watched her out of the corner of my eye, holding the question inside, but I couldn't wait any longer.

"Have you ever felt Lizzie here?" I asked.

"*Here?* In Maine?" Chloe asked.

"Yes. In the house."

"That's a sick question." A huge gust of white breath came from her mouth and she looked wounded, as if I'd slapped her.

"Last night I felt as if she was here," I said.

"Was that before you upset Mom or after?" she asked.

"Both," I said, remembering Mrs. Porter's furious force, grabbing the letter. "I think it's why your mother got so mad. Because Lizzie came to me, not her."

"Way to be losing your mind, Em," Chloe said. "You're hallucinating."

"Who wouldn't, being forced to sleep in her dead friend's bed?"

Chloe's lips thinned.

"I really did feel her there," I said steadily.

"Good for you."

I wondered why she wasn't more curious, but maybe she was too busy being hurt/angry. "How would Lizzie know about Sarah Royston?" I asked.

"School Sarah?"

"Yeah. And Town Sarah. Considering you moved here after . . ."

"Did you ever stop to think about *why* we moved *here*?" Chloe snapped. "Why of all the places in the world my parents could have chosen to bring Lizzie back to life—through you, and you're doing a rotten job of it, by the way—they picked here?"

Actually, I hadn't. I'd just figured Royston was so far and so different from Black Hall, all rocky angles and spiky trees, compared to home's soft marshes and gentle estuary light, that it would take them away from the sharpest, daily-est memories of Lizzie. Or maybe they had just thought it was the perfect middle-of-nowhere location to hide a kidnapped girl.

"Why did they come here?" I asked.

"That's for me to know and you to find out."

"Who put her letter . . ." I started to say.

Usually it was just Chloe and me at the bus stop, but I heard feet crunching through the snow's crust. I looked out the snow fort's window, and there was Casey coming down his driveway.

"Whoa," Chloe said in a low voice. "He never takes the bus. His dad doesn't like him walking along the road, it's too narrow and traffic goes too fast. So he always drives him or gets someone else to."

"Why is he taking it today?" I asked.

"No idea," Chloe said.

"Hi, Chloe, Lizzie," Casey said when he reached us.

"Hi," I said.

"Cool fort," he said. "Did you guys build it?"

"Carole and I did," I said.

"It's not that great," Chloe said. "It was super easy to spy on them and attack them with snowballs."

I stared at her and remembered how she'd hid behind the holly bushes. So she'd heard me and Carole talking about Casey and his mother, and Sarah Royston. And then the letter had appeared. I gave Chloe my best *I know you did it* squint. She held my stare for a few seconds, then turned her back on me.

The bus was a few minutes late. I stood close to Casey, and when it arrived, we got on and sat together. He faced me, and I knew he was seeing only my shadow, the Emily part of me, and it made me feel settled, the way I had at his house, but also awkward, because being around him had started churning me up inside.

"I was thinking, I should get a guitar, so I can practice," I said to fill the silence.

"You can use mine," he said. "Come over anytime."

"That would be great," I said, now trying to sound casual.

"After school I'm heading over to Mark's, to the Christmas tree farm," Casey said. "We're going tobogganing. You should come."

He was asking me to do something. My heart smashed into my ribs like a car wreck. There was no way Mrs. Porter would let me. Even if she wanted me to act as much like a normal kid as possible, there was last night and the letters, and her frozen-river eyes this morning. Visiting Casey's house was different—he lived right next door, and she could keep an eye on me. But somewhere else? Forget it.

"Sounds good, I'll try," I said.

"You have to come," he said. "I mean, you really have to."

I glanced at Chloe, sitting across the aisle. I knew she'd been listening, and I saw her shake her head hard, just once, letting me know the answer would be no. As if I didn't know already.

I watched the snowy woods go by, feeling Casey's arm jostle mine every time the bus went over a bump. I had a brief, glimmering fantasy of high-velocity flying down snow-covered hills with him on a toboggan, his arms around me from behind, the north wind in our faces.

"This is the first time I've seen you take the bus," I heard myself say.

"Yeah," he said.

Why? I felt like asking, as I'd asked Chloe. But by the way Casey was leaning into me, the way his breath was shallow and my heart was pounding, the truth was, I knew. He'd wanted to see me.

"You *are* coming to Mark's," he said.

"Yeah, I am," I said, hating the lie.

When we got off the bus, we stood there, on the sidewalk outside the school, for a whole minute. Icy snow fell on my face, tiny pricks of cold, as Casey leaned so close to me—even closer than in the room filled with shelves of honey—I could feel his breath on my forehead. Then the bell rang to signal the start of classes, and I walked away fast, because all I wanted was for him to kiss me right there, that exact moment. I couldn't believe how crazy it felt to have these feelings for a boy in the midst of everything that was happening to me.

As soon as I got to homeroom, I got a message that Mrs. Morton wanted to see me. Any blip in my routine filled me with both hope and dread. I walked down to the principal's office, through the dark hall with stained glass ruby light sparkling the floor. Sarah Royston had lived here, and then girls without homes, and somehow they were all connected to both Casey and Lizzie.

I entered Mrs. Morton's office, stood before her desk.

"Lizzie, your teachers have been telling me you've caught right up with your class, even after missing the first part of the semester," Mrs. Morton said.

"Thank you," I said.

"Remember I mentioned how great it would be if you could tell the school about your travels? Well, what would you think about doing that tomorrow afternoon?" she asked. "I know it's not much notice, but Ms. LeBlanc has to go to a teachers' conference and it seems everyone on my entire list of substitutes has the flu. Would you consider filling the class time and regaling us with tales of Europe?"

"I'm not sure anyone really wants to hear me," I said.

"Oh, believe me, they'll love it. And so will I. What do you say?"

I hesitated, then nodded. What choice did I have? I had learned to adhere to the rules, the schedules, trying to be the Lizzie everyone expected me to be.

At noon, right after Carole and I sat down with our lunch trays, Mrs. Morton made an announcement over the loudspeaker that tomorrow afternoon instead of sixth period, Lizzie Porter would be giving a presentation about attending high school in Paris and traveling through Europe.

"Whaaaaat?" Carole asked, her head snapping toward me.

"I know, it wasn't exactly on my agenda."

"Wow. This is going to be amazing. Even I don't know about your fabulous travels, Ms. International Woman of Mystery."

"Oh, you know, I just don't want everyone getting jealous of my partying on yachts on the Riviera."

"Tell all," she said, leaning close.

"Just joking," I said.

"I bet. I'm sure you're saving the juicy stuff. I guess I'll just have to wait till tomorrow to hear along with everyone else."

I steeled myself to think of what I was going to say, but it was okay—Lizzie would be giving the talk, not me. If I could split in two, I'd be fine. Emily could sit back, check out, and Lizzie could spin the stories and be the center of attention. Every day since being taken, I'd practiced being two different people.

"Hey, Lizzie," Angelique said, walking toward our table.

"Hi, Angelique," I said, surprised she'd talk to me.

"So, giving a talk, that's dope," she said. "And I hear you're quite the budding guitarist. Planning to join the band?"

"I'm just starting to learn," I said.

"We need more woman power," she said, plunking her tray across from me and Carole.

"That's the way," Carole said. "You should do it, Lizzie. Poor Angelique, all alone onstage with the boys."

"Women for women," Angelique said.

"Like Sarah Royston," I said.

"Ah, the mythical Sarah," Angelique said. "Casey's ancestor."

"Lizzie Porter has a connection to her, too," I said.

"Do you always talk about yourself in the third person?" Angelique asked, and Carole glanced at me quizzically, too.

"Ha-ha, out-of-body experience," I said quickly. "Anyway, I'm not trying to be in the band. You're incredible—I'm barely starting."

Angelique shrugged, trying to be modest, but when you played violin like that and looked like an actual angel, there was no point. She had a salad, and she ate it piece by piece with her fingers. She made eating a salad with pointy fingertips look like the coolest thing in the world. I watched how she took each lettuce leaf, held it above her mouth, then lowered it in.

"You can learn to play well, too," she said, wiping raspberry vinaigrette from her lips with the back of her hand. I was in awe of her confidence, the way she seemed to be inventing a whole new set of manners that, instead of thinking they were rude, everyone would want to imitate. "In fact, I'll help you."

"Well, Casey is," Carole said. "He's teaching her."

Angelique tossed her long, wavy strawberry blond hair and gave me a fake-sweet, secretive, verging-on-devious smile. "Good luck with that, and I totally mean it! But be forewarned, he loses interest the minute he starts something."

"Yeah, I'm sorry you two broke up," Carole said, deadpan. Under the table, she banged my knee with hers.

"Love, break up, love again," Angelique said. "We have our patterns, the dear boy and I. I need my space and I'm not the possessive type. Anyway, he and I traded instruments for a while. I coached him on fiddle; he got me started on mandolin and guitar. Strings are strings, frankly. Anyway, I'd love to help you. Woman power, right. Hey, maybe I should quit Sapphire Moon, and you and I should be the Sarah Roystons!"

"There's only one Sarah Royston," Carole said.

"Right, that," Angelique said. "Later, ladies." She blew air kisses at Carole and me, left her tray on the table for us to bus, and walked over to where Casey was sitting with Mark and Hideki.

"Not possessive," Carole said, shaking her head. "The way she made you switch seats with her in the car that time. So she could sit next to 'the dear boy.'"

"She was being really nice just now," I said.

"That dig about 'love, break up, love again'?"

I shook my head and laughed. "Guess what?" I asked. "Casey asked me to go to Mark's today."

"That's so great!" Carole said.

"You're going, right?" I asked her.

"Oh, yeah."

"I wish I could, but I have something I have to do at home . . ."

"No," Carole said. "No way. You are not getting out of this. We are going to have too much snowy, cozy fireside fun for you to miss out. We clear on that?"

I laughed, and she took that as a yes—I had to find a way.

The bell rang. The rest of the day dragged. I couldn't wait to get out of school, and I had the feeling I was already tobogganing— sledding down a rutted hill, my whole spirit leaping with every bump. The big question was: What would happen if I went? How far could I push Mrs. Porter? What would she say? For once, I wished it was one of her volunteer days so I could see her in the hall, try to convince her.

Lizzie's useless phone sat in my pocket. Between the last two periods, I went to the office, made the same old lame excuse about forgetting my charger and told Mrs. Baker, the administrative assistant, that I had to call home. She pointed to a phone on the empty desk across the office—not much privacy.

"Hello?" Mrs. Porter answered.

"It's me," I said.

"What's the matter? What's wrong?"

"Nothing. I just . . . some friends are going to Mark Benjamin's after school. His family has a tree farm, and I'm invited to toboggan with them. I wondered if I could go." I spoke slowly, feeling bold for even asking, considering the incident with the clock.

"That's a good idea," she said.

"It is?" I asked, actually shocked.

"Yes. It's just what you should be doing. Getting into the mainstream."

"Okay. Thank you."

"You love sledding, sweetie," she said. Her words were nice, but they sounded as if they were coming between gritted teeth. "You always have."

That was true. Whoever she was talking to—Lizzie or Emily—we had both loved winter sports. She might have been happy to see the smile on my face when I hung up, just like a normal kid, making plans for after school.

A bunch of us climbed onto the bus. No sign of Angelique. Casey grabbed my hand, pulled me into the seat beside him, across from Beth and Jon, two kids from our class.

"Where's Angelique?" I asked.

"She didn't want to come."

"Why?" I asked.

He gave me a long, steady look. Then he slid his arm around my shoulder, and I felt his answer in my skin.

The bus meandered up and down some steep hills, over a frozen river, along a deserted road with only two houses on it, each with red barns. I'd been by here on the way home from school, and I spotted Mark's place right away: the BENJAMIN FAMILY TREE FARM sign, and hundreds of trees, but also the most incredibly over-the-top light display I'd ever seen.

It was nearly dark by the time we got there. The big white house glowed, lined with thousands and thousands of tiny white lights. They encircled the porch rails, the window frames, the roof line, the chimney. A row of illuminated candy canes led to the barn, itself blindingly decorated with colored lights—pink, green, amber, red, blue—blinking on and off. A sign above the barn said ENCHANTED HOLIDAY VILLAGE!

A few cars and pickups were parked in the lot, and slews of little kids ran straight for the barn door. I peeked inside. As wildly bright as the outside was, indoors it was holiday on steroids.

Music jingled out, and there were at least a million white lights; illuminated angels with tall and feathery wings; two gigantic menorahs with blue bulbs; Santa Claus with a fluffy white beard sitting in a big red velvet chair; a kinara candleholder holding red, black, and green candles to represent the seven principles of Kwanzaa; and Mrs. Claus and a bunch of elves passing out cups of cocoa and hot cider and plates of sugar cookies. Two black Lab dogs with fake antlers on their heads slept by a wood stove in big soft plaid beds.

"That's usually my job," Carole said, pointing at the elves and Mrs. Claus. "On days I work here, I'm on cookie duty."

"I thought you sold trees," I said.

"Consider me support staff. I'm not the stand-in-the-cold-wearing-a-big-husky-jacket type. So I get to play with the kids while their parents decide on the perfect spruce."

Electric trains ran in two directions along the perimeters of the floor and the ceiling. Behind snow-frosted windows were illuminated tableaux: one of antique dolls in beautiful gowns, another of white mice sitting down to a feast, and—my favorite—four teddy bears at a tea party.

"That one was my mother's," Casey said, coming to stand beside me.

"You mean one of the bears?"

"All of them. She designed that window. Before she died, she and Mrs. Benjamin were best friends. Mom helped her create this whole holiday world, but the teddy bear tea party was all hers."

I looked at the bears and wished I could touch them through the glass. Their velveteen coats were threadbare. Their eyes were old-fashioned; instead of plastic buttons, they were made of thread stitched in a circle. Their colors had faded in time and light. The bears sat at a low wooden table covered with doll-size teacups and teapot.

"She inherited them from her great-aunt," Casey said. "So they're very old."

Her great-aunt—Sarah Royston's daughter, I thought. "Nora?" I asked.

"Yes," he said.

"Did you play with them when you were little?" I asked.

He nodded. "Yeah, but mostly they sat on a shelf in our dining room having this same tea party, all through my life."

"What made your mother and Mrs. Benjamin do this?" I asked, gesturing around to the holiday displays.

"The tree business wasn't doing that well," he said. "Local families always bought their trees here, but this is such a small town. My mom had the idea of pulling people in from far away. Now just about everyone in Maine makes a trip here to see the display and, while they're at it, buy things."

"That was really smart of her," I said. "And she was a good friend."

"My mom was both," he agreed.

"I'm sorry you lost her," I said.

"Thanks," he said. "She was the best, and losing her was the worst. She took amazing care of me, and I wish I could have done better for her."

"What do you mean?"

We just stared at the bears for a while before Casey answered. "She fell one night—in the dark, a dumb thing, taking the garbage out. My dad was away, I should have done it, but she wouldn't let me—she was always afraid I'd bump into something. Anyway, she twisted her ankle really bad, and it turned out she had a hairline fracture. They gave her oxycodone at the clinic."

"Painkiller?"

"Yep. She was only supposed to take it for a few days."

My heart skipped. I already knew what he was going to say.

"She told the doctor the pain wasn't going away so he refilled the prescription. And then again, and then I'm not sure how she kept getting them, but she did."

"I'm so sorry," I said, feeling a pit in my stomach.

"One day she took too many. She never woke up."

"Casey . . ." I said, my mouth dry.

"I tried to stop her, all along. I'd find her pills, throw them out. But she'd always get more."

"I . . ." I began, looking for the words. "My mother drank. We used to hide her bottles. It was so hard to see her checking out—she was awesome till she took that first drink of the day, then it was pure oblivion."

"I had no idea," he said. He thought I was talking about Mrs. Porter. I'd never even seen her have a glass of wine. He held my hand.

"Yeah. The minute she drank, she just . . . went away," I said.

"My mother did, too, with the pills," he said. "I would have done anything if she'd quit."

"But that's the thing about addiction," I said. "There's nothing anyone can do until the person wants to stop. They have to do it on their own."

"My mother couldn't," he said. He blinked, looking at me.

"Do you get mad at her?" I asked.

"How do you know?"

"Because she didn't stop. You wanted her to, begged her to, but she didn't. It's a disease; we know that, but still. It took her away. It took mine away, too. I was so angry all the time."

"Me too," he said. "When she'd be high, she'd cry. She'd say she hated herself, ask me to forgive her. She'd get all maudlin about stuff like I'd never get a license, I could never play on sports teams. As if I cared. But it started to feel she was looking for excuses for why she was using."

"But she taught you to play guitar," I said. "And she trained you to keep bees."

"Toward the end, she never thought that was enough. There was nothing I could do to stop her, or help her," he said.

"You both look so happy in that picture in your kitchen. All I see is love," I said, meaning it more than one way.

"That's all I see, too," he said.

He was staring straight at me. It pierced my heart, told me he felt the same way.

Suddenly the cheerful scene around us felt too noisy and close. We walked outside into the clear, cold air. I wanted to be alone with Casey—there was so much I wanted to say to him— but all the others were waiting for us outside the barn. Mark had gotten out the toboggans.

My mind buzzed. We all started marching along a trail into the pine forest, up a steep hill. It was so dark in the trees, a few kids snapped on their phone flashlights. But Casey seemed to know where he was going without light. He and I held the same cord, pulling our toboggan behind us. I stumbled on a rut, and he caught me.

"I know the way," he said. "I've been coming here since I was five. I know every bend, every tree. You'll be fine—don't worry."

Implicit in those words was that he was protecting me. In another place and time, I might have bristled; I'd always thought of myself as strong woman personified, the tough younger sister of a big Irish clan. But everything I'd been through had made me feel insecure and threatened, and it felt good to have Casey there for me.

When we got to the top of the hill, we stepped out of the woods into a big clearing. There was a rustic hut, and someone had already lit a bonfire. It crackled and sparked, orange flames shooting straight up into the star-filled sky. The other side of the hill gave onto a long, wide slope. Looking around in a 360-degree circle, there was not one house visible. There were no streetlights. This was the wilderness, the most peaceful place I'd ever been.

"Who's first?" Mark asked.

"We'll go," Beth said. She and Jon piled on, shoved off, and we heard their shrieks of exquisite terror and delight as they went sliding down. They disappeared below the last ridge, and then came Hideki and Roxanne, a girl who was a senior.

Mark, Carole, Casey, and I stood by the fire. I took off my gloves to warm my hands. I watched Mark put his arms around Carole, standing in the dark circle just outside the glow.

"Want to take a run?" Casey asked me.

"Sure," I said.

We maneuvered our toboggan onto the hill's crest. I settled on the hard wooden seat, and Casey sat behind me. His legs were tight around my hips. We braced our feet on the curved piece in front. Then we both used our hands to shove off, and we went flying down the slope.

The frosty air filled my mouth and eyes. Every bump sent us airborne, but we used our weight and balance to stay centered and not topple over. The wind rushed past us. The faster we went, Casey's arms came around me and held me tighter. I leaned back into his chest, and my heart was thrashing so hard I was sure he felt it. We careened around a bend, instinctively tilting left as if we were one person. Then a right turn, and his arms tightened again and made me feel so thrilled I forgot to lean, and we spun out and soared into a snowdrift.

We landed in a lump, arms and legs entwined. The opposite of hurting, tickled by snow crystals. We laughed just a little at first, then hysterically. We cleared snow off each other's faces. I'd lost my hat, and he smoothed my hair.

"You okay?" he asked.

"Great, you?"

"Better than great."

Which, considering the fact we'd just crashed into the hillside, struck us as incredibly funny, and we both started laughing again. Then all at once the laughter stopped, I looked into his eyes, and he kissed me.

The world fell out from under me, and I was floating in space, held up by Casey's arms. And I was holding him, too, with all my might. The smell of pine trees and crisp snow surrounded us, and we lifted above the earth. His lips were soft and the kiss was hot, and I forgot I had a body and a life—and I was part of Casey and he was part of me.

Casey took off his glove. He raised his hand, touched my cheek. His fingers felt warm.

"I wish I could see you," he said. "*Really* see you. The details, the way your eyes look, every single thing, not just the shadow."

"You already do," I said. "More than anyone." I had to say it; I couldn't have stopped the words if I'd tried. "You see the real me. Not my Lizzie disguise."

"You're incognito?" he asked. He thought I was joking.

"Yes," I said.

"Then who are you really?" Still joking.

"You know," I said, my voice breaking. "You already guessed it. And I've been wanting to tell you you're right."

"Right about what?"

"You know how we talked about our mothers before? I meant my real one."

"Your real one?" he asked, frowning.

"She's waiting for me in Connecticut. She misses me. I'm so afraid that if I don't return to her she'll start drinking again. Maybe she already has . . ."

Casey slipped his arms around me. The smile left his face, and his eyes were suddenly solemn. I felt him realize that this wasn't a joke, that I was being serious. My heart began to gallop. There was no containing what I felt. I heard the sound of my blood rushing. We were perfectly still, but the darkness around us seemed alive, the constellations tilting overhead.

"Who are you?" he asked.

"I can't say it out loud," I whispered. "Something terrible will happen if I tell."

"You're the missing girl," he said, saying it for me.

"Yes," I said, and a door in my heart opened. "I'm Emily."

I hadn't meant to say that. The words just slipped out. Or maybe deep down I had intended to tell him—because I couldn't stand it anymore. Keeping the truth inside was killing me.

"Why did you run away?" he asked.

That was the question that stopped me, brought me to a screeching halt against the force of reality. Should I go all the way, tell him the whole truth, ask him to help me? Mrs. Porter, my mother, the knife. My mind fought with itself over what to say.

"I . . ." I began.

"Your family misses you; it's been all over the news," Casey said. "The drinking—you were talking about your real mother. Not Mrs. Porter."

"Yes," I whispered.

"Don't you want to go home?" he asked.

"More than anything."

"This is why you're worried your mother will start drinking again?"

I nodded.

We were still lying in the snowdrift. The sky had stopped spinning. We sat up and held each other. My head was on his shoulder; I could feel him breathing hard. I couldn't bear the idea of letting go.

"I'll help you," he said. "Are you afraid your parents will be mad?"

"No," I said. "Not at all. It's something else."

"Then let's call them, right now. Tell them you're okay," he said, reaching into his pocket for his phone. He handed it to me. My hands were shaking. I was too overwhelmed to think straight. My fingers dialed our house number.

This is what I'm not sure about: Would I have gone through with it if the call had actually worked? I heard the line ring—I was sure of that. But then it went dead. I looked at the bars on Casey's phone—two verging on one, one verging on zero. We were too far from any cell tower for the call to be completed.

"No reception," I said.

"Then let's go back to the barn," he said. "We can call from there."

We stood up, started pulling the toboggan up the hill. Carole and Mark zoomed by, going the other way. I barely noticed them. Bare branches overhead scraped in the wind. They clawed at the stars. I felt menace in the universe.

We crossed the clearing, entered the trail heading back to the farm. Casey held my hand.

"Why are you living with the Porters?" he asked. "Calling yourself Lizzie?"

"It's complicated," I said.

"Chloe acts like you're really her sister," he said.

"We've been close for a long time," I said. How could I explain it to him? Did I even want to? The emotion of our kiss, of night sledding, of him telling me how his mother had died, then seeing the real me, had overcome what I'd known all along, what I'd been committed to do—maintain the facade, keep up the lie, not only for my survival, but for my mother's.

"Why haven't her parents called yours to let them know you're okay?" he asked.

"They . . . the Porters . . . are taking care of me," I said.

"It seems weird," he said. "They have to know your family is going crazy. And your mother . . ."

"The Porters . . ." I began, searching for words to justify what the Porters had done, but I lost it. I heard a voice shrieking in the woods. Then I found myself holding Casey—not in a romantic way but clutching him for dear life, as if I was being swept away by a mad river. The voice was mine, crying with all the panic and despair I'd kept bottled up for sixty-seven days.

"They don't take care of me. They kidnapped me, forced me into their van," I said. "On my way home from school, in October. They locked me in a basement; they're making me pretend to be their daughter."

Casey frowned. "Lizzie?"

"Yes, she was my best friend, and she died of cancer, and her mother lost her mind from grief; that's why she's doing this . . ."

"I don't care why she's doing it," Casey said, holding me so hard I could barely breathe. "She's a kidnapper. They all are."

I started crying harder then, because what he said was true, and hearing someone say it out loud made me realize what I'd been going through.

That might sound strange; you think when you're actually experiencing something, you know it and are keeping track of what it's doing to you. But I'd turned into stone along the way. I'd blocked out the worst just to live.

"We can call the police," he said.

"But that's just it," I said. "We can't."

"Why? They're criminals, L . . ." He started to say *Lizzie*, then switched to *Emily* and it came out *Lemily*.

"Even so," I said. "I have to go along with them."

"You can't. You don't belong with them. They're hurting you already, and it could get worse."

"Yes, much worse," I said. "She's told me what she will do. I've seen it, how close she's come."

"She?"

"Mrs. Porter."

"What can she do that's half as bad as kidnapping you?"

"Kill my mother. She has a knife . . . she's going to use it."

"What?" Shock filled his voice and face. I wondered if he even believed me. Why would he—how unreal was this to someone who didn't live it every day?

"There's a video," I explained. "Mrs. Porter at the marsh with my mom. The blade is right there, pointing at my mom's back. And I've seen the knife itself—she showed me that day at Jeb's, when we first met you. She was afraid I'd talk."

"You almost did," he said. "I felt you wanting to say more." Extra-sensory Casey.

I nodded. "That's why we can't tell anyone. She'll go straight to my house."

Casey shook his head. "She won't have time. The police will arrest her right now, put her in jail. There's no way she's hurting your mom."

"If I do what she says, everything will be fine," I said, almost pleading with him. "All I have to do is go along with her. That's all. I'm getting used to it; it's not even that hard anymore. She feeds me; she's letting me go to school. Even tonight—it's a big step, letting me come here with you."

"Do you hear what you're saying?" he asked. "You're making it all right. They're criminals, and who knows what part Chloe's playing, and you're defending them. It's Stockholm syndrome, Emily."

"What syndrome?" I asked.

"That's something when a person gets abducted or imprisoned and her mind gets so twisted from being controlled that she starts feeling grateful to the kidnapper."

"I'm not grateful to her!"

"You just said she fed you."

That struck me hard—he was right.

"It's just that I've worked it out in my mind," I said. "I'll know when I can leave, when the threat is less, but it's not right now."

"Let me help you. Tonight."

"You don't know what she's like!" I said, almost boiling over with panic because he didn't get it; he was going to mess everything up and put my mother in more danger than she'd been in all along.

"I think I do. She's someone who'd take a kid, lock her up, force her to be Lizzie when she's really Emily. She'd torture your family, letting them think you ran away, not knowing where you are. That could almost kill them. Being that worried could change them forever. You're right—it could trigger your mother to drink again." The words tore out of him with passion that echoed my own.

"I know!" I said. "Mrs. Porter made me lie, say in the email I knew my mother had gone back to drinking. But I swear— Mrs. Porter wants it to happen. She told me my mother will get so desperate with me gone that she'll start again. The stress will make her . . ."

"Start leaning on substances to cope. I get it more than anyone," Casey said.

"She's sober. At least I think she still is," I said.

"I hope so," he said. "I wanted that for my mom so badly. For all of us."

I nodded, leaned into him. This was why I'd been able to tell him everything: Kids of addicts and alcoholics have their own special hyper-alert understanding of life, of how the world is eternally unpredictable, how you can't count on anything to stay the same. Even ordinary, everyday safety and comfort.

"Mrs. Porter told you one true thing—your mother could drink again," Casey said softly. "And if she did, it could end her life."

I thought of Casey's mom. Then I pictured the times my mother had fallen, passed out, thrown up, wept with despair. He was right.

Casey put his arm around me, began leading me back down the trail. I started to hurry, pulling him by the hand, because suddenly I couldn't wait to call the police. I imagined them driving into the parking lot, their blue-and-red strobes flashing. But then I saw in my mind—exactly as if it was happening in real time— Mrs. Porter slowly cruising down the road, as she always did. Keeping an eye on me.

She would notice the police cars, see me and Casey being interviewed.

Then she would turn her van around and start driving south.

But that wasn't to be—not at all. Approaching the holiday village from the back side, I saw a minivan idling outside the Christmas tree farm, white wisps of exhaust ghostly in the cold air. Mrs. Porter was at the wheel. She was already there.

"Casey," I said, tugging his arm, stopping him from walking farther.

"Is she here?" he asked. "It doesn't matter. You don't have to leave with her. We'll go through the back door, call the police from inside. She won't know what's happening till they have her surrounded."

Maybe that would have worked. If I'd caught sight of her ten seconds earlier, before Casey and I had left the darkness of the trail and entered the brightly lit perimeter of the barn, all those lights sparkling. If I hadn't given her the chance to spot me, we could have tried his plan. But as it was, she had fixed me with her gaze. It was almost like being hypnotized.

"I have to get in the van," I said.

"I'm not going to let you," he said. He put his arms around me. I saw Mrs. Porter staring.

"Just for now," I said. "Keep my secret for me, please? You're the only person who knows. Please don't tell anyone. Your dad . . ."

"He's not home, or I would tell him. He's doing a gig at Mohegan Sun. He'll be back in two days."

Mohegan Sun was a casino in Connecticut. It was in the eastern part of the state, not too far from Black Hall. My eyes scalded with tears to think of Casey's dad so close to my family. I could be in Connecticut tonight, too. All I had to do was let Casey help me. But there was Mrs. Porter, her frozen-river eyes glaring at me, pulling me toward the van.

"Give me until then," I said. "Till your dad gets home. To let me figure it out. To plan the right move. I have to do the thing that will keep my mom safe. I need to time it when Mrs. Porter won't know. Please?"

Mrs. Porter got sick of waiting for me. She stepped out of the van and came toward us.

"Please?" I asked Casey as she approached.

"Emily, I hope I'm not making a mistake. Okay, I'll go along with you, but just till my dad gets here. Promise me you'll let us get you out of there then?"

I squeezed his hand, my way of saying yes.

"Well, hello," Mrs. Porter said, putting on a big fake smile. "Casey, how nice to see you. It's a school night, time for Lizzie to come home. Would you like a ride?"

"No," he said, no hint of friendliness or politeness in his tone.

"All right," she said, sounding taken aback. "Whatever you want, that's just fine! We'll see you back on Passamaquoddy Road. Let's go, Lizzie."

I hesitated, facing Casey. This was the night of so many things: my telling him the truth, his telling me about his mom, my first *real* kiss. I wanted to stay with him another minute, hold him, kiss him, make sure he was going to keep his word. But Mrs. Porter grabbed my arm firmly and tugged.

In the van, even before we left the lot:

"What did you say to him?" she asked.

"Nothing! Why?"

"The way he spoke to me. I saw that cold look in his eyes. As if he knows. He doesn't, does he? Tell me exactly what you said to him! I'll hear in your voice if you're lying. I want to know every word!"

"We just went tobogganing, exactly what I told you we were going to do. We were tired from climbing the hill, that's all." I paused, then for effect, "Can't we please go home? I'm freezing. Can I have a snack? One of your cookies?"

I watched her shoulders, tensed up around her ears, drop slightly with a sort of relief.

"Well, he was very rude," she said.

"He just didn't need a ride," I said.

"I saw you holding hands. I watched him put his arms around you. I don't like that, Lizzie. He is not the boy for you."

Yes, he is, I thought.

"You deserve someone much better. You are a special girl. The fact he's living in that big falling-down house with a father who cares more about music than him and a mother who overdosed . . . it's damaged him. You can never count on a person like that. Just like that *other* mother. Who drinks herself into a stupor."

She meant my mother. I wanted to attack her, but I held my feelings inside.

"People need a good upbringing, constant love, encourage-ment, to be good, to have a lovely life," she said. "Like the way I love you, Lizzie. That's why you are so perfect. It's the reason you excel, the reason people always comment on your beauty, your goodness. My love is making you good."

"I know," I said.

"Aren't you going to thank me?"

"Thank you."

"Thank you . . . who?"

Stockholm syndrome. Kidnapped people being grateful to their abductors. "Thank you, Mom," I said.

She gave a tight smile. We drove along the dark road, under tall pines. I closed my eyes. I felt Casey's hand on my cheek, heard his voice. He had promised me, and I had promised him. The last lines of Lizzie's favorite poem filled my mind:

The woods are lovely, dark and deep,
But I have promises to keep,
And miles to go before I sleep,
And miles to go before I sleep.

Promises to keep.

CHAPTER FOURTEEN

DAY SIXTY-NINE

The things you tell yourself to make it through two more days:

Act normal.

Go to school.

Give the talk in front of everyone.

Think of Casey.

Remember the promise we made.

Two more days.

LESS than two more days.

You can do it. You only have to pretend to be Lizzie for another forty-seven hours, fifty-three minutes, and seven seconds.

All I had to do was figure out how to save my mother's life along the way. That was all. No big deal. My head ached because I'd been awake all night trying out different versions of how I could get Mrs. Porter occupied with Something-Very-Important to distract her while, oh, I called the police on her.

Or let Casey call the police on her. For kidnapping. For taking me.

I wanted Casey to kiss me again.

To keep myself from thinking thoughts that were, really, going nowhere and just driving me insane, I rehearsed the talk I would give in just a few hours. The Lizzie Porter Magical Tour of Europe. Get through that, a half day gone, only one and a half more to go.

My mind seemed to be working only in fragments and half sentences.

At breakfast that morning, with everyone around the table, I almost felt the others weren't there. The Porters were disappearing before my very eyes. I ate my waffles, silently rehearsing the things I would say in front of school:

I went to Paris.

I went to Rome.

In London . . .

On the way to Brussels . . .

I did not tell the Porters that today was the day of Lizzie's travelogue. I kept that to myself. I didn't want to hear a million reminders from Mrs. Porter. It wasn't one of her scheduled volunteer days, and the last thing I wanted was for her to show up at school, to make sure I was saying everything just right.

I told myself I was looking forward to this. I wasn't nervous to talk in front of everyone: I loved theater, standing on a stage, acting in plays. I had read, or at least looked through, all the travel guides Mrs. Porter had given me, tried to memorize the notes she had made. But mostly I remembered and dreamt of the wonderful stories Mame had told Lizzie and me about visiting Hubert in France. This wasn't real life; I was acting, I was playing a role.

Give the talk, another half day gone. One and a half left, then I'd go home.

All I had to do was figure out how to save my mom's life.

That was all. Just that one thing.

Casey wasn't on the bus. I panicked. Was he mad at me for not doing what he'd wanted? Did he resent my making him promise to do it my way? Being so on edge made me realize this was different: I had crossed a border. I was in another mode from being Lizzie. Casey had gotten me hoping, wishing, believing I might actually make it back to my family.

But where was he?

I went to homeroom. First-period geometry. Second-period English. Third-period colonial American history. Lunch.

Carole and I sat together. I ate my chicken Caesar salad without tasting it. She had packed her own lunch.

"Almond-and-apricot Kind Bars somehow have the power to completely transform me into a good mood and all-around better person within two seconds, honestly," she said. "I have an extra." She pushed it my way.

"No, thanks," I said.

"This is not natural," she said. "No one says no to a Kind Bar."

"I'm not that hungry."

"Freaking out about the talk?"

"Not really."

"Oh, do I detect butterflies of love?"

"What?" I asked.

"From last night. You and Casey conveniently disappeared in the middle of the soiree. Nothing like being ice cold on a toboggan run to get the blood flowing, am I right?" She smiled. "You have to tell me."

I was supposed to confide in her, to tell her about the kiss, but I couldn't. Where was Casey? I was half frozen with fear. What if he'd taken matters into his own hands, called the police on Mrs. Porter? He had no idea who he was dealing with.

Finally, it was time to head to the assembly. Carole and I finished eating, and we walked down the hall together.

"You don't seem okay," she said as we approached the auditorium.

"I'm fine."

"It's a big deal, speaking to the school. I know you must be nervous."

She was wearing an oversize white wool sweater and black leggings, her pale blue Uggs, and a gold chain with her initials on it: *CD*. Standing there in the hall, she unclipped her necklace.

"We'll trade, just for the assembly," she said. "You wear mine, and I'll wear yours. It'll make you realize I'm right there with you."

That made me feel better. "Thank you, I love that," I said, glowing.

"Well, it's just in case you turn shy telling those stories about parties on the yacht."

"Ha-ha," I said.

Almost instantly my palms turned sweaty. I reached behind my head, swept my hair away, but my fingers slipped on the clasp of Lizzie's anchor necklace. Carole undid it for me. Then she slid her CD chain around my neck and made sure it was fastened right. She carefully put on my necklace.

I stared at Lizzie's gold anchor nestled against Carole's sweater and tried to swallow. Walking down the hall, my thoughts began to swirl. I felt unsteady and actually bumped into her.

"Oops," I said. "Sorry."

"You'll do great," she said, giving me a big hug. She opened the auditorium door and let me walk in ahead of her.

Like all of Royston High, the large room made me feel I had stepped back in time. The stained glass windows glinted with red-and-blue light, and the dark walls with their intricately carved mottos and motifs climbed to heavy beamed ceilings. Delicate cat etchings were placed beside every door, even in here.

I thought of Sarah Royston, of how she had cared so much about girls who were far from home, who had lost their way. At that moment, I felt no one had ever lost her way more than me.

Carole took a seat on the aisle, and I walked toward the stage. All the kids I'd met and was starting to know filled the chairs. I spotted Mark and Hideki, Angelique and Beth, nearly everyone from my class. Chloe sat with Mel, Junie, and a cluster of other middle school kids. With every step I took, I felt I was disappearing down a tunnel. I told myself I was entering Lizzie Land. I felt weird because I was shedding all my Emily-ness to get through this.

Mrs. Morton stood on the stage, beaming as I approached. Suddenly there was Casey—he was sitting on the aisle, second row. He grabbed my hand as I walked by.

"Where were you?" I asked.

"I missed the bus," he said. "I stayed awake all night thinking about you, about everything, and I overslept."

"You kept the promise?" I asked.

"Of course," he said, giving my hand a firm squeeze. It flooded me with relief, but that feeling lasted only a few seconds.

I climbed the stairs up to the stage. I pushed memories away from my mind—rehearsals and performances of *A Midsummer Night's Dream*, *The Crucible*, and *Ghost Girl*. That had been Emily. I tried to channel Lizzie, the times she'd read her poems in English class and, once, in a state poetry contest. I gazed out at everyone. My eyes found Casey again. His half smile looked worried. My stomach clenched.

Mrs. Morton introduced me. I stared down at Casey and felt him watching me. I knew he'd sat so close so he could see me better, so I would be more than a shadow. Mrs. Morton's introduction echoed in my head, like I was hearing her words from far away. They reverberated, sounding distorted, as if they were coming through gauze.

"And here, with no further ado, is Lizzie Porter to tell us what it was like to live in Europe."

"Thank you, Mrs. Morton," I said. My mouth was so dry my lips stuck together. I took a minute, trying to breathe the way I'd learned in theater class. Deep breaths, fill my chest, feel my diaphragm lift.

"At the beginning of freshman year," I began.

I heard myself recite: *I went to Paris. I lived with my grandmother in a seventeenth-century building on the Ile St. Louis. Every day I would walk to school along the Seine, and I attended classes in an old convent just off Boulevard St. Germain, where Hemingway and other writers hung out at the cafés, and I felt as if I was an expatriate, too, an American living in Paris, just like them.*

This was the script I had worked out with Mrs. Porter. I knew it almost by heart, with just enough room for improvisation—built in from remembering Mame's stories—to sound halfway natural. I scanned the room, saw all those faces of people I was getting to know. Kids who believed I was who I said I was.

Then I looked into Casey's beautiful turquoise eyes, and I paused. See, once the secret is out—even to just one person, someone you trust enough to keep it from the rest of the world until you're ready—it's completely out there. The secret has left, and there is no getting it back.

I steadied myself, hands on the podium.

Casey watched me intently, nodding his head. I felt him telling me I could get through this. He was counting the hours with me—just make it till his dad returned, then we would tell, and then I could go home. I imagined this was how a prisoner feels: her last day behind bars. I read once that the last few hours before freedom are the hardest to endure.

Carole was sending encouragement to me, too: I found her in the crowd, saw her beam at me, and touch the anchor necklace. *Oh, Lizzie. That chain that hung around your neck, even to the end.*

These people, these new friends, Carole and Casey and all the other students, people I already cared about were watching me. Something in me had broken. The part of me that had been able to swallow the truth had washed away in the feelings that were storming through my chest.

"Paris," I said, trying to continue. "Paris in freshman year ..."

I was supposed to say more about the Left Bank, the Musée d'Orsay, going to the Gare Montparnasse to catch the TGV, the high-speed train to the southwest of France, over the Loire River, to Mame's country house. But the lies about France wouldn't pass my lips. Other words spilled out, ones I had no control over. The dam had burst and they came in a river, raging through me.

"In the beginning of freshman year," I said, starting again. "My best friend got sick. At first we didn't know what was wrong, but she had a rare cancer. It spread so fast. There were so many tumors. She went into the hospital, and she never came out. We were almost as close as sisters, we had always spent every possible minute together, and she was so sick, and she never got better. My best friend's name was Lizzie, and she died," I said. "Lizzie died."

I started to cry, so hard the room blurred and swerved. Panicking, I looked for Casey in the front row, but he had already bounded out of his seat. He jumped onto the stage to catch me. Just as I staggered into his arms and tried not to collapse, I saw Mrs. Porter standing in the back of the hall. Her eyes and mouth were wide with shock and fury. She screamed, "No!"

And then I blacked out.

* * *

When I came to, I didn't know where I was. I was lying on a narrow bed. The walls were pale green, no windows. I heard chimes ringing, and a doctor being called over a loudspeaker. A needle was in my arm.

A woman with kind eyes leaned over me, listening to my heart with a stethoscope. She had dark brown skin and wore a white lab coat, and underneath I saw a soft coral sweater, pearls at her throat.

"Ah, you're awake," the doctor said. She looked into my eyes with one of those examining lights, taking her time, her hands gentle on my face. "You're wearing contacts," she said. "Let's take them out." And she did. I barely flinched.

"Am I in the hospital?" I asked.

"Yes, in the emergency room," she said. "You came by ambulance about forty minutes ago. Do you recall that?"

"No," I said.

"What is the last thing you do remember?"

I blinked, trying to clear my mind. A bag of clear liquid hung over my bed, a tube drooping down and flowing into the needle in my arm—an IV drip, just like Lizzie's. "What's that for?" I asked.

"We're just making sure you're not dehydrated," she said. "I'm Dr. Dean."

"Carole's mom," I said.

"Yes," she said. "Carole is out in the hall with Casey Donoghue and Mark Benjamin and your family. They're very worried about you, along with everyone else. Now tell me, what is the last thing you remember?"

It all came back, and with the memory, my eyes filled with tears that ran down my cheeks, hot and salty, into my mouth. I'd been honest. I'd been unable to help myself—nothing in the world could have made me tell the lie with Casey sitting right there, knowing my real identity—and the truth had just burst out of me. It was all over: The nightmare had ended. No matter what happened, the truth was out. And in spite of that relief, all I could think of was the knife, Mrs. Porter keeping her word, driving as fast as she could to Black Hall right now.

"What family is out there?" I asked.

Dr. Dean was focused on shining the light in my eyes.

"How much time has passed since I fainted?" I asked, pushing her away as I struggled to sit up. Dr. Dean touched my shoulder, very tenderly pressed me back onto the gurney.

"Don't worry about that," she said. "We're taking care of you now."

"You don't understand, I have to protect . . ."

"What's going on inside you?" she asked. "Why did you say . . ."

"My mother!" I said. "You have to make sure she's okay. It's an emergency! Please, listen to me, and . . ."

"She's fine," Dr. Dean said. "She's right here with you. Now, you're safe here, but will you tell me something? It's very important. Why did you stand on the stage and say 'Lizzie died'?"

"She's very metaphorical," came the voice. I felt poison dripping into my veins, instant horror. "She's a poet, my girl, and when she left for Europe, she got a little dramatic." Mrs. Porter stepped out from behind Dr. Dean.

"It was more than a little dramatic, Ginnie," Dr. Dean said.

"Well, I'm sure she's still affected by that virus. It was a fever—you know how fevers can be. I'm going to wring my brother's neck for saying she was well enough to return to school. I should have had you check her out first."

"Why did you say that?" Dr. Dean asked, looking directly at me. "That 'Lizzie died.' What did that mean?"

Mrs. Porter didn't give me a chance to answer. "Well, clearly she meant—in her poetic way—so the new one could be born—otherwise, how could she have left home, to go away in the first place? We're such a close family. Her dad, Chloe, and me. Isn't that right, sweetie?"

"Is that true?" Dr. Dean asked me. "Is that the reason you said 'Lizzie died'?" Her expression was concerned.

"Of course it is, Pamela," Mrs. Porter said. "You know, when I first met you, how terribly I longed to have Lizzie come back from Paris. I almost couldn't bear having her gone from home, but I had to stay brave so she could have the time of her life. That Xanax prescription, hello."

"Is that what you meant?" Dr. Dean asked me.

Mrs. Porter's eyes were cold steel. They bored into me, pure rage.

"Yes," I whispered.

"Carole said you were very emotional, up there, starting to give your talk," Dr. Dean said.

"I shouldn't have let her go to school this morning," Mrs. Porter said, placing a hand on my forehead. "She said she had a stomachache, but she's such a good student, missing a day just isn't something she does."

"Ginnie," Dr. Dean said. "I'm going to ask you to step out of the room."

"She's my daughter, Pamela. I don't like your tone."

"Be that as it may, I need to speak to this girl alone."

Mrs. Porter glared at me. She squinted her eyes, tapped her pocket. The knife pocket.

"Please leave the room, Ginnie," Dr. Porter said.

My heart should have soared, but it didn't. It was a dead thing in my chest, and my blood was a frozen river. I lay still, staring at the ceiling. I knew Mrs. Porter was hovering just outside the door. Or maybe she was on her way to the car, her knife sharpened and ready.

"Tell me what happened," Dr. Dean asked, pulling a stool close to my bed, sitting down beside me. "There's no one else here. Now, I don't think you would have said 'Lizzie died' just to express how it felt to leave home for a year abroad. That doesn't sound right to me."

I was stunned and dizzy, listening for Mrs. Porter outside the curtain.

"Are you depressed?" Dr. Dean asked. "Depression is not unusual among high school students—it can happen to anyone, really, and there's nothing to be ashamed of if you have it."

"I'm not depressed."

"Have you been thinking of hurting yourself?" she asked.

"No."

"No suicidal thoughts?"

"No!"

"Have you taken anything today?" She peered into my eyes. I didn't have to ask what she meant: The school nurse's office both here and at home were full of posters and pamphlets about the opioid crisis. I thought of Casey's mom and nearly cried.

I shook my head. "I don't take drugs."

"Then it's something else. Tell me."

Her voice was gentle but insistent. She was ready to believe me, whatever I told her. I stared into her eyes. They reminded me of Carole's.

"Your eyes are blue," she said. "But you wear green contacts."

"I like green eyes."

"Why did you say Lizzie died? Isn't that your name? Are you telling me you're not Lizzie?"

I heard the curtain rustle and knew Mrs. Porter was pressing close, hearing every word. Knowing she was right there removed every choice. This was how I sold myself out. This was the moment I dug a hole, so full of mud and stones and worms and slugs, that I would never get out, that I was buried, part of the earth now, that I would never see light again.

"My name is Elizabeth Porter," I said, my voice an ugly croak.

"Why did you cry onstage, Elizabeth? Why did you say 'Lizzie died'?"

"You heard my . . ." *Gag.* "Mother. I can be dramatic. And she's right. I had a stomachache this morning. I didn't feel good. Something just came over me—I got scared, in front of all those people."

"I can get someone for you to talk to. It might be a good idea."

"What do you mean?"

"A counselor. A therapist."

I shook my head. "But I'm fine."

"Girls don't just pass out for no reason," she said.

"I didn't have breakfast. Because of my stomach. And I was so nervous . . ."

She checked the drip going into my veins. The bag was pretty much empty. She wrote some notations on a chart. "Your temp is normal," she said. "And your other vital signs are fine. I'd like to keep you overnight."

I nearly moaned. "I'm fine," I said, forcing my voice to stay steady. "I just want to go home."

She stared at me as if she knew I was lying. Had she seen the news with my story featured? Were there bulletins and alerts, did people at the hospital keep up with missing children? Was she recognizing me even at this moment?

But she didn't, or she wouldn't have smiled. Seeing her capitulate, give up her suspicions and decide to believe me, made me feel that Emily really died. And she was never coming back.

"I'm going to release you, Lizzie. But I'm worried. I want you to see a therapist. That's the price of my letting you go home now. I'll give your mother some names. And you're going to come to my office in a few days for a checkup."

"Okay," I said.

"And don't skip breakfast anymore."

"It's the most important meal of the day," I said.

Mrs. Porter was waiting outside the exam room for me. While Dr. Dean signed my discharge papers, Mrs. Porter removed Carole's *CD* necklace from my neck. I felt her cool fingers undo the clasp, then replace it with the anchor chain she'd obviously taken back from Carole. She supported me, arm around my shoulders, just like a loving mother, as we walked past my friends. Without a word, she handed Carole her necklace.

Casey reached out, to brush my fingers with his, but I kept my hand in my pocket. I was shaking so hard, I couldn't let myself look at him. I would have flown into his arms if I had.

I stared straight ahead as I walked out the hospital door, through the parking lot, into the minivan, into what felt like the end of my life.

CHAPTER FIFTEEN

DAY SIXTY-NINE

It was easy for them to keep me home from school. Mrs. Morton and the entire administration thought Lizzie was obviously sick, and she needed to rest and recuperate.

Mrs. Porter locked me in my room. She didn't come downstairs once. They didn't feed me for an entire day. The steeple clock's chimes reminded me.

At first I wasn't hungry. Even if I had been, I wouldn't have given them the satisfaction of eating. I did feel a certain agony, though. I worried that I'd pushed Mrs. Porter over the edge. She'd drive to Black Hall to stab my mother and leave me to rot in this cinder block dungeon.

Soon my stomach began to growl. It grumbled and gnawed, and the harder I tried not to think about it, the more I did. A few hours without food isn't that long, I told myself. Explorers, people lost on mountains or in the woods, went much longer than that. I'd seen the movie *Into the Wild* with Mick and Anne, and I thought of how Chris McCandless had stayed in his bus in the Alaska bush for months, not eating.

Then again, he wound up dying of starvation.

My namesake, St. Emily de Vialar, deprived herself of food because the poor didn't have enough to eat. Monks went on long fasts. In church, we said "offer it up." Meaning: Offer up any suffering to the greater good—like world peace or finding a missing girl. I offered up my hunger to my mother's safety. And to my family finding me. Was that selfish? I was too hungry to care.

If I thought I had been weak and wobbly onstage, it was nothing compared with this. I started to hallucinate. I became convinced that my mom was dead, and that I was going to die here alone. I'd never see another person, never see my family. Casey must have thought my disappearance negated our pact. He wouldn't come for me.

By the time the door finally clicked open, I was lying under the covers, whimpering.

"Em."

I rolled over, saw Chloe standing there with a bowl of soup. She walked slowly toward the bed, being careful not to spill it. She sat down beside me and waited for me to sit up.

"Here," she said, handing me the bowl. "It's tomato, your favorite."

And it was—Emily's. Lizzie's favorite had been chicken and rice.

My hand trembled as I tried to hold the spoon. When I touched the metal to my mouth, my teeth chattered so much the hot liquid spilled down the front of my nightgown. Chloe grabbed a wad of tissue and dabbed it off me.

"Eat fast," she said. "You need your strength."

I put the spoon down and used both hands to drink from the bowl. It should have tasted delicious, but it made me retch. I had to wait, let my stomach settle, before trying again. Then I thought: arsenic.

"Is this supposed to kill me?" I asked.

"No," Chloe said. "I made the soup myself. Well, I opened the can. My parents just left—they had to go to a meeting at the school, to talk about you. But I don't know how long they'll be gone."

"What about me?" I asked.

"About what happened in the auditorium. You know, everyone's asking, 'What's wrong with Lizzie?'"

"How are your parents going to answer that?"

She seemed agitated; she checked her iPhone. "They've got it all figured out. The same old thing about how traveling wore you down, and you got that virus, and you're so drained and 'emotionally exhausted'; that's what they're going to say. And they'll say you have to get treatment, that 'Uncle Jim' the doctor is arranging for you to go to a hospital. They're not sending you back to school."

"Then . . . what?"

"They're going to keep you in here," she said. "Lock you in this room forever. They'll say you're going to the hospital to get well, and when you get back, they're going to homeschool you. That's the story."

"I can't," I said, trying to set the bowl on the bedside table, missing the edge, dropping it on the floor. The china shattered and the soup splashed everywhere.

"They know you can't be Lizzie out in the world," Chloe told me. "You proved that when you lost it and said Lizzie died. But they still think you can be Lizzie here in the house. With us. Well, my mom does."

"No," I said, staring down at the floor and the soup spreading around my feet, shaking my head. "It's impossible."

"I know," Chloe said. "Get dressed."

"What?"

"Hurry," she said, throwing some clothes at me.

They were mine—my wonderful, comfy, non-Lizzie clothes. In a blur, I threw on my old jeans, my Martha's Vineyard T-shirt, and my ratty sweater and green army jacket. Chloe must have pulled them out from wherever her parents had hidden them. My sweater sleeve was frayed. Lizzie would never have worn anything so shabby. Her clothes were always perfect. It's strange the things you notice even when you're moving fast.

"Come on," Chloe said.

Chloe and I ran up the stairs. With the Porters gone, the living room felt empty, cold and dank, as funereal as if another death had occurred in the family. Chloe went to the window, looking left and right, up and down the street.

"Let's get going," she said. "I should never have taken the time to give you that soup, but I didn't want you fainting again."

"Where are they really?" I asked.

"School, I told you!"

My heart seized. I didn't believe her.

"They've gone to Black Hall, haven't they?"

"Aren't you listening to me?"

"She's going to kill my mother!" I said. Just then we heard tires crunching the snow outside. The car stopped behind the back door, between the house and the barn. In a minute, the Porters would walk into the kitchen.

"They're back," Chloe said. She grabbed my hand, pulled me toward the front door.

"They'll see us."

"Just hurry!"

Was she really helping me? Or was this a sick trap? She opened the front door, let me out, then muted the latch as she silently closed it behind us. I had no choice, so I followed her down the steps.

"Where are we going?" I asked.

"Casey's. He's waiting for us. But if we cut through the trees, they'll see our tracks."

The yard was three feet deep with snow. Every second felt eternal, and I imagined the Porters' eyes on our backs as we ran down the hard-packed driveway toward the street.

Circling around the woods and thicket between our houses seemed to take forever. It was late afternoon, and the light was fading. The snow was purple with long shadows. I felt the encroaching darkness trying to hide me.

We tore up the trail to Casey's house, and I looked for his father's SUV. That had been half our deal: We would wait for Mr. Donoghue to get home, and for the Porters to be busy, and then we'd call for help. But the vehicle wasn't there, and the Porters had probably already discovered that I wasn't in the basement and were anything but distracted.

Casey's front door was open. I saw smoke wisp out of the chimney, dissolve in the frigid air. Chloe and I ran up the steps. Casey was inside waiting. With one hand he slammed the door behind us and with the other he pulled me close. My heart was pounding so hard I couldn't breathe.

"She's not safe!" Chloe said, pacing the front hall. "They'll figure it out; they'll be here in a minute."

Casey double-locked the door. He led Chloe and me through the living room, turning off lights behind him. We climbed two creaky flights of stairs. The third floor was frigid, like walking into a freezer. The walls weren't insulated; you could see lines of blue ice through the cracks between boards. But there were storage chests tucked under the eaves, and Casey pulled out two blankets. He gave one to Chloe, wrapped the other around me and himself. Shivering, we knelt by the small window facing the Porters' house. Even though I knew we were up in the mansard roof, and the attic was dark and we wouldn't be silhouetted, I imagined Mrs. Porter with supernatural eyesight, homing in on me, coming to get me.

"I should go back," Chloe said. "I can play dumb."

"No, she'll get it out of you," I said.

"I will never tell," she said.

"Why are you helping me? They'll be so mad at you."

"Because Casey said you told him everything," Chloe said. In the half light streaming through the tiny window, I saw her eyes pool with tears. "He told me what it's doing to you."

You've been living with me, seeing it all along, I wanted to say. *Why didn't you help before? Why didn't you see it's been killing me?* Instead, I took her hand, filled with a surprising rush of love.

"What are we going to do now?" Chloe asked.

"Wait for my dad," Casey said. "He's driving back from New York. When he gets here, he'll help."

I snuggled against him under the blanket. His arm was around me. The heat between us made a force field, a safe shield, and no one could get through. But then I saw the Porters' back door wink open, just long enough for a splash of orange light to spill onto the snow, then disappear. Through the rattling old window glass I heard someone running.

"Lizzie! Get back here right now!" Mrs. Porter's scream sliced through the cracks in the walls.

It was too dark to see what she was doing. Was she on the way here, to Casey's? I imagined her flying straight onto the roof like a witch, oozing her way into the attic, enfolding me in black robes and hiding me forever. But then I saw car lights flickering through the branches and thick pines. I imagined something even worse than the witch coming here: She was going to Black Hall. I jumped up.

"She's leaving! We have to stop her!" I said. "Chloe, you know where she's going to go."

"Here," Chloe said. Her hands were trembling as she handed me her cell phone. "Call your mother and warn her."

Just the idea of being able to call home shoved a sob into my throat. I was shaking so hard, my fingers slid all over the numbers and I couldn't dial. Car lights flickered closer to Casey's house—had Mrs. Porter driven straight next door, coming to find me at the Donoghues's house? But they weren't just headlights; the pulse of blue strobes sparked the black sky. A police car sped into Casey's drive. It stopped short, and two police officers got out.

"What's going on?" I asked, staring into his eyes. "Did you call them?"

"No," he said. "I promised you I wouldn't. Did you, Chloe?"

She shook her head. "No." Her voice came out in a whisper.

I had no idea why they were there, I didn't even think about it, but I ran downstairs so fast my feet slipped, and I slid halfway down the second flight, barely catching my balance, my hand on the banister. Casey was right behind me.

The doorbell rang, and he stepped forward and opened the door. The officers stood there, a man and a woman. They wore thick black uniform jackets and watch caps. The woman's brown hair was pulled back in a ponytail.

I waited in the dining room, but I peered around the corner.

"We're looking for a missing girl," the officer said.

Casey was silent.

"She's from Connecticut. Have you seen anyone like that?"

Still, Casey said nothing.

"Two nights ago, a call was made. It pinged off the cell tower on Deer Rock Road, up near Benjamin's tree farm. Were you up there?"

"Yes," he said.

Night before last, tobogganing. Casey had handed me his phone on that hill in the wilderness, and I'd dialed home, but the signal was dropped. I'd thought the connection hadn't been made.

"The Connecticut State Police traced the call to a cell phone registered at this address," the officer said. "Did someone here try to call Mary Lonergan in Black Hall, Connecticut?"

I walked out of the dining room, stepped around Casey.

"I did," I said.

"What's your name?" she asked.

"Emily Lonergan," I said. "I'm Emily. I'm the missing girl."

And then I started to cry.

CHAPTER SIXTEEN

B ut there wasn't time to be emotional.

"This is life and death," I said to the woman officer. I read the name tag sewn on the breast of her black Royston Police Department jacket: CLARKE. "I know that sounds crazy, but it's true."

"What do you mean?" she asked.

"The people next door—they're going to kill my mother!"

"Okay, hold on, slow down."

"No, you have to go there now, right away. If they see you here, they—well, she, Mrs. Porter—is going to go to Connecticut and murder my mom. Please hurry, stop her now."

Officer Clarke just stood there, an expression of apprehension on her face. The male officer, Peterson, had circled around to stand behind Casey and Chloe. I felt as if they were trying to herd us together.

"Why don't we all go down to the station," Officer Peterson said. "And we can sort it out there."

"You don't get it," I said. "We have to do something *now*."

"Emily, why did you run away?" Officer Clarke asked.

"I didn't," I said, trying to keep my voice steady and low, in case Mrs. Porter was lurking in the bushes.

"She didn't," Chloe said.

"Who are you?" Officer Clarke said.

"Chloe Porter."

"And you?" she asked Casey.

"Casey Donoghue," he said. "That was my phone Emily used to try to call her parents—to ask for help. This is my house. Mine and my dad's."

"And you helped Emily run away? You've sheltered her?"

"You're not listening!" Casey said. "She didn't run away; she was kidnapped. We were just waiting for my dad to get here, so he could call you and the people next door wouldn't know."

"That's what I'm telling you," I said, boiling over with panic. "They're going to hurt my mom. Please go there now—she, Mrs. Porter, is probably already on her way. I'm sure she saw you pull in. She swore to me if I told, she'd kill her. Please let me call my mom, I have to warn her . . ."

"Okay, okay," Officer Clarke said. She pulled out her radio. It crackled, a voice came on, and Officer Clarke said a bunch of numbers, Casey's address, then, "more units." She turned back to me.

"Who kidnapped you?" she asked. I swear, her eyes looked more suspicious than understanding. I would suspect me, too: It must have seemed to them I'd been free to leave at any time. They hadn't discovered me in the locked basement, but right here in Casey's house, no kidnappers in sight. I shuddered so hard my teeth chattered, and I couldn't speak.

"My parents did," Chloe said. "They took her."

I turned to look at her. Tears were pouring down her pink cheeks. She gazed toward the grove between the houses, as if she could see through the trees, straight to her mother.

Things started happening fast after that.

Two more police cars sped up the street, sirens wailing, blue lights flashing. Casey's dad had arrived, just turned into the driveway, but an officer stopped the SUV, wouldn't let him come closer.

Casey's arm was around me. On the other side, I pressed against Chloe. She was shaking and cold. Officer Clarke went out to talk to the newly arrived police. Mr. Donoghue was speaking to them, too, animatedly, pointing at the house, wanting to come to us.

I was dying. They were all just standing there talking. Why were they wasting their time here instead of stopping Mrs. Porter? I grabbed Casey's hand.

"I have to get over there," I said.

"Come on," he said. While Officer Peterson was talking on his radio, Casey, Chloe, and I backed surreptitiously out the front hall, walked quietly into the den, and flew out the side door. Officer Peterson called after us. The snow hadn't been shoveled. There was no trail between the houses. The heavy pack was iced over. The ice held in places—it was like skating on a frozen river—but then the crust broke and I sank into snow thigh-deep. I ran through as if it wasn't there. Casey and Chloe were right behind me.

The first thing I noticed: The minivan was parked next to the barn. That was a blast of relief until I realized Mrs. Porter might have had another vehicle hidden nearby. She had said she had secret ways of getting to my mom. I thought of the shoe on my bed, of her sneaking into my mother's closet to get it. She could be driving the secret vehicle right now.

All three of us tore into the house.

Casey and Chloe began searching the first floor. I heard Mr. Porter's voice calling down from one of the bedrooms. Mrs. Porter wouldn't be up there. I knew where to find her. I walked down the basement stairs.

She was sitting on Lizzie's bed, holding one of the pillows. She clutched it to her chest. Her face was screwed into a knot of pain. When she looked up, saw me standing in the door, the anguish relaxed. It didn't go away entirely, but she gave me a small, broken smile. She looked surprised and guardedly happy to see me.

"You came back," she said.

"I thought maybe you . . . would have been on your way to Black Hall by now," I said.

"No," she said.

"But my mother," I said. "You said . . ."

"She's safe," Mrs. Porter said.

My eyes teared up with relief.

"The police are here," I said.

"I know," she said. "I saw their lights. This pillow"—she buried her face in it—"still smells like Lizzie. It's from her shampoo, I suppose. That you wash your hair with."

"Mrs. Porter," I said. "We should go upstairs."

"We will. In just one minute. Stay a tiny bit longer, talk to me, just so I can take the memory with me, remember it always. Please."

Reluctance kept me rooted in the doorway, but she was looking at me with such warmth and sadness. I saw the old Mrs. Porter, the one I used to love, who had always been kind, had always cared about me, the one I'd felt so close to for so long.

She held up the letter I'd found in the clock. I could see Lizzie's handwriting, the envelope addressed to Mame.

"I chose this town because of Lizzie," Mrs. Porter said. "There were so many places we could have moved after she died. But she had such a fascination with Royston, her connection to Sarah through Mame. And I thought . . . wouldn't Lizzie love it here? Wouldn't she be fascinated to live right next door to the house Sarah had built for herself and Nora? Another mother and daughter who were so close, looked after each other. Right here! And this house was for sale, so it seemed meant to be."

She held out the envelope for me to take. I stepped closer, hesitating. I was on high alert, listening for voices and footsteps upstairs. A door opened and closed softly; I imagined Officers Clarke and Peterson, the other police officers, too, in the house now, asking where I was.

"Take this," Mrs. Porter said, handing me the letter. "I want you to have it. It's good to have a talisman. An object from this place, from this precious time on earth, to take with you where you're going next."

"Thank you," I said. Her words were bizarre. Going next? Home, Mrs. Porter—to my family, to Black Hall. But I was eager to read the letter, and I tucked the envelope into my jacket pocket.

"Could I ask you one more favor?" she asked.

"What?" I asked.

"Sit with me until they come for me. Be Lizzie for one more minute."

My throat caught. I felt a wave of nausea, thinking of the nights she had hovered over me, watching me sleep. I knew I should hate her for everything, but in that moment, she was so calm, her voice so normal—erasing the evil Mrs. Porter and bringing back the old one I'd loved.

"I can sit with you, but I can't be Lizzie again." I eased down on the edge of the bed. Our elbows were lightly touching. She leaned against me, put her head on my shoulder. I felt physically sick.

"Your hair smells like her. It's the same color. If I close my eyes, I can pretend it's her. Do you know what that's meant to me? You've given me the greatest gift. I told myself you wouldn't mind, that you'd come to accept being Lizzie." She turned to me, brow furrowed. "I'm sorry it's been so hard."

"That's okay," I said, even though it wasn't. The point was, this was almost over. My heart galloped, wanting to get upstairs. But I told myself as long as she was right here, sitting still, she wasn't on her way to my mom. Everything would be fine now.

"Will you say it one more time?" she asked. "I'll close my eyes, and you say it, and I'll hear it forever, wherever I go."

Mom. She wanted me to call her that, but there was no way, never again. That request broke something inside me, whatever had been holding me in suspended animation, and I knew if I didn't get out of there I'd throw up or scratch her face off.

"Let's go now, Mrs. Porter," I said.

"Please, say it just once more. Will you call me by the right name? It will make this so much easier . . ."

This? Going to jail? Suddenly the insanity in her expression was back, and I started to jump up. But she clawed my wrist, nails digging into my skin, pulling me back down.

"Lizzie," she said. "Lizzie, we're going together."

"I'm going home," I said, trying to yank myself free.

Then I saw her other hand.

Her fingers were closed around the knife with the silver blade, the one I'd seen in the video, and in her pocket, and so many times in my nightmares.

"I am doing this because I love you," she said, her voice soothing, almost honey sweet. "This life is unbearable. The cruelty of losing the people you love, of having them die and being left here alone. But we won't have to lose each other again. There's eternal peace. That is what I am giving you."

"No, you're not!" I screamed.

I fought her. I hit her as hard as I could, heard my fist crack her cheekbone. I tried to kick her, but she'd leapt up from the bed, gripping my wrist, and my foot missed. She was waving the knife, stabbing the air, but I kept ducking, trying to pull away.

"You brought this on," she said, her eyes red with tears. "You made me do this. We could have been happy, if only you'd tried harder. We could have been a family again. This is the only way."

I put everything I had into it, and I tried to shove her again, but the knife got in the way. It felt like a punch in my chest, not sharp at all. But I heard my bones splitting, and I felt my insides melting. My heart sped up, and with every beat, I heard a gush of my blood, saw the bright red stream pulsing onto the floor.

Voices surrounded me. Chloe's, Officer Clarke's. Mrs. Porter's. Mrs. Porter was crying, "Let me die with her; I want us to die together."

My spirit started to rise. My body stayed crumpled on the floor. I could see it—my eyes open, glassy, staring at nothing. Blood so fresh with oxygen it was scarlet pouring out of my chest. My spirit felt light as air. It looked like gauze, a shapeless wisp spiraling toward the ceiling.

Casey practically dove at me. He cradled my head in one arm. Then he eased me down, flat on the floor, pressed his hands straight into the stab wound, trying to keep the blood inside my body. I heard blood gurgling through his fingers; I swear I felt him holding my heart. All of a sudden my spirit was back in my body. I looked into his eyes, the color of the sea. They were so bright.

"You're not going anywhere," he said. "Emily, you're here with me."

EMTs rushed in. They pushed him aside. An oxygen mask was slapped onto my face. They cut off my jacket and sweater, applied intense pressure to my chest. Someone was saying my name really loud, "Emily, how you doing there? Emily, you're going to be fine. Stay with us, Emily."

And then another voice: "Virginia Porter, you are under arrest for the kidnapping of Emily Lonergan. You have the right to remain silent, you have the right . . ."

Chloe was weeping as the handcuffs were clicked around Mrs. Porter's wrists. Then they handcuffed Chloe.

"No, not Chloe!" I tried to say, but I was choking on blood as they led her away behind her mother.

My whole body had been numb, but now I could feel, and every nerve ending was a sharpened dagger stabbing me again and again. The pain was a wildfire raging through my entire body, taking over my mind, until nothing else existed. I was no longer a person; I was just pain.

"Emily," came Casey's voice. He held my hand, his fingers sticky with my blood, and in the quietest voice you can imagine, with his mouth against my ear, he whispered my name over and over.

CHAPTER SEVENTEEN

They say your life passes before your eyes when you're dying.
Mine did. I saw my parents, my brothers and sisters. Casey,
Carole, their faces full of fear and sorrow and love. I hovered
above them as they took turns sitting by my bedside in intensive
care. Detectives in blue suits stood just outside the room, ques-
tioning Casey and Carole about the Porters, taking notes. They
tried to talk to me, but Dr. Dean told them it wouldn't be possible
for a long time.

If I survived.

My parents huddled close to me, on either side of the bed,
holding my hands. My mother, my beautiful mother with her blue
eyes, so full of love and worry, as if she'd lost me and found me
and was afraid of losing me again.

Mrs. Porter hadn't killed her. She was here. I kept thinking
that. Hot tears scalded my cheeks.

"Oh, Emily," Mom said, her voice breaking. She bent down to
hold me, even though I was bandaged and stuck with a thousand
tubes.

I tried to stay awake. I heard my mom and dad say how much they loved me, how they knew I was strong, how I had to fight to want to live and return home. I felt flooded with love for them. I focused on my mother's blue eyes, my father's wide mouth, his hand so rough, her voice so tender.

"Live, Emily," my mother said. "Please, I love you so much."

I love you, too, I tried to tell her, but the words wouldn't come out. *Do you know what I did to save your life? All I ever wanted was to go home. I prayed you wouldn't drink. I just want everything to be okay.*

But a breathing tube ran down my throat, and the best I could do was croak.

"Emily," my mother said over and over. "Emily, my Emily . . ."

I stared at her as long as I could, before my eyelids got too heavy to stay open, before they fluttered closed again.

Morphine kept me in a sick, sleepy twilight state. That meant I was mostly aware but not totally, and not quite sure whether I was dead or alive. My life hung in the balance—literally. That's a dramatic phrase you hear on soap operas, like the ones Lizzie and I used to watch on snow days, and it meant the person was in a coma, balancing on the tightrope between living and dying. Fall, and you never get up again. The state of my aliveness was minute to minute.

When the EMTs put me in the ambulance, I was legally dead. Casey kept my blood pumping as long as he could, but my heart stopped, and so did my breathing.

I heard Dr. Dean tell this to my parents. She told them that my brain was deprived of oxygen for over a minute, so even if I lived, I could have brain damage. I didn't think I did because my thoughts were pretty clear and my imagination was more vivid than ever.

Or maybe this was just how it felt to be dead.

My parents were generous, I heard Dr. Dean tell me. Some families don't let friends visit the patients in intensive care because visiting time is so limited—only a few minutes each hour because the patient needs her rest. But my brothers and sisters were here in Maine, and each one took a turn with me.

And every three or four times, Casey came.

I longed for those times.

His touch was so gentle, the way he smoothed my hair, stroked my arms. His long hair brushed across me, tickled my face when he lowered his head to kiss my forehead, press his cheek to mine.

"Patrick and Bea told me a lot about you," he said. "Things I didn't know. Because we haven't had enough time."

He was holding a library book. I could see the protective clear plastic wrapping, the sticker on the spine, but his hand covered the title. "Patrick says you like plays. You write and perform in them, and I can't wait to see one. Maybe you'll write one about what happened here."

I will, I thought. *It will be a killer, not just because the girl was kidnapped and stabbed and lives through it, but because she fell in love with the boy next door.*

"I know you can hear me, Emily," Casey said. "Some people are saying you can't, the coma is too deep, but I feel you. You have so much energy, it's filling this room. The whole hospital is humming with it. So I thought, since you love plays, I would read one to you. That means I have to play all the parts, so try to forgive me because I'm no actor, and I'm sure you've read this a few times already, but it, well, it's a love story."

He started to read:

"Act One, Prologue, Two households, both alike in dignity, In fair Verona, where we lay our scene . . ."

Romeo and Juliet.

The breathing machine, the thick tube down my throat and taped to my mouth, kept my respiration steady, a constant rhythm that didn't vary. But if only Casey knew how fast my heart wanted to beat. The fact he chose this play to read me, the way he'd said, *Well, it's a love story.*

I wiggled my fingers. He didn't see, because they didn't actually move. But inside me, where I was most awake and alive, my spirit most restless, they did. They were signaling to him that I loved his choice of plays, I loved the way he read each character with such feeling, and I loved him.

"She lives!" Iggy said.

He and Mick happened to be the ones at my bedside when my eyelids fluttered open and didn't close again right away, when I started gagging and pulling at the tube in my throat and the little plastic oxygen prongs in my nose, trying to rip the needles from my arms.

"Whoa, sweetheart," Mick said, restraining me with his entire 6'4" heft. "No going crazy here. Calm down, there you go.

Look at those eyes, look at those gorgeous blue peepers. You know how worried you've had us? Well, I've said all along, 'She's a fighter, she's a trouper, no one has more Irish in her than Emily Magdalene Bartholomea Lonergan.'"

I couldn't wait to tell him I saw him crying when he said all that, big tough Michael Lonergan, older brother. Ha-ha, saw your tears, big guy.

Iggy walked into the hall to tell the family that I was awake. They all rushed in, completely ignoring rules about two visitors at the most at a time in the ICU. They surrounded me, every single one of them either touching my legs or arms or literally, like my dad, picking me up. He held me in his arms, cradling me against his chest, probably just like when I was a baby. Bea got right into the bed with me. She lay beside me, just like we did on cold winter nights when we'd giggle and tell stories, when we'd entwine feet to stay warm and wind up in a pillow fight. I felt her breath on my cheek, and it calmed me down a little.

But I quickly started struggling again. I wanted to untube myself and get out of there. A nurse came in. I liked her—Nina, with dark hair and long eyelashes and a way of telling me about her rotten boyfriend while I slept on. She herded my family out the door and talked to me while she took my vital signs, told me the jerk had had the nerve to show up at her apartment with a cactus—a cactus!—three days after she'd found out he was cheating with his upstairs neighbor.

The story slowed my heart rate, and if I could have laughed at the cactus, I would have. By the time Dr. Dean arrived, I was ready to breathe on my own. She and a resident and two nurses removed the thick tube, hurting my throat as if it had been sliced with razors, but giving me so much relief I felt freed from yet another prison.

Only an hour later, the agents showed up. I had thought they were detectives, a man and a woman, in the suits and solemn expressions, but they were FBI. I couldn't believe it.

"I'm FBI Special Agent Chase," the man said. "And this is Special Agent Madison." He gestured to the woman.

"The FBI?" I rasped.

"Emily, we are investigating because you were allegedly taken across state lines," Special Agent Madison said. "Can you tell us in your own words what happened?"

I wanted to laugh. I knew Bea was out in the waiting room, and she would have gotten it: Special Agent Madison was a woman in a pretty blue coat, with fair skin and blond hair. The kidnapper of my mother's nightmares. But instead of laughing, I shrieked. I guess the medication had made me a little sensitive, and the reality, the nightmare of what I'd been through came roaring back. Having the FBI at my bedside made it realer than real. There was no way I could even start to tell what happened, what it was like in the basement.

"You're not ready; it's okay," the agent said, when my shrieking got louder, when I felt myself going insane. Then I exhausted myself—my mind went totally blank as if all the bad memories were erased. I stopped screaming and became totally silent. I stared into space, not seeing anyone or anything, just blankness.

"We'll come back," Special Agent Chase said.

* * *

"Chloe is toast," Carole said. Other than Casey, she was the first non-family visitor once I'd moved from the ICU to a room on a medical floor.

"What do you mean?" I asked.

"They're in prison," Carole said. "All three of them. Mr. Porter's in the Maine Correctional Center, Mrs. Porter's in the Women's Center, and Chloe is in the Casco Bay Development Center, which is another way of saying jail for kids."

"But she didn't do anything," I said. "Other than what they forced her to."

"It's sad, I agree, but she had a choice," Carole said.

"Not really," I said, remembering how focused and controlling Mrs. Porter had been. "She went along because her mother needed her to."

"If her mother had needed her to kill you, would she have done that?" Carole asked.

"No," I said. "She helped me to get away."

"Well, yes," Carole said. "But only after you were there for over two months. By the way—two *months*? You couldn't have told me?"

I stared at her. She was wearing a huge blue L.L.Bean fleece that I knew belonged to Mark, her gold *CD* necklace, and a cream-colored cable-knit cashmere watch cap. She looked both hurt and reproachful.

"I'm sorry," I said.

"It's not just because we're friends," she said, "but I could have helped you. I keep thinking back, wondering if you tried to give me secret messages. Did I miss them? Did I let you down?"

"No, not at all!" I said, wishing I could leap out of bed and hug her.

"Okay," she said. "But I'm so worried I did."

"You didn't."

Carole nodded, then patted my hand. "Anyway, half the school wants to start a defense fund for Chloe, and the other half wants her to rot in jail."

I thought about it, remembering moments with Chloe: when she'd lured me into the van, when she'd forced me to watch her mother's FaceTime and send the email, when she'd brought me soup and led me to Casey's house.

"I don't want her to rot in jail," I said. But I was confused about exactly what I did want.

"Yeah, well," Carole said. "The FBI will sort it out. They're in the hall, salivating to interrogate you some more."

"I know," I said, because they'd already been in to see me again and again. I was tired of talking. There was only so much I could say about what I didn't understand.

A resident I'd never seen before entered my room. She was tall, thin, with curly red hair, hazel eyes, and surprisingly perfect makeup. She wore blue scrubs and I noticed the hot pink collar of a wool blazer peeking out. It was pretty and matched her blush.

"How are you today?" she asked.

"Fine," I said.

"Really?" she asked.

"Kind of," I said.

"I'm Dr. Daniela," she said. "I'm a psychiatry resident. Do you mind if I ask you about how you feel? Maybe you can tell me what happened?"

I watched her pull a stethoscope out of her pocket. With one hand, she warmed the round metal piece they put on your chest. But she didn't press it against my heart. She just stood there holding it.

"Start from when the Porters took you," she said. "What was it like?"

"Well," I said, feeling uncomfortable. "I didn't expect it."

"I can imagine! Tell me more." She moved closer. I looked into her eyes and had the weirdest feeling: She looked hungry but very excited, as if she had just come upon some delicious food, as if I were her meal.

"Where's Dr. Dean?" I asked.

"Oh, she's busy with other patients," she said. "Now, what part did Chloe play? Is it true she lured you into the van? Did they drug you?"

I'd had therapists after Lizzie died. I'd seen a psychiatrist. They always asked you about how you felt—not about what actually happened. Also, why was she holding a stethoscope? Why was I getting such a creepy feeling?

"Um, is my mother outside?" I asked.

"She's getting coffee," she said. "Now, about Chloe. I'm hearing that she was every bit as guilty as her parents, and . . ."

The door opened. My brother Tommy walked in. He stood between me and the woman, glowering at her. "I'm studying journalism and I appreciate that you need to get the story," he said. "But you can't bother my sister."

"The story?" I asked.

"This is Daniela Starkey," Tommy told me. "She's a reporter for a local station. She's been trying to interview the family, just wanting to do her job, but she can't do it here. Do you understand, Ms. Starkey? Don't bother my sister again."

"I'm sorry," the woman said. "I truly am. But if you want to talk, Emily, when you're ready, I'm here."

"Got it," Tommy said, his voice hard, leading her to the door. "But I swear you'll be sorry if you come back."

"You're threatening me?" she asked, holding her tape recorder toward him.

"I'm telling you we'll call your editor. We'll get you fired for harassing a very badly injured girl."

She clicked off the recorder and scuttled away.

Tommy returned to me, sat on the edge of my bed. "What a sleaze, trying to trick you. She must have missed the part about respect in journalism school."

"What does she want with me?" I asked.

"Em, you're the biggest story in the country right now. Every single TV station and newspaper wants your story. Have you looked outside?"

He put his arm around me, helped me out of bed. My chest was bandaged. My breath was shallow, because it hurt every time air went in or out. Just a few steps to the window felt like a mile on the track, but Tommy held me up.

Lining the street and filling the hospital parking lot were more trucks than I could count. They all had logos painted on the side—TV stations from NBC to the BBC—and satellite dishes on the roofs. People were standing outside the vehicles, bundled up against the Maine winter cold, staring up at my window. As soon as I leaned my forehead against the glass, a bunch of flashbulbs went off. Tommy eased me away, closed the curtain.

"I bet Daniela's stethoscope was a microphone," Tommy said. "She was trying to get the dirt on Chloe and the Porters. You can talk whenever you want, but we'll help you. The whole family's behind you, Em. These reporters are sharks, and . . ."

"I'm shark food," I said. "I get it."

I certainly felt like it.

I had seven surgeries within the first three weeks. The knife had nicked my left lung, barely missed my heart. My ribs were cracked. The wounds and incisions contributed to a lot of pain, way too much anesthesia, and, yes, opioids. I wasn't quite allergic to the drugs, but they made me really sick. I was always throwing up. Casey could visit me lots more now that I wasn't in intensive care, and it was great, but what wasn't great was having the dry heaves with him sitting there.

"It's okay," he said, grabbing for the little curved plastic pail on my tray table.

"Not in front of you," I said.

"Em," he said just as I let go and spewed into the pail.

"That didn't happen," I said.

"Already forgotten," he said.

Tears began leaking from my eyes. He wiped them with his thumb. The worst part about trying not to be emotional was that I always wound up emotional. He was kind of the best. No, he was the total best.

It turned out the reason I wasn't getting better faster was that I had "confusion"—that was an actual medical term. It meant I had tachycardia—a too-fast heartbeat, over one hundred beats a minute—and dropping blood pressure. Dr. Dean did another sternotomy—she cut straight through my sternum—to find that Mrs. Porter's knife had actually touched the left ventricle of my heart. Only the very point of the blade had penetrated, an almost microscopic incision, but that was enough to cause internal bleeding. My blood oxygen level had dropped, so they had me on oxygen again.

That meant I had to go to Boston, to the best cardiac surgeon in New England.

Dr. Cho wasn't just in Boston—he was at Lizzie's old hospital.

Because it was an emergency, there was no time for good-byes to Carole and other friends. Casey had been in the OR waiting room with my family, waiting for news about my condition, when the decision was made to airlift me. They let him see me, but they made him wear scrubs, including a funny-looking cap and surgical mask.

"Dr. Donoghue," I said through an oxygen mask as he approached my gurney.

"You're not leaving," he said.

"I know, I refuse," I said.

"Well, it turns out you have to," he said.

"Stop," I said. "It hurts to cry."

"I sent an audio file to your phone," he said.

My real cell phone—the one I hadn't had the last two and a half months.

"It's a bunch of music I played, some I wrote," he said, "for you to listen to while you get better."

"Thank you," I said.

"And I have an app for texting, so you'd better text me back."

"I will."

The pilot and medical staff who would take me on the air ambulance—that's what they called the plane that would transport me to Boston—were ready, so they came to get me. Anne and Bea, and Iggy and Patrick, all with surgical masks on, started to lift my stretcher, to carry me into the ground ambulance. Casey helped, too. The five of them hoisted me.

"When are you coming back?" Casey asked.

"As soon as she gets better, she can make plans," Anne said.

"The minute the surgery's over," Bea said. "The second she's ready, she'll be in touch with you."

"When will that be?" Casey asked.

"Tomorrow," I said, through the oxygen mask. A doctor had slapped sensors on my chest and hooked me up to a heart monitor. A blood pressure cuff was inflating and making my bicep sore. A nurse checked my IV. Casey kissed my forehead, then the staff hustled me away. The ambulance sped to the airport. I was loaded onto a private jet, we took off and banked over the Maine woods, and that was the last I remembered until I woke up in Boston.

The surgeries weren't exactly a piece of cake, but they were a lot better because the OR staff let me wear headphones during all of them. Casey's music took me completely away, to a place of peaceful feelings. Sometimes the anesthesia made me hallucinate. I'd see people, strangers and friends, and imaginary creatures, including an octopus with twenty legs and pink wings. I'd see Mrs. Porter's green eyes, but not her face, and I'd scream, but no sound would come out. Once I dreamed of flying knives. They were aimed at my mother, but I had superpowers and was able to stop each silver blade before it hit her.

Chloe often appeared to me through the haze of surgical drugs. I'd see her in that place, Casco Bay. I hated that she was locked up. Sometimes I'd forget I was in Boston and wonder if I was back in Royston. I would feel Chloe standing beside me. We were ice cold, just like all those mornings at the bus stop in the snow fort, sheltered from the wind. We'd both be stamping our feet to stay warm, listening for the school bus to come down Passamaquoddy Road, waiting in comfortable silence, almost like sisters.

Almost.

PART TWO

CHAPTER EIGHTEEN

I wasn't the same.

Twenty-five days had passed since I escaped from the Porters, and I didn't know who I was.

Is this really where I live, this house in Black Hall, where I grew up? I found myself thinking. *I love my family so much, more than ever. But I am different than I used to be.*

The experience of being kidnapped, of being held captive for two months, changed me. No one, no matter how they try, could understand. For the first time in my life, I felt separate from my family. I actually started to wonder if I belonged.

My first night home, I slept between my parents in their bed. Nearly every other since then, I slept in Bea's bed. She was always careful, turning over gently, trying not to jostle me. My chest still hurt, as if the knife was still in there. It would have been easier to sleep alone, but I needed my sister's closeness.

Otherwise the nightmares were too bad. When I woke up, Bea would be right there, telling me everything was okay, no one would ever take me again, no one would ever kidnap her little sister, Emily, again. Ever.

Bea said my name a lot, as if she could erase the fact that for two months I was supposed to be Lizzie.

I always thanked her. What I didn't say was that I didn't feel like Emily anymore.

The only thing that soothed me was thinking about Casey. His long silky hair, his gaze, the feeling of his lips on mine, his sea-glass-colored eyes. I tried to remember every word we ever said to each other. The feeling of his arms around me when we flew down the toboggan hill, when he held me after Mrs. Porter stabbed me, until the paramedics came.

Maybe I should have known that when I saw him at Royston Hospital, before they put me on the helicopter to Boston, it would be the last time—or it felt like the last time. He didn't drive, and never would. I didn't have my license yet. There were hundreds of miles between us.

So I lived for our texts. Some of his were audio files he sent me. My favorites were the ones where he played music.

> *Last night I dreamed of the mountain*
> *And our cottage in the dell,*
> *And I dreamed a love story,*
> *Of the girl I knew so well.*

I shivered—it was the first song of his I'd heard, when Chloe and I had hidden, listening to him and the band playing in the woods. Even though it seemed crazy, it felt as if he had written the song for me, long before we'd met, even before we'd known each other existed.

One afternoon, lying on my bed in the room I shared with Bea, I got a new text from Casey.

> **Casey:** How are you?
> **Me:** Not sure.
> **Casey:** Why not?
> **Me:** Home doesn't feel like home anymore.
> **Casey:** Then come back here.
> **Me:** Not sure the fam would be wild about that idea.
> **Casey:** They can come, too.

I smiled.

Then I heard footsteps in the hall. Seamus, our golden retriever, lay on the floor beside me and lifted his head to see who was coming. My stomach tightened, the way it did when I'd hear Mrs. Porter approaching. Noises did that to me—they triggered an avalanche of memories and set me on guard, always ready to defend myself.

There was a knock on the door, and Patrick and Bea were standing there, looking so alike with their black hair, lightly freckled skin, and Atlantic Ocean–gray-blue eyes.

"Let's go," Patrick said. "You need to get out of here."

"Where?" I asked.

"A ride. The beach, Gillette Castle, anywhere but your room," he said.

"We'll disguise you and spirit you past the reporters," Bea said.

"No disguise!" I said, louder than I intended, thinking of the months I'd spent wearing Lizzie's hair, face, clothes.

"Okay," she said quickly.

I wanted to jump up, be the same excited, enthusiastic younger sister who'd always followed Bea and Patrick anywhere. But it was as if the bed was a magnet and I was an iron bar: I couldn't move. I didn't move. Neither did Seamus. He barely left my side lately. He knew I needed him.

"I don't want to go out," I said to my brother and sister.

"You've been cooped up too long," Bea said. "You're depressed, Em."

"Can you drive me to Maine?" I blurted. "Then I'll be undepressed."

"The scene of the crime? I don't ever want to go back there again," Bea said. "I can't imagine why you would."

"Casey," I said.

"Well, of course," she said. "Duh, I'm an idiot. Well, he'll have to come visit you here."

"I get why you don't want to be disguised," Patrick said. "So we'll sneak you out the back door, into the car. You can duck down so the reporters won't see you."

"My little celebrity sister," Bea said.

The press. The media. Exclusive interview. *Celebrity*. How could you get to be a celebrity for something you hadn't done yourself? Getting kidnapped and stabbed? It seemed disgusting. Everywhere I went there were news trucks—at both hospitals, here at home in Black Hall, outside the doctor's building, outside the therapist's office. Some of the news trucks were like fancy mobile homes, with lounges for the reporters to relax in and studios for them to edit and transmit footage.

They did whatever they could to get shots of me. Their cameras zoomed in, trying to see through our curtains. They caught me biting into a piece of toast, a glob of strawberry jam sticking to my chin. When I walked outside, from our side door to the car in the driveway, they followed my every step. They yelled my name.

"Come on," Patrick said, sitting beside me on the bed. "Please? I'm worried about you. You're supposed to start school Monday, but how are you going to do that if it's so hard even to take a ride with us?"

"I'm not going back to school," I said.

Bea and Patrick just stared at me. They'd told me the journalists hovered just off school property, shouting questions at them. Reporters went to my older siblings' colleges, to my dad's job sites, and into the marsh to stalk my mother walking Seamus. Seamus, the greatest watchdog in the world, would apparently just wag his tail at them.

All I wanted to do was stay right here on my bed. It was comfortable. It had a squishy pillow-top mattress. The color of my comforter was persimmon—somewhere between red and orange—warm and bright and cozy. My side of the room was painted Tuscan gold with dusky lavender window trim. I used dark ink to draw tendrils and vines of English ivy, the leaves outlined with real gold leaf, a technique I'd learned in set design class. I'd copied the colors and design from the lobby of the Nehantic Theater, where I'd acted in a play the summer of eighth grade; the colors were the opposite of Lizzie's black-and-white and earth tones palette, and they used to make me feel so happy.

"Look," Patrick said finally. "I don't want to pull age rank, but I'm about to. Seamus needs a walk. You need fresh air. Bea and I need coffee. I'll carry you to the car if you really want me to."

"I'll walk," I said. I stood slowly, and my ribs screamed. I caught a glimpse of myself in the mirror: My hair was two-tone. The bottom half was Lizzie black, and the top two inches were Emily reddish-blond. My eyebrows had finally grown in, and I thought they looked pale and boring without the kohl. And this fact weirded me out: I felt naked without the beauty mark. Now that I didn't look like Lizzie anymore, I also didn't look like myself.

Even though we tried to escape the press people, they spotted us leaving the house. Their shouts made me block my ears.

Emily! Over here! How are you feeling? Do you hate the Porters? What was it like? Why didn't you try to escape? Why didn't you run away when you were at school? Will you testify against the Porters? Will you testify against Chloe?

Their words rang through me as if I was a hollow bell. The word that hurt the most was *Chloe*. Bea, Patrick, and I herded Seamus into the station wagon, backed out of the driveway, and headed down Shore Road toward town. Patrick drove fast, backtracking down dirt roads to shake our pursuers. The news trucks must have not wanted to get their fancy tires all muddy, so they dropped away.

The radio was on. Patrick sang loudly to Bon Iver's "Flume," and I felt this crazy fondness—my brothers always sang at the top of their lungs without knowing they were awful. We rounded the corner by the Congregational church and stopped at Black Hall Roasters. The café was on the first floor of a yellow Federal-style house with white columns. Bea and I stayed in the car, and Patrick ran in to get three black coffees. The Lonergans are hard-core; no milk or sugar for us.

"What do you think will happen to Chloe?" Bea asked me, turning around in her seat.

"I don't want to talk about Chloe," I said.

"Was she really part of it?" Bea asked.

"I told you! I really don't want to talk about her!" I said, a little too loudly.

Bea stared at me with an air of older-sister disappointment, letting me know that snapping was unacceptable.

But her questions reverberated in my mind. Chloe had lured me into the Porters' minivan right here, on this exact street. She had made me write that first email to my parents. She had reminded me about her mother and the knife. Yet I wouldn't have gotten out of the basement without her.

I stared out the window.

"Em," Bea began. There was silence while she struggled for the words. "Why *didn't* you?"

"Didn't I what?"

"Run when you could. Why didn't you call us when they let you go to school?"

"Gee," I said, feeling sarcastic and miserable. "I don't know, Bea. But what a good idea. Why didn't I think of that? Why didn't I just escape?" I glared at her. "Why didn't you find me? Look harder? When I sent those emails, why didn't you trace me?"

"Emily. We tried. But the IP address came up as somewhere in Iceland, then Australia. The FBI said . . ."

"I know," I said, deflating, all the anger toward my sister going out of me, along with all the air in my lungs. Evil Mrs. Porter and her fake proxy server, her virtual private network. As Chloe had said, her mother had thought of everything.

Patrick came out with the coffees. Seamus let out an impatient yelp. He was ready for his walk. We drove down to Old Granite Neck, parked in the lot, tried to ignore the reporters who pulled up next to us. Patrick opened the tailgate, and Seamus bounded out, running along the trail to Long Island Sound.

Bea opened the back door, waited for me.

I shook my head.

"A walk on the beach," she said. "You know how much you love that."

"Not today," I said. "I'm just going to stay in the car and drink my coffee."

Bea stared at me for a few seconds. She didn't follow Patrick

and Seamus. She stayed with me, to protect me from the reporters. We sat in the car, not talking. I felt numb. I felt encased in a
hard shell—me soft as a snail inside, everyone else on the outside.
They couldn't get to me, and I couldn't get to them.

I tried not to remember how it used to be, when my sister and
I would be talking and laughing so fast and constantly, tripping
over each other's words. Since returning home, I'd barely had any
conversations at all.

More weirdness:

Being back in Black Hall, you'd think I'd want to text and see
my old friends, my lifelong friends, catch up with them and get
back to where we'd been before I was taken, right?

We texted, but I'd see their names on my phone, and my heart
would do nothing at all. No feeling of happiness.

I lurked on Instagram and Facebook, not posting anything,
scrolling back through the months to see what people had said
about me. To my shock, Dan had posted all these photos of the
Ghost Girl play, including a shot of us kissing.

My girl Em, he'd written under one.

Whattttt?

Then a slew of girls from our class commented: *Oh, poor Dan!
My heart is with you. She WILL come home. You have to heal. Can
I help?*

He didn't reply to any of them, just posted another picture of
me—he'd obviously taken it during rehearsal, me standing
onstage pointing and looking kind of bossy: the director I was.

Dan texted me, too.

Hey its Dan u free for a sec to talk?

This would have been my greatest dream a few months ago.
And I was free, but I couldn't talk. I just couldn't.
Sorry, busy, I wrote.

Dan: R u well? Will u tell me?
Me: Yeah, I'm fine.

I didn't want to be a jerk, but I didn't have that much to say. I
knew that what everyone—including Dan—really wanted was
to talk about THE KIDNAPPING. To ask what it was like to
be abducted. To delve into the creep factor, of me being forced to be
Lizzie. My friends, like everyone in Black Hall, wanted to know
why I didn't bolt.
But Casey and Carole got it.

Carole: What r u doing?
Me: Not sure. What's the meaning of life?
Carole: Ur so existential
Me: That's me. Changing my name to Françoise Sagan.
**Carole: Bonjour, Tristesse. Best depressed girl novel ever.
U depressed?**
Me: Massively.
Carole: Gee I wonder why
Me: A mystery

Carole: Could be fact u were held captive by lunatics? Just a thought.

Me: Ur a genius

Carole: *sigh* the cross I bear. Ok, gotta go. Class. Ms. LeBlanc.

Me: What r u reading now?

Carole: Chaucer. The Canterbury Tales. Ur my favorite pilgrim.

Me: Ur mine.

And then there was Casey.

Did you really write that song for me? I asked after yet another new tune.

Casey: I write them all for you.

Me: Why?

Casey: Because L.

Me: L?

Casey: You know what I mean.

Me: Not really. What?

Casey: It's the first letter in a word.

Me: How many other letters?

Casey: I'll let you take a guess on that.

He didn't give me an actual answer on that, but the next song was titled "Three Letters." The first line of the song was:

In case you're wondering, they're O-V-E.

I had to admit, those two texts made everything much, much better for the next few days.

One cold January morning, my mother and I were the only ones at home—my dad was at work, Bea and Patrick at school. Mom and I were in the kitchen when the phone rang. My mom answered, listened to whoever was on the line with a frown on her face, then started to smile. When she hung up and came over to me at the kitchen table, she was beaming.

"You're about to get a special delivery package," she said.

"What is it?" I asked.

"It's a surprise," she said.

The word *surprise* lodged like a hard black walnut in my chest. It hurt and made me feel on edge. I had stopped liking anything spontaneous. I wanted to know what was going to happen every minute. I didn't like not seeing around the corner. My mother must have spotted the worry on my face, because she leaned over and hugged me.

"You're home safe, honey. Nothing is going to hurt you here."

I shrugged. Couldn't she imagine what it was like to be snatched off the street, ten minutes from our house, by people I'd known and loved? Was that really so alien to her? I stared into her face, the smile lines around her gray-blue eyes. She wore the same necklace Mrs. Morton had; I counted the children charms. Seven. Each had birthstone chips. Mine was topaz. A November baby, like Lizzie.

"What did you do on my birthday?" I asked.

Despair flashed in her eyes. "Oh, Emily. That was a hard day."

"But what did you do?"

"Honestly? I couldn't get out of bed. I tried to sleep all day because every time I opened my eyes, you weren't there. I tried to pray, but I felt there was no one listening. I couldn't hear God talking back to me. The priest from All Souls Church came, but I told your father not to let him in."

"I'm sorry." I wanted to feel something, but my heart had turned to stone. This was my *mom*, she was gazing at me with the purest love in the world, and I could see how much she wanted the old me back.

"What can I do to help?" she asked.

"Nothing," I said.

"I'll do whatever it takes. Getting through this next part—healing from the surgery, getting ready for court—I know it's terrible for you. Believe me, Emily—I want to go to Maine right now, straight to prison, and I want to see the evil for myself, and I want to rip her throat out. I swear, I hope they never let her free."

Mrs. Porter.

My mother had my attention, but I was still numb.

"I won't do it, of course," she said.

"I know."

"What I *will* do is protect you," she said.

But you couldn't before, I wanted to say. But I held back, because I knew how badly it would hurt her. She pressed her forehead to mine, and I couldn't help sniffing the air for alcohol. Since returning home, I hadn't seen her drinking, hadn't heard the bottles clinking.

She caught me doing it and tilted her head back.

"I'm sober, Em," she said.

"Sorry, I didn't mean to act like I think you're not."

"It's normal that you'd wonder," she said.

"They told me you were drinking," I said. "That you thinking I had run away would make you start again."

"The Porters?" she said.

"Yes."

She shook her head hard. "No, Emily. Having you gone made me even more determined to stay sober. To keep my mind clear, so I could find you. Except for that day when I couldn't face the world, your birthday, I never stopped looking. I was the biggest thorn in the police's side—I called every day. And I knew you hadn't run away."

"How did you know that?" I asked. I stared at her. My mom was tall and thin. Her dark hair was streaked with silver. I loved those little lines of sun and weather around her eyes when she smiled, but they had disappeared along with her smile.

"Because I know you," she replied. "That one time you did leave, when Lizzie helped you hide, you were giving me a message, telling me you couldn't take my drinking anymore. And things were so different after I got home from rehab. You trusted me again. And I one hundred percent trusted you the whole time you were gone. I knew you'd been taken." Her voice broke. "I knew someone had forced you to send those emails."

"I would never have sent them on my own."

"I know," she said.

"Are you mad because I didn't try to escape?"

"Sweetheart, no."

"But I could have. They let me go to school."

"You had to survive, Emily. The FBI told us the younger a person is when she's taken, the easier it is for the kidnapper to brainwash her. The Porters held you prisoner psychologically, not just physically."

And then she did cry, big tears running down her cheeks. She hugged me. I wanted to melt into her, but my body was stiff. That hard shell was still around me, especially hearing that I'd been brainwashed—wasn't that something that happened in spy movies? I was smart, I had always trusted myself. But practically as soon as I got to Maine, Mrs. Porter had started to warp my thinking. And she'd succeeded.

That made me feel incredibly hollow.

"You're going to have all kinds of moments," Dr. Dean had said when I was still in Royston Hospital, "ones that make sense and others that don't."

"No, I'm going to be fine as soon as I get home," I said.

"You've been through a trauma," she said. "And your mind and body have some extraordinary, mysterious ways of protecting you from reliving it, remembering it too vividly."

"Like what?" I asked.

"Some people block it out," she said. "Kids who've been kidnapped, people who've been through a violent attack, sometimes try to forget that it happened."

"No one will let me forget," I said, lying back in the bed, my chest taped up, the IV needle in the back of my hand making it ache. "It's all anyone wants to talk about."

"Well, when things quiet down. You'll see how you feel. But

you might find yourself going numb. Some people describe it as going into a deep freeze. An uncomfortable stillness. If that happens, I want you to talk to someone. A counselor back home in Black Hall. Or at least your parents, for starters."

"Okay," I said.

"It's serious, Emily. It might not feel that way—because, honestly, you might not feel *anything*. But it's a big deal. It can cause problems later on if you don't deal with your emotions."

"Problems?"

"Depression is a big one. Isolation, cutting yourself off from friends, from whatever used to make you happy. Substances to keep the feelings at bay. Drinking."

"Never," I said. "I will never drink."

"Just talk to someone. When you need to."

But I hadn't believed her, that I would need anything like that. I had thought I'd be normal, fine, ready to get on with things. But it was as if there was a big wall between me and everyone else. It was made of glass: I could see through it, hear voices, talk to them. But I felt separated from them.

A knock sounded at the door. I hung back, in the kitchen. I heard voices and finally peered into the living room. Mr. Donoghue stood there holding a battered leather guitar case. I stepped forward.

"Emily!" he said, spotting me. "I bring greetings from Casey!"

"Thank you," I said. My heart sparked, hearing Casey's name.

"I was passing by on my way to a gig in New York, so it seemed the right thing, to stop and see you. He wanted me to."

I smiled, a genuine smile that I felt all through my body. Casey had kept this news to himself, not mentioned it to me.

"How is Casey?" my mother asked. "Our family hero."

"He'd be happy to hear that. He's, um . . . hard to say."

What part was hard to say? I wondered. And why was Mr. Donoghue gazing at me while he spoke?

"He's working on some new songs, surviving winter in Royston," he continued.

"Speaking of winter," my mother said. "Let me get us some hot coffee." She ducked into the kitchen, and I heard her running water, filling the pot.

"Casey wanted me to deliver this to you," Mr. Donoghue said.

"'This'?" I asked, not understanding.

He handed me the guitar case. I looked at him with surprise, then laid it on the hardwood floor and clicked open the brass fasteners. Inside was a red guitar. It said *Takamine* on the headstock. And on a manila tag, tied to the low E string, was a note. I recognized Casey's writing but didn't read it yet.

"He misses you," Mr. Donoghue said.

"I miss him," I said.

"He's messed up, Emily."

"Is that what you meant before? When you said you're not sure how he is?"

"It's totally not your fault," he said. "But he misses you badly."

"How does that mess him up?" I asked.

"Not many people know what it's like for him, since you left," Mr. Donoghue said. "His mom was pretty much everything to him, to both of us. It's not easy for him, me being on the road all the time, but music is how I support us. I wish I could stay home and do something normal and pay the bills. Every time I leave, I see the disappointment in his eyes. Sometimes worse than that."

I stared at him, unsure of what he wanted me to say.

"That expression got a hundred times deeper after you left. It was almost despair. He wanted you to go home, of course, but he's lonely without you."

That hit me hard, because it was just how I felt—surrounded by my family, who I loved so much, I felt lonely without Casey. Having him next door, feeling he was somehow looking out for me, just knowing he was there, had helped me get through. And then there was the fact I was in love with him.

"He'll be in your band someday," I said. "Like you said that time. Then you won't have to be apart."

"I think he wants to be in a band with someone else," Mr. Donoghue said. "In fact, I know it." He pointed at the note written on the small cardboard tag, and I read Casey's words:

Keep playing, Emily. I wish you were here so I could teach you, but find a teacher there so you can come back and be in my band. Well, you already are in my band. Well, actually, you ARE my band. And I'm yours. Do you hear the music? That's me playing a song for you, just like I do all the time. You've heard some of them in my texts—there are a lot more I'll play you in person when I see you. You should know this about the guitar: When you think of someone while you're strumming, that person can hear, or at least feel, the song. I hope you feel mine right now. O-V-E, Casey.

I said the missing letter out loud: "L."

I finally felt everything I'd been holding inside. Tears scalded my eyes. That block of ice, otherwise known as my heart, melted a little. With the guitar still lying in the case, I gently brushed the strings. My mother brought out mugs of coffee, and she and Mr. Donoghue sat at the table. I heard her telling him how much she and my dad loved his band, how they had every record Dylan Thomas Revisited had ever made, how they'd seen them perform at the Newport Folk Festival.

"We are so grateful to Casey," my mother was saying. "The way he helped Emily escape, what he did for her after the attack. Dr. Dean told us he saved Emily's life."

"I'm very proud of him," Mr. Donoghue said.

"You should be. We want to see him again," my mother said. "As soon as possible."

"Will you be returning to Maine for the trial?" he asked.

"Yes, and the pretrial hearings," my mother said, lowering her voice. "They will be in Portland, in federal court. The Porters took her across state lines, so the United States is prosecuting them. We'll show up for every single hearing. I want Ginnie Porter to see me in the courtroom, look me right in the eye. We were friends! She knows how much I love my daughter! How could they have done this to Em?"

"I never suspected," Mr. Donoghue said. "I had no idea the Porters were anything other than a normal family. Casey was just waiting for me to get home that day, to take Emily out of there. Emily was afraid Ginnie would hurt you—that's why she stayed. To protect you."

They kept talking, but I focused on the guitar. I held it in my arms. With the fingers of my left hand I made triangles on the strings, just as Casey had shown me. With my right hand, I strummed softly. I made up a song and got lost in it.

I wasn't very good. My fingertips slipped, and my chords twanged and jangled. I had a long way to go. But the song filled my heart. Playing the tune, I wasn't completely numb. Every minute, I thawed a little more. For the first time since getting out of the hospital, I could feel.

Some words ran through my head, not lyrics, exactly, but they kept coming, over and over, like a mantra or a prayer. I heard the melody, sweet and sad with a lot of E minor. And one name that kept running through my mind, out my fingertips and up and down the strings.

Casey, Casey . . .

And also: the letter *L*.

CHAPTER NINETEEN

The morning I was to return to school, my parents sat me down at the breakfast table. My mom had made my favorite oatmeal with cranberries and pecans, and my dad had squeezed fresh pink grapefruits straight from my uncle in Florida to make a tall glass of juice. Patrick and Bea were going to drive me to school; they waited in the living room so my parents could have this discussion with me.

"Are you ready for this?" my dad asked.

"I don't know," I said. "I guess."

"Your friends will be so excited to see you," my mom said. "And I'm sure you will be to see them, right?"

"Of course," I said.

"One thing we've been worried about," my dad said, "is the media. They're going to follow you. We've got an idea how to stop that, but we want to make sure it's okay with you."

"What?" I asked.

"Everyone wants an exclusive interview," he said. "Lots of different news outlets have offered us a lot of money for the chance to talk to you first. Your mom and I have refused all along, wanting to protect you, but now we wonder if it's something you might want to do."

"Take money to tell what happened to me?" I asked. I felt so sick, I nearly threw up. "No, never, please don't ever mention it again."

"You wouldn't have to take the money for yourself," my mother said. "You could decline to be paid, or you could donate the fee to charity. Or you could put it toward your college. It's up to you. And if you don't want to give an interview at all, that would be fine, too. We just thought it would get the press to go away. You could control your story, tell it the way you want, and then there'd be nothing for them to hound you for. It would be out in the open."

My story. It all haunted me, but one part more than the rest. The question everyone screamed the loudest was: *What about Chloe? What part did Chloe play? What was it like to have your friend's sister as one of your captors?*

I shivered, thinking of Chloe in the Casco Bay Youth Development Center. It had a positive-sounding name, but as one official said in an interview, "It's rehabilitative, but it's also jail." She was under arrest and couldn't leave. Her parents were in the adult jail. All three of the Porters were incarcerated, waiting to be put on trial for kidnapping me. I hated picturing Chloe there. I imagined how scared she must be.

"I'll think about it," I said.

"Okay," my mom said, hugging me. "No pressure, not one bit."

"That's right," my dad said. "We'll go with whatever you want to do. But for now—as if I have to tell you—don't talk to any of them."

"That's one thing you don't have to worry about," I said.

I headed out the back door where the reporters couldn't see me, toward the car to meet Patrick and Bea. But there was a gigantic surprise. Every single one of my siblings was there: Mick, Tommy, Anne, and Iggy stood in the driveway. When they spotted me in the doorway, they began to cheer. Mick and Tommy hurried toward me. I hugged them, and they swooped me up in a king's chair and held me off the ground.

"What are you doing here?" I asked, smiling.

"You think we weren't going see you off to school today?" Mick asked.

It made me think of how they had all walked me—the baby of the family—to school my first day of first grade. They'd all gathered around me at the hospital, kept vigil until I started getting better. But now they were back at college, beginning their second semesters. Now they were grown up. We all were.

"You didn't have to come," I said.

"It would have been really funny to see you try to stop us," Tommy said. He half threw me up in the air. I laughed and righted myself, arms clamped around both his and Mick's necks until they lowered me to the ground.

Anne stepped forward. She held out a scarf woven from the softest red-jewel-colored yarn, and she wrapped it three times around my neck.

"I made this for you, little one," she said. "To keep you warm and so you know I'm with you always. You can do it."

"I thought I was ready," I said, my eyes flooding as I stared into my oldest sister's steady gaze. "But now I'm not sure. Everyone's going to ask too many questions."

"And you don't have to answer," Anne said, and her eyes started watering even more than mine. "You're as brave as ever. And you're a Lonergan, as stubborn as your four big brothers and two big sisters. You have an Irish heart. Just remember that."

I nodded. I was a Lonergan. I was Emily. I wasn't fake Lizzie Porter. I wasn't a rag doll dressed in my old friend's clothes, parroting her words, with her mole dotted on my cheek. I wore a knit cap to cover my roots growing out. I'd tucked the longer black part up underneath.

I knew all that, but I wasn't sure I could count on my Irish heart. I wondered if I had stopped, in some permanent way, having the Lonergan strength the night the Porters had locked me in that room.

"I should have fought harder; I should have escaped when I could," I said.

"No, Em," Mick said, and I was shocked to hear his voice choked up. "You should have stayed alive, exactly what you did."

"You were perfect," Tommy said.

"You're with us now," Anne said.

"*Faugh a Ballagh,*" Mick said.

"Clear the way," Iggy said.

"Here comes Emily," Patrick said.

Bea took my hand. She and I climbed into the back seat of the car while Patrick got into the driver's seat. As we pulled out of the driveway, Mick, Tommy, Iggy, and Anne cheered and waved. I looked for secret worry in their eyes and saw none. They believed in me. I swallowed hard and tried to feel their strength. So far, no luck.

At school, most people circled me at a safe distance. It seemed they thought I might be dangerous. I felt stared at, like a creature at the zoo, as if I wasn't quite human. Maybe they were right and I had turned into another species. Jordan and Alicia came straight over, though. They glued themselves to me while I put my coat in my locker.

They looked different. Jordan had cut her platinum-blond hair really short—feathered around her face and the nape of her neck. She had gotten a pair of Harry Potter–style black-rimmed glasses, even though I was pretty sure she didn't need them. She'd started wearing a shark tooth necklace that she never took off. Alicia had spent Thanksgiving with her cousins in Mexico City and gotten a tattoo of Our Lady of Guadalupe on the inside of her wrist.

"I couldn't sleep last night, I was so excited to see you, Em-girl," Alicia said.

"I was excited to see you, too," I said, a semi-lie. *Nervous dread* better described my feelings the night before.

"For once, my grades are the only part of my life that aren't a mess," Jordan said. "Nothing lower than a B minus so far this semester! On the other hand, Kirk is such a Scorpio, and I just can't."

"Kirk?" I asked.

"OMG, you haven't met him!"

"Her latest obsession. Prepare to hear everything," Alicia said with an exaggerated sigh.

Jordan shrugged and smiled. "He moved here from North Carolina just before Christmas. He had a minute with Monica, but what can I say? He saw the light."

"You're going out?" I asked.

"Yes, if I can overcome the Scorpio-ness of it all," she said.

"What about Eric?" I asked, trying to keep things straight.

"The never-ending saga of Jordan's boyfriends," Alicia put in, rolling her eyes.

"Eric and I ended before Thanksgiving. Whatever. Kirk gave me this." Jordan touched the shark tooth.

Whatever. I heard the word and remembered the email Mrs. Porter had written for me to send home, how she'd made me sound like somebody else—like Jordan, or anyone. Just not myself. I felt sad to think no one had noticed. My family, who knew me so well, hadn't caught the fact I'd written a word I would never have used in a million years.

The bell rang, and Dan walked straight over to me.

"Hey," he said. There was excitement in that syllable, so much, it took me aback. He stood a little too close. There was almost no space between us. He looked straight at me with a slack mouth but eyes searching and full of—what? Not questions, but happiness to see me. And behind that—wow—care.

"Hey," I said.

"For so long," he said, "we didn't know."

"You didn't know what?"

"If you were okay. Where you were. It wasn't like you to run away."

"No," I said.

"I knew you hadn't." He put his hand on my shoulder. It was a gesture both comforting and odd, something a parent or teacher would do. Then he pulled me against him, so hard he almost crushed my not-quite-healed ribs, but I didn't cry out. I felt his chest shaking with emotion. Dan was crying. I just squeezed my eyes tight and knew that in another world, a lifetime ago, this would have made me happier than anything.

The bell rang, and the tide of everyone streaming toward class tore us apart. He lowered his eyes, as if ashamed of showing his feelings, or maybe upset that I hadn't returned them. He went his way, and I walked into American history class.

Jeff Woodley sat in the third row. My first instinct was to pretend I hadn't seen him and walk to a desk across the room. Instead I took a deep breath and went to sit beside him. I could only imagine how he felt about the fact I'd just spent the last few months as a warped version of Lizzie. He was wearing the chain around his neck, her ring dangling from it. Our eyes met.

"I'm sorry," I said. "I never wanted to be her."

"Em, I know that. It freaked me out, but only for your sake. It must have been horrible."

"It was."

"You were in *People* magazine. They did this creepy compilation photo, your face merged with Lizzie's."

"Are you serious?" I asked. My family had shielded me from that one. "When did it come out?"

"Like two weeks ago."

"I'm sure my parents won't show me, but I kind of want to see." I took out my phone.

"Okay, call me obsessed," Jeff was saying, "but I couldn't stop looking at it. Seeing Lizzie, well, it was a little like having her brought back to life."

I started to look up the article on my phone, but then he slid the magazine out of his backpack and opened to the page. I stared at the bizarre photo—it was like of those M. C. Escher drawings, where a flock of birds transforms into a school of fish. Half Emily Lonergan, half Lizzie Porter.

It was hugely disturbing, but I couldn't tear my eyes away.

"I don't want to look at it anymore," Jeff said. "Now that you're back."

"Me neither," I said.

He ripped the page from the magazine and handed it to me, and I shredded it into tiny pieces, balled them up in my hand, and walked them to the trash can in the front of the room. When I got back to my desk, Jeff reached across the space between us and linked his fingers with mine.

Ms. Fowle began lecturing on Lieutenant Colonel William Ledyard, a local soldier who had fought during the Revolutionary War. Kids in our area had grown up with the story; most of us had visited Fort Griswold on class trips or with our families. I felt relieved that this was a familiar lesson, that I could ease myself back into studying with facts I already knew.

"September 6, 1781, the Battle of Groton Heights," Ms. Fowle said. She was small and compact, with straight dark hair and tattoos of roses on her wrists. She wore a fringed black leather vest over a flowing beige tunic, with leopard-print leggings and pink cowboy boots. Her big brown eyes were kind. Rumor had it she reenacted local battles and also that she was obsessed with zydeco music.

"Colonel Ledyard refused Benedict Arnold's command to surrender Fort Griswold," she was saying. "The British had eight hundred soldiers, Ledyard had about a hundred and fifty. The Americans held the British off for nearly an hour." She paused. "Now, Benedict Arnold. We all know his name is synonymous with what?"

"Being a traitor!" Liana Hagen called.

"That's right. He was born twelve miles from the fort in Norwich. He was a Connecticut native who became known as the Dark Eagle—why would he have been given that name? Anyone?" She looked straight at me.

"Because he switched allegiances," I said. "Because he pretended to be one way, but he switched sides, fighting against his neighbors and country for Britain. He burned New London, a city he must have known well. It was the ultimate . . . going to the dark side. Hating. Abusing everyone's trust."

"That's good, Emily," Ms. Fowle said.

My mind reverberated, just as if I'd been in an intellectual earthquake. Trust, pretending to be one way, going to the dark side: the Porters. I struggled not to squirm, not to think about anything but this class.

"In any war, with all battles, there are legends," Ms. Fowle said. "Accounts written, passed down through word of mouth. Some battles inspired poetry. At the centennial of the Battle of Groton Heights, they read a poem by New Haven poet Leonard Woolsey Bacon. Here's a line: *Where the foe had entered the fort, / Lay Ledyard, gallant knight, / His bosom gored by his own brave sword.*"

I heard the word *gored*, and my whole body hurt.

"What does that sound like to you?" she asked.

"They killed him with his own sword," Marty Lambert said. "Benedict Arnold did."

A horrible gasp filled the classroom. Whose voice was that? I looked around, along with everyone else, then saw that the entire class turned to look at me.

"Great," I said, to Jeff, trying to laugh.

"Yeah," he said. "Your first class back, and the subject is stabbing."

I made it through the rest of the class without making a sound, and I am pretty sure I kept a smile on my face, even at the kids who kept staring at me. It made me sad. They didn't get it. They didn't get me.

Home, even though it still didn't quite feel like home, was my refuge.

The guitar began to feel right in my hands. I got used to the rhythm of strumming, and the strings started to sound melodic instead of discordant. Holding the guitar made me feel as if I was embracing something, someone, alive. The wood was fine and contained warmth. The shape curved into my body. When I played, I'd feel a slight, comforting vibration, almost like a heart beating against mine.

"Do you have schoolwork?" my mother asked, poking her head into my room before dinner.

"A little," I said, fingerpicking the strings.

"I know you'll get to it," she said.

"I will," I said.

She smiled. "You sound good."

I smiled back. "Thanks," I said.

Our words were mother-daughter normal. So were our smiles. But so much had changed. The song I had in my head was full of mourning and anger. I had no idea those two emotions ever went together.

The song was about a ghost girl, but that spirit was me—the ghost of my old self. I half wanted to sing it to my mother, but I held the words inside and just focused on the notes.

That night Casey and I FaceTimed. He sat in the living room of his house in Royston, surrounded by his father's instruments. I sat on my bed. He held his mandolin; I held the guitar.

At first, we just stared at each other. It was such a relief to see him. I reached toward the screen as if I could touch his face. He was bundled up in a down vest with a plaid scarf around his neck. I saw and heard the fire crackling behind him.

"You look cold," I said.

"You look beautiful," he said.

I blushed and shook my head. "I've been practicing," I said, lifting the guitar.

"Let's hear you," he said.

Of course I felt nervous as soon as he said that, but I started off with an A chord, then E, then D, and next thing I knew, he was playing with me. I made a lot of mistakes, but he was slow and patient. After a while, I sounded better. Playing with him lifted me up—both my spirit and my ability.

"Do you have lyrics to that song?" he asked.

"Yeah," I said.

"Want to teach me?" he asked.

A huge *bang* and *crash* startled both of us. Casey's phone moved, and the camera showed that the front window had cracked open—the curtains were blowing wildly.

"What happened?" I asked.

"Another shutter came off in the wind," he said. "Smashed into the glass."

I watched as he ran over, out the door, and I heard him on the porch and saw him trying to get the shutter back into place. With no pane, the icy air had to be howling through the house. He returned a few minutes later, shivering, holding his upper arms.

"Can you fix it?" I asked.

"My dad's on his way back from a gig," he said. "We'll get it replaced then. Man, this house needs work. I might have to become something other than a musician to get it repaired right."

"It's too cold for you to stay tonight," I said. "Can you go to Mark's?"

He shook his head. "No, I have to stay here to make sure the pipes don't freeze. They did last winter, and that was a mess, and it cost a fortune to fix. You know what's weird?"

"What?"

"Chloe helped me last year. My dad was playing a show in Washington, and I was alone here. See, the water inside the metal pipes expands when it freezes, and if I didn't melt it somehow, the pipes would burst—and leak once it thawed. So I missed school because I had to open all the cabinets under the sinks, literally light candles in the small spaces to try to heat the pipes enough to keep a trickle of water running through them."

"That sounds dangerous," I said, picturing the old wooden house going up in flames from one of those candles.

"It was. Chloe stopped over when she got off the bus, to make sure I was okay. She found me running back and forth between the kitchen and bathrooms, checking on the candles. And she wound up staying with me till after dark, helping me keep an eye on them."

"So you both saved the pipes from bursting?" I asked.

"Most of them, yes, but I forgot about the one that went to the back bathroom upstairs. After the thaw, we had a huge leak—it ran through the ceiling, and there was plaster everywhere. But still, it would have been much worse if Chloe hadn't been here." He paused and glanced at the door. "I'd better go, nail up a tarp over the broken window for now."

"Okay," I said. "I wish we lived closer so I could help."

"So do I. I miss . . ."

"What?"

"Having you next door. But that's probably not cool to say."

"It is. It's fine."

"L," he said.

"L," I said.

When we ended the call, I kept playing. I thought of Casey in that old ramshackle house. I pictured him and Chloe lighting candles. Even the small warmth from each one had made a difference. Just a little helped.

The library was my second-favorite place to study in school—after the Apiary. I loved the smell of books, the stacks that reached to the ceiling. I used to be happiest when I needed a volume from the top shelf and would get to wheel over the small oak ladder and climb it. Lizzie and I each had a favorite carrel.

I pulled out Lizzie's envelope addressed to Mame, removed the letter, and smoothed it on the desk with my hand. My idea was to research Sarah Royston. Even though she was prominent in Maine, and this was Connecticut, I had the feeling there hadn't been many women mill owners or industrialists in the nineteenth century. Our library had a big section on New England history.

I could have gone online, of course, but for this, I wanted to read real books, find actual pages. I wanted to hold dusty volumes in my hands, have the authors' words right in front of my eyes instead of filtered by a screen.

Instead of starting to work, I texted Casey.

Me: Are you there?

Casey: Always.

Me: Big sigh of relief. I wish I were in Maine.

Casey: I wish I were in Connecticut

Me: Hmmm.

Casey: Did you hear about Chloe?

Me: What?

Casey: She got attacked in her cell.

I froze to read those words, to think of what had happened to her. My hands were shaking when I typed again.

Me: Is she okay?

Casey: Yes, aside from a black eye. Another inmate beat her up.

Me: Why?

Casey: Her nickname there is "Kidnapper." The other kids think she should be punished for what she did to you.

Me: I don't want that.

Casey: I know.

There was a long silence between us. My stomach flipped. I felt sick, thinking of Chloe locked up, as I had been, beaten up and unable to get away and go home. Unlike me, she had no home to go to.

Me: What will happen to her?

Casey: There's a hearing on Friday, to figure it out.

They're going to send her to a group home. They're
saying she's not really a criminal, that in some ways, her
parents abused her, too.
Me: Where's the hearing?
Casey: Portland

The biggest city in Southern Maine. It was where the United
States district court was located—the place the Porters would go
on trial. And I knew the Casco Bay Youth Development Center
was near there, too.

Me: I want to go to her hearing
Casey: I was thinking of it, too
Me: Let's try
Casey: If you're going, consider me there.

I was sixteen now; I could get my license, but I needed to
take driver's ed, get some practice driving in before that could
happen. I looked up and noticed Dan in the library. He stood in
the earth science aisle, trying to catch my eye. BR—Before
Royston—I would have been over the moon. But now it didn't
matter.

I googled *Portland, Maine* on my phone. I saw images of the
Atlantic Ocean and a bay full of small islands, brick buildings on
the waterfront, a planetarium, and six different lighthouses.

Then I searched for the *Casco Bay Youth Development Center.*
I pulled it up on Google Earth, looked at the tall walls and small

windows, the narrow outdoor recreation area. I read an article about how the youth offenders attended high school inside. Bullying was rampant. Passing notes—incarcerated kids' version of texting—wasn't allowed. It was called illegal mail.

There was no question I would attend Chloe's hearing on Friday. I just had to find a ride.

CHAPTER TWENTY

On Wednesday, Bea and I went to the Apiary. It was the last room on the second-floor corridor, with its comfy chairs for studying and glass bubble that contained the beehive. In spring, bees flew in and out from the outdoors, forming a colony and making honey. Now, during the winter, the bees clustered on the frame, deep in hibernation.

The bees were in a state of suspended animation. I stared at them, immobile in their cells. Each cell was private, enclosed. I wondered if the bees felt trapped, if their wings twitched, longing to fly. Did they remember that each year spring came again, that there were meadows and flowers and wild thyme? I suddenly felt sure, as positive as I'd ever been about anything, that these were Casey's mother's bees, that they had swarmed down from Maine, joined the colony already living in the hive. They were safe right here in my school.

Bea scrolled through her phone and made an impatient-sounding exhalation.

"Mom, jeez," she said.

"What?" I asked.

"She joined Twitter and now she's following all our friends."
"Mom?"

"She's replying to people," Bea said. "To anyone who posts about you."

Since getting home, I'd decided to close all my social media accounts. As much as I'd missed being online when I was away, I knew it wouldn't be good for me now. "I don't want to see what people are writing about me," I told her.

"Well, a lot of people are curious about you," Bea said, scrolling. "'How's she adjusting to being home?' 'What is she saying about Chloe?' That's their big thing—they want a feud between you and Chloe."

"There's no feud," I said.

Bea looked up. "Em, how can you forgive her?"

I knew Bea was being loyal to me, but I really didn't want to talk about Chloe. Maybe that's why I uncovered Lizzie's letter on the table, so she'd see.

"Is that Lizzie's handwriting?" Bea asked. She leaned forward to take a closer look.

"Yeah," I said. "I'm doing my project on this amazing woman she found out about. Sarah Royston. She used to own the biggest mill in Maine, and . . ."

"Royston?" Bea asked. "As in the town? Where they took you?"

"Yes," I said.

She frowned. "Why are you focusing on it?"

"Not the town—Sarah. Lizzie was fascinated by her. After Lizzie died, that's why the family moved there. It was one good thing they did—a way to honor Lizzie. And that's why I want to do my report on Sarah. She was a major business woman in a hard-core man's world, and she donated her house to help troubled girls . . ."

I stopped short. I thought: *Chloe.* Maybe some of the girls who'd lived in Royston Home for Wayward Girls had been nineteenth-century versions of her, had had parents who'd committed crimes, leaving them with nowhere to go.

Bea leaned forward. "Em! Put that place and those people out of your mind! Royston and the Porters, just forget about them!" she said.

"Forget about them?" I asked. "You think I can?"

"I swear it would be better if you ripped up that letter and did your project on shipbuilding in Black Hall, something nice and local and so what if it's boring? At least it won't *traumatize* you," Bea said.

"What *traumatizes* me is not thinking about it," I said. "Pretending it didn't happen. Why can't you understand that? And can't you let me have my own feelings about Chloe?"

I glared at Bea, and my heart fell. Tears were running down her cheeks. She took my hand.

"I'm trying," Bea said. "But you don't know what it was like. Missing you. Worrying every minute that you were never coming home. That you were dead."

"Oh, Bea," I said. I hadn't thought of it from her perspective, not like this.

"When we found out you were alive, I was overjoyed. But once it came out that the Porters had taken you, and everything they did to you, I went crazy. I want them to pay for what they did to you—even Chloe. And it kills me that you're doing a report on Royston—to me, it's the worst place on earth."

"I'm so sorry," I said. "For not realizing what it was like for you."

She wiped tears from her cheeks. Then she reached over, stroked my head. "Even your hair," she said. "They changed the way you looked. They tried to make you into someone else. Every time I look at you, it reminds me of what they did."

I looked at my reflection in the convex apiary window. She was right—my hair was two distinct colors: my own, and the black dye. The police and my parents had taken plenty of photos documenting all the Lizzie-isms—the hair, the mole, my eyebrows, the green contacts, so I didn't have to worry about preserving the evidence or anything. But it was taking forever for my hair to grow out.

"I want to cut the black part off," I said.

"Then the rest will be really short," Bea said.

"I don't care," I said. "Will you do it for me?"

She began to smile. "Seriously?"

"Yes."

"Okay, when we get home."

"No, now," I said.

Bea stood up and ran out of the room. She came back a few minutes later with a pair of scissors.

"Go for it," I said.

And it was strange, but as soon as she started to snip, I began to feel really anxious. I heard the scissors clicking—*sharp object alert*. Bea caught the clumps of hair as they fell. I'd always had long hair, below my shoulders, and it suddenly felt so light and weird. I checked my reflection again. She had gotten about halfway through.

"Keep going," I said. "Make it look good for Friday."

"Friday?"

"Chloe has a hearing, and I want to be there for it. To make sure she doesn't get sent somewhere horrible. Casey is going, too."

Bea was silent. I waited for her to say that Chloe should stay in jail, that she didn't deserve my support. The scissors kept snipping. I gazed at the bees. They were so still, no signs of life. But they were beautiful: tiny, perfect yellow-and-black bodies, waiting in suspended animation. Being in that cell block room had been a type of hibernation. I had been waiting to be rescued. The bees were waiting to wake up.

"What time is the hearing?" Bea asked.

"I don't know," I said. "I'll have to ask Casey." I paused. "Do you really think I'm crazy to want to go?"

"I think you were driven a bit mad, being locked up and controlled. But, Em, you're stronger than anyone I know. Do you realize that?"

Slowly, I nodded. I'd learned that I had within myself a power I couldn't completely understand—it was the opposite of Mrs. Porter's cruelty and domination. I thought again of Sarah Royston. She was someone who'd had a terrible experience and made things better, not only for herself, but for girls who'd needed help.

"It takes someone really strong to care about a person who hurt her as much as Chloe hurt you," Bea said. "So yeah, you might be a little crazy, but I think you're amazing, that you want to go to court for her."

"Thank you," I said.

"You do realize one thing, though, right?" Bea asked. "It's been hard for you to leave the house, to walk past the reporters. They'll be all over you, once they figure out you're going to Maine. Please be sure you're ready for this, Emily. I don't want you to have any setbacks—you're doing so well."

She put down the scissors, leaned over to embrace me from behind. I grabbed her hands. Holding tight to my sister, I stared at the cluster of bees in the hive. They huddled together on the frame, immobile for the winter, till spring's warmth woke them. But as I watched, a small miracle: One moved. The small striped body, the translucent wings. The bee shifted, crawled over the others. It was still full of life. Winter was just an interlude. It would end, and the bees would fly again.

So would I.

CHAPTER TWENTY-ONE

The next night, I waited until after dinner, until Bea and Patrick went to their rooms to do homework, to help clean up the kitchen and talk to my parents.

"There's something I want to do," I said, putting away the wooden salad bowl. "And it's very important, and I need a ride."

"Let's sit down," my mother said. She poured coffee for my dad and herself, and we all took our seats at the table.

"There's a hearing about Chloe's welfare on Friday," I said. "The Porters are obviously unfit to take care of her, and once she gets out of that Casco Bay place, the State of Maine is going to send her to a group home."

"It's true," my dad said. "The DHHS—Department of Health and Human Services—stepped in. They determined Chloe is in jeopardy—clearly, her parents are in prison—and she's going to be placed."

"How do you know?" I asked.

"We're keeping track," my dad said.

"Why?"

"Because the case involves you," he said.

"And because she is a child," my mother said. "Who doesn't have anyone."

That was true, and exactly how I felt. I'd been worried they'd only see Chloe in the worst light.

"She loved her parents, and just like them, she was grieving for Lizzie," my mother said.

"She was," I said.

"Parents can be the best guides in the world," my mother said. "Or they can be the worst, and hurt their children so badly." Her lips thinned as if she was trying to hold her feelings inside. "I know from experience."

"You didn't do anything bad!" I said.

"I can't bear to think of how many times I almost got behind the wheel after drinking, sweetheart. And I wasn't present—I was passing out, causing our family so much worry. You protected me, hid the bottles, tried to get me to stop. In that way, I understand how Chloe is affected by her mother."

"I do, too," I said. "She was being loyal. She's only thirteen."

"Emily," my dad said. "You could hate Chloe for the part she played. But you don't. You forgive her."

"Yeah," I said. "I do."

"We're proud of you," he said.

My eyes filled with tears. "I care about her. I'm worried about what will happen to her."

"So are we," my mother said.

"I really want to see her," I said.

"Well, we can," my dad said. "We'll go to the hearing together."

"There's something else," I said.

"What?"

I took a deep breath. "I want her to come live with us."

Total silence. My parents looked at each other. Their expressions were grave. I could almost read them telepathically communicating to each other. They were certain that I had lost it, gone bonkers. Then my mother took my hand.

"That's not possible," she said.

"Why?"

"It's too much," she said. "After what you've been through. It would be a constant reminder."

"Mom, the alternative is that I'll be thinking of her in some horrible place, all on her own."

"You're the best girl ever to care so much," she said. "But your well-being comes first. As much as we care about Chloe, we can't let her jeopardize your progress."

"My progress is fine," I said.

"She has a court-appointed lawyer," my father said, putting on his half glasses to look at his phone. "Jane Manwaring. Your mother and I will talk to her, make sure Chloe is being looked after. I'm sure Jane will be at the hearing tomorrow. We'll make a point of meeting her, letting her know we're all behind Chloe."

"That won't be enough," I said, with that heart-sinking despair that had become so familiar. "It's just one more horrible thing to come from the Porters. Chloe's life will be ruined."

"We can't think like that," my mother said. "After some point, we have to just trust the process. That her lawyer will fight to get her into a good place."

I closed my eyes. I pictured a house that was clean enough, warm enough, decent enough. I imagined it full of strangers that Chloe wouldn't know. I pictured the Royston Home, back in the day, full of wayward girls.

But Chloe wasn't wayward. She was someone I knew. And for over two months, she had been the closest thing I had to a sister.

"We'll let the court sort it out," my dad said. "But one thing is for sure—on Friday, we're going to Maine."

My parents said we had to leave at 4:00 a.m. because it was a long drive and court started at 10:00. I'd texted Casey, made sure he was still going. I didn't hear back, which seemed really strange, and it took forever for me to fall asleep. I drifted off in a whirl of emotions, so when my phone buzzed, I thought it was the alarm.

"Hello?" I said, fumbling in the dark.

"It's me," Carole said. "Have you heard?"

"Heard what?"

"About the fire."

"What fire?"

"Em, prepare yourself—it's bad. There was a fire at Casey's house."

My heart tore loose. "Is he okay?"

"He's safe. So is his dad. But the house is badly damaged. They're saying it was a spark from the wood stove."

"Where is he now? I have to call him," I said, scrambling to get up.

"You can't," Carole said. "He was in such a hurry to get out he had to leave his phone, and it burned up. It was so scary, it happened really fast."

"Did he get hurt?"

"Not badly. My mom checked in him and his dad at the hospital. They both had minor smoke inhalation, but they'll be fine."

"Where are they?" I asked.

"A hotel till they can figure out what to do."

"Which one?"

"I don't know. There aren't any in Royston," she said. "Maybe somewhere on Route 1."

"Will you tell me as soon as you find out?" I asked.

"Of course, but I'm sure he'll be in touch with you before anyone else. As soon as he can. I just wanted to tell you before you saw it on the news or anything."

"Thanks, Carole," I said. "I miss you."

"Miss you too, so much."

I never got back to sleep. All night I veered between imagining what it must have been like for Casey, smoke billowing and fire engulfing his home, and wondering how it would feel to see Chloe again. What it would be like for her to see me.

We hit the road before dawn. My dad wore a suit, and my mom dressed the way she did for church, in charcoal slacks and a beige blazer. I wore a dark green plaid dress and my best, least scuffed Doc Martens. I kept checking my phone for a message from Casey, but there was nothing.

Once the sun came up, I watched the highway carefully,

wondering if it would remind me of driving north with the Porters. But I had been drugged then, so none of it looked familiar.

We made it through Massachusetts, and the New Hampshire coastline went by fast, and as soon as we took the arched bridge over the wide Piscataqua River into Maine, I started breathing differently, faster. We were getting close.

Portland is a redbrick city. It glowed in the morning sun. GPS led us directly to the courthouse, an imposing gray granite building with columns. My dad wanted to drop off my mom and me while he parked the car, but I said no, I wanted us to stick together. From the parking lot, I could see the harbor, dark blue with whitecaps, with tankers and freighters and a big ferry boat bound for Nova Scotia.

My parents were heading toward the steps when I saw them: Casey and Mr. Donoghue coming from the opposite direction. I began to run. So did Casey. We met in the middle and he hugged me so hard, my bones melted.

"You made it," I said. "I never thought you would, Carole told me about the fire . . ."

"I told you I'd meet you here," he said. "I'd never have let you down."

"Are you okay?" I asked, studying his face.

"Yeah," he said. "The house is gone, so are my dad's guitars. And my mandolin. But he and I are fine. It was really bad, Em. We were up on the second floor, and the fire was roaring in the living room. My dad wanted to save at least one guitar, he'd been sound asleep, and he wasn't thinking straight at all. I had to literally drag him out the back door. I was afraid he'd die." He swallowed hard.

"Pretty stupid of me," Mr. Donoghue said. "But how am I going to support us now? Well, never mind. One thing at a time. I can always get a job flipping burgers."

"Dad . . ." Casey said.

My parents walked over, and they both gave Casey a big hug.

"We're so sorry to hear about the fire," my mother said.

"Thanks," Mr. Donoghue said. "We'll get through it."

"No doubt about that," my father said, smiling. "You're Dylan Thomas Revisited."

"Come on, everyone," my mother said. "It's time for court."

We walked up the big steps and into a big hall. Austere portraits of judges lined the walls. Heavy oak doors led to the actual courtrooms and antechambers. One door was marked VICTIM'S ADVOCATE. Another said CONFERENCES. Casey and I held hands. While my parents and Casey's dad spoke to a woman in a cherry-red suit, we leaned our heads together. His hair smelled like wood smoke.

"Whoever would think the happiest I've ever felt was standing in a courthouse in Portland?" he asked.

"Me too," I said. "This is definitely without a shadow of a doubt the one hundred percent best thing in the world."

"But when we have to leave later will be the worst thing," he said.

"I know."

"My dad and I are staying at a motel right outside town," he said. "We knew we were coming here, and our house is gone, so we figured, why not head to Portland? What I'm thinking is, why don't we just move to Black Hall? Find a place near there so you and I never have to be apart again."

"Definitely!" I said. And for that moment, I let myself believe it could actually be possible. Holding Casey's hand, electricity ran from his fingers into mine, lighting up all my bones and cells, making me feel almost too excited, as if I couldn't quite breathe.

"Emily Lonergan?"

At the sound of a familiar voice, I turned. The woman had shoulder-length brown hair, and she wore a dark blue dress and black heels. She had kind, bright brown eyes behind tortoiseshell glasses.

"Marcela Perez," I said.

Our family's favorite newscaster, from back in Connecticut. It seemed so odd to see someone I'd been watching on TV most of my life standing beside me. Since my return to Black Hall, she'd been outside our house and just off school property with the other news crews, but she'd never gotten so close. I saw the same gentle, slightly sad expression she'd had on camera while reporting so many Connecticut stories. It made me shiver, to feel it directed at me.

"I'm here to cover Chloe Porter's hearing," she said. "I have to admit I was hoping you might come to testify. I would love the chance to talk to you."

"Please leave me alone," I said.

"I'll respect that," she said, handing me her card. "But if you change your mind, just call or text. My mobile number is there . . ."

Just then a group of other media people, clustered at the end of the hallway, came hurrying toward us.

"Are they going to put the hearing on TV?" I asked.

"No," Marcela said. "Cameras and audio aren't permitted in the courtroom. So, you're safe there." She gave me a wry smile. "If you hear clicking, it's all of us live tweeting. That's allowed."

"Thanks for telling me," I said.

Casey put his arm around me, and we walked quickly toward his dad, avoiding the reporters. My parents were still talking intently to the woman in the red suit. Casey's dad led us past the crowd into what at first looked like an empty courtroom.

But it wasn't quite empty.

There, at a table in the front, sat Chloe. She looked so small in the vast room. I had thought she would be wearing an orange jumpsuit, like prisoners on TV shows, but she was dressed in regular clothes—green cords, a yellow sweater. A young brown-haired woman in a gray business suit sat beside her.

Chloe must have heard the heavy door open. She turned toward the sound, and when she saw me, I heard her gasp. I walked toward her, pulled, as if the courtroom had an undertow. She stood. The woman at the table put her hand on her wrist, tried to get her to sit down, but Chloe wouldn't.

We stood facing each other, a thick waist-high mahogany rail between us. Her skin looked very pale. She had a bruise on one cheek that she'd attempted to cover with makeup. Her eyes filled with tears. I guess mine did, too, because I felt them rolling down my face.

"You're here," she said.

"I am."

"Why?"

"Because," I said. I could have spent an hour explaining, but the way she was looking at me, I knew I didn't have to. They say people who've been through a disaster together are bonded forever.

"I'm sorry," she said. "For everything."

"I know that," I said. "So don't say it again. Ever."

That made her smile. Nothing like a bossy older almost-sister to set things straight. Her eyes flicked up, looking over my shoulder. My parents and the woman in the red suit had entered the courtroom, clustered together, and now other people were filing in, too, including the reporters.

"Your parents are with my lawyer," Chloe said.

"Jane Manwaring?" I asked. "Do you like her?"

"She's okay. I've talked to a lot of lawyers since that last day. Jane's my main one, Millicent is her associate." Chloe gestured toward the young woman standing beside her.

"They're going to help you get into the best possible place," I said.

"A group home, I know," she said.

"I wish you didn't have to go to one," I said.

"It'll be better than jail," Chloe said, her hand unconsciously drifting to her bruised cheek.

"I hope so," I said.

"Do your parents hate me?" she asked, watching them.

"No."

"Hate is such a weird word," she said. "I've said it more in the last month than in my whole life. You know who I say it about?"

"Who?"

"My parents," Chloe said, her voice breaking. "For what they did to you." She threw herself into my arms, and we held each other, the mahogany rail between us, until two uniformed court officers came to pry us apart.

Then a gavel sounded, and a judge with long silver hair falling down the shoulders of her black robe came to take the bench. A brass nameplate said THE HONORABLE REBECCA STORRICK. Chloe turned away from me and sat down, and I hurried to sit between Casey and my mother.

From the minute the judge began speaking, I heard reporters' pencils scribbling on their notepads, thumbs clicking on keyboards. I stared straight ahead, my jaw set tight. I didn't want them to see any emotion when the judge assigned Chloe to somewhere in the Maine foster system.

"Couldn't they at least send her somewhere in Connecticut?" I whispered to my mother. "So we could visit her?"

But my mother didn't respond because Jane Manwaring had started to speak. She stood at the table, while Chloe remained sitting between her and Millicent.

"Your Honor, I'd like to be heard on the matter of Chloe Porter."

"Go ahead, Ms. Manwaring," Judge Storrick said.

"As you know, an order has been filed for the release of Ms. Porter from the Casco Bay Youth Development Center, and today's hearing is to determine placement through Maine Child and Family Services." She nodded across the aisle. "Ms. Ling is here to make sure that is carried out."

A tall woman with shoulder-length black hair stood. She wore a tailored dark gray suit and black boots, a heavy silver necklace at her throat, and my first thought was that Lizzie would have loved her outfit. Chloe half turned, caught my eye. We held back smiles, and I knew she was thinking the same thing—Lizzie's style.

"Yes, Your Honor," the woman said. "Daria Ling for the State of Maine."

"What do you propose, Ms. Ling?"

"Well, here is the release order for Chloe Porter," she said, striding to the bench, heels ticking on the wood floor, to place a paper before the judge. She also gave a copy to Chloe's lawyer.

"All right," the judge said, reading the single page. She glanced up at Chloe. "Chloe, you're officially free from custody of the Development Center, but our job to care for your welfare is not over. It's up to this court—with the guidance of Ms. Ling and Ms. Manwaring—to determine where you will live. Do you understand?"

"Yes," Chloe said, standing.

"Because you are a minor."

"And because my parents are in prison," Chloe said.

"Yes, they are," Judge Storrick said.

"I wish they were here right now," Chloe said. "So they could hear me apologize for them, for what they did." She turned toward me. "I know you told me not to say it again, Em, but I'm so sorry."

I couldn't help responding. "You didn't do anything bad, Chloe," I said. "You love them, they told you what to do." I thought maybe the judge would stop me, say "Order in the court" like on TV, but she didn't. "You helped me get to Casey's. Without you I wouldn't have gotten away."

"Thank you, Emily," Jane Manwaring said, giving me a smile. "Now, Your Honor, that brings us to the reason we are here today. Chloe's placement."

"Yes," Judge Storrick said. "Ms. Ling, what is your recommendation?"

"We had secured a spot for Chloe at St. Cleran's, a group home in Yarmouth, but as of this morning, we have a better possibility."

"What is that?"

"Ms. Manwaring informed me that a family has offered to take Chloe in as a foster child. They are not registered with my office, and we'll have to do background checks, a thorough investigation, but it is my opinion that this is a much better option."

"And who is this family?" Judge Storrick asked.

"The Lonergans," my father said, and both he and my mother stood. "I'm Thomas, and this is Mary. We're Emily's parents."

"Mr. and Mrs. Lonergan," Judge Storrick said. "While I commend your compassion, considering all that has gone on, surely it would be too traumatic for Emily to share her home with Chloe."

"It was Emily's idea," my mother said.

The court was completely silent except for the sound of all the reporters tapping out their tweets.

"We were licensed as foster parents in Connecticut," my mother explained. "It's been nearly twenty years since we have taken in a child, and we realize we'll have to reapply for certification. But we've known Chloe since she was born. We understand, probably better than anyone else will, what she has been through. My husband and I consider her to be a victim of her parents, just as our daughter was. We'll do everything we can to make sure she gets whatever help she needs."

"We love her," I said.

Chloe turned to look at me, and our eyes met and held.

"She's like my sister," I went on. "Please let her live with us. Please don't send her anywhere else. She needs us. And I need her."

"I need you, too," Chloe whispered.

The judge was silent, gazing at Chloe, then me.

"Well, that's compelling," the judge said after a few minutes.

"I would like to request that Your Honor give us a week to work with the Department of Children and Families in Connecticut," Ms. Ling said. "Perform home visits, determine whether the Lonergans' license can be renewed, and, if warranted, transfer the case from Maine."

"A week?" the judge asked. "And where would Chloe live during that time?"

"St. Cleran's is ready to take her today," Jane Manwaring said. "We agree with that as a temporary measure."

"This is a very unusual case," Judge Storrick said. "I can't think of another like it, but that doesn't mean this isn't a good solution. I'm hoping you can resolve this expeditiously—not only for Chloe, but for Emily."

"So, she can come live with us?" I asked, my voice barely a whisper.

My mother's arm slid around my shoulder, holding me tight. Casey squeezed my hand on the other side.

"If everything works out the way we all hope it will," the judge said, "yes. She can live with you."

I nodded, so choked up I couldn't say a word. My parents hugged me hard. They had taken in foster kids, after all. They had taught my brothers and sisters and me to care about people, to not let them suffer when we could do something about it. And they had named us after saints; that had to count for something.

"Ms. Ling, report to me your findings in one week's time," the judge said. She banged her gavel. "Court is dismissed."

We all went to Chloe. My parents, Mr. Donoghue, Casey, and I. We reached for her across the rail, and then a court officer unlocked a gate so she could come through and we could give her real hugs.

"I can't believe this," Chloe said.

"Way to come through, Mom and Dad," I said.

"We wouldn't have it any other way," my mom said. "Chloe, are you sure you want to do this?"

Chloe's lower lip wobbled. I saw her eyes flood with tears again. "I wish, more than anything, that I could go back in time. Before everything fell apart. That Lizzie could be alive, that our family could still be together. But since I can't have that . . . yes, I'm so happy you want me."

"We do," I said.

Then my parents talked to her quietly, saying they understood it wouldn't always be easy for her, that they knew how much she'd miss her mother and father.

"Can we come live with you, too?" Casey asked me in a low voice.

"I wish," I said.

"I'm only kidding," he said. "Sort of. I think."

"Where will you go?" I asked him.

"I'm not sure, but don't worry. My dad will figure something out. He has one guitar in the shop, getting the neck repaired. And I can work after school. I can probably get a job at Mark's tree farm."

"It's not Christmas anymore," I said.

"No, but they have to take care of the trees, right?" He smiled. "I'll get a new mandolin, and I'll write songs and sing them to the baby trees. It will make them grow."

I was listening to Casey, but my heart was starting to pound with a new idea. I grabbed Casey's hand and pulled him toward the back of the courtroom. It was basically empty except for a few reporters, including Marcela.

"Emily, I want to warn you," she said, stepping toward me. "Everyone will be waiting on the steps with cameras—they're allowed to photograph you there. If you speak to the officer, he can take you and your family out the back way."

"Actually, I came to talk to you, to ask a question," I said.

"Anything," she said.

"My parents said news organizations would pay for my story," I said bluntly.

"Em!" Casey said, sounding shocked.

Marcela studied me, her eyes warm and possibly amused. "Our station doesn't," she said. "Because it would compromise our journalistic integrity. But I'd still love to talk to you."

"I can't," I said. "Not without money."

"Whoa, Em," Casey said.

"It's not for me," I said, clutching his hands. "It's for you and your dad. I never wanted to talk about what happened, not ever. But if telling my story can help you pay for a place to live, I'll do it."

A bunch of the other reporters had crowded around, but Casey pulled me really close. My heart was trying to beat out of my chest.

"I won't let you," he said. "You're the best person in the world, but I know how you feel about your privacy, and you can't do this."

"There might be a way," Marcela said.

CHAPTER TWENTY-TWO

We decided to do it in the Apiary.

It was thirty-one days after Chloe's hearing, the Friday before April vacation. Everyone in school was excited about spring break, but I knew they were also revved/curious/weird about what was happening with me.

Yesterday I'd stood alone in the Apiary, figuring out where everyone would sit, where the lights should go. I staged it like a play. Although I hadn't written a script—there was no point, we each had our own stories, our own points of view—I felt it was a type of theater. There had been a first, second, and third act. We had each played a role.

Bea and Patrick drove us to school. My parents were in the car behind us.

"This is the last time we'll see the TV trucks," Patrick said, pulling into the parking lot.

"Good riddance," Bea said.

"You ready for this?" Patrick asked. He and Bea were in the front seat, and his eyes met mine in the rearview mirror.

"I think so," I said.

"Definitely," Casey said from beside me.

"Can I let you know after it's over?" Chloe asked from my other side. "Ha-ha."

"You'll be fine," I said, squeezing her hand.

When we got out of the car, Casey and I kept Chloe in between us. We walked so close together, our shoulders were touching. I felt protective of Chloe, and it made me feel like an older sister, let me know how my siblings felt about me.

When Chloe had first moved in, Mick, Anne, and Iggy had all come home from college and grad school to welcome her. Only Tommy was missing because his internship wouldn't give him the time off, but he'd sent her a UC Berkeley hoodie and told her he'd see her soon. We'd had a big turkey dinner, a sort of make-up Thanksgiving, with all our favorite dishes and two of Chloe's that the Porters had always served and we hadn't: sweet potatoes with maple syrup instead of marshmallows, and Lizzie's special M&M pie. We'd wanted Chloe to start feeling as at home as possible right away.

She'd sat next to me, her head bent down through most of the meal, and I saw two big tears plop onto her plate. No one called attention to it. We all just had our typical big family banter, with lots of teasing and laughs, and a rousing chorus of "Jingle Bells," because we had a tradition of taking strange joy in mixing up holiday tunes. My heart relaxed when I heard Chloe singing quietly and letting loose with *Oh, what fun it is to ride in a one-horse open sleigh—hey!*

Now, entering Black Hall High, she pressed closer to me. She had turned fourteen in Casco Bay Development Center, and my parents had enrolled her at middle school, just across the playing fields—the one she'd attended before the Porters had moved to Maine—to finish eighth grade.

"Lizzie should be here," Chloe said. "This was her school."

"I know," I said.

"Being here, I can feel her. Where was her locker?"

"We'll pass it on our way to the Apiary."

"The Apiary," Casey said. "Bees?"

"Yep," I said. "That's why I chose it for the interview. Because you can't just rebuild your house—you have to fix up the bee-hives, too."

"Em, you don't have to do this," Casey said, for the millionth time. "Sell your story."

"I don't think of it that way," I said. "We're *telling* it."

Heading up the stairs, it seemed that just about everyone had come to check out Casey and Chloe. Some kids acted cold and rude toward her, but most gave her smiles and hugs and told her how good it was to see her back. I couldn't help noticing she was wearing Lizzie's anchor necklace. I was glad.

When we got to Lizzie's locker I stopped and pointed. I didn't have to say a word; Chloe just knew. She brushed her fingers over the dark gray metal, gave the dial—now programmed with some-one else's combination—a gentle rattle. Then we walked along.

Marcela Perez stood at the end of the hall, right outside the Apiary. The camerawoman stood behind her, and bright lights illuminated the hallway. Marcela wore a blue suit today. She'd told me not to wear white, that it tended to bounce on TV, and she said stripes would vibrate. So, I wore a blue dress printed with pots of honey—I'd found it at the Nearly New Shop and thought it just right for the occasion.

"You did an amazing job setting up," Marcela said. "The chairs are angled just right, and I like the way you placed the table. If I didn't know better, I'd swear you were a television producer."

"She's a playwright and a set designer," Chloe said. "She knows her stuff."

"That she does," Marcela said. "This is going to be brilliant."

"It was your idea," I told her.

"Well, it was the only way we could accomplish everything," she said. "It's my get, the program will air on my network. We're sticking to our rules and not paying for your story."

"But wait," Chloe said, turning to me. "I thought this was going to help Casey and his dad rebuild their house."

"It is," I said. "But since I'm interviewing you and Casey, and since we're telling what happened on our own, we can charge a fee. We're setting up a nonprofit, and this will be the first donation. The Sarah Royston Foundation."

"Really?" Marcela asked, taking notes.

"Yes," I said. "Casey and his dad live in a historical house. It was Sarah's. The Donoghues will have the top two stories, and the town is going to open the first floor as a museum to her work, tell everything about what she did for troubled girls."

"You mean wayward girls, like me," Chloe said.

"Like us," I said. "Girls who wind up far from home."

"And find our way back again, sort of," Chloe said.

"That's really good," Marcela said. "Will you remember to say that on camera?"

"I don't think so," I said. "That was just for us. But I've got my questions ready, and we'll tell everything else that happened. Right?"

"Right," Chloe said.

"Definitely," Casey said.

Then the three of us walked into the Apiary and sat in the chairs I had arranged. I'd made sure to set them up facing the beehive. The lights were bright, and the camerawoman had gotten into position. I stared past her.

It was spring now. The air was getting warm and the bees had started flying outside, collecting pollen and nectar from the season's first flowers, then returning to the colony. Their wings glittered, iridescent in the sunlight. I thought of Lizzie, felt a shiver of missing her. I hoped she could somehow know that Chloe was going to be okay.

That I was, too.

Casey, Chloe, and I exchanged one last look. Casey squeezed my hand.

"L," he said.

"L," I said.

"What does that mean?" Chloe asked.

"L for 'love,'" Casey said.

"And for Lizzie," I whispered.

And then I let go of Casey's hand and sat up straight in my chair. I cleared my throat. The camera began to film.

And starting at the very beginning, we told our story.

ACKNOWLEDGMENTS

I am so grateful to my brilliant, kind, and insightful editor Aimee Friedman. Everyone at Scholastic has been endlessly supportive and creative, including David Levithan, Ellie Berger, Lori Benton, Alan Smagler, Elizabeth Whiting, Betsy Politi, Nikki Mutch, Sue Flynn, Tracy van Straaten, Brooke Shearouse, Rachel Feld, Isa Caban, Lizette Serrano, Emily Heddleson, Anna Swenson, Mariclaire Jastremsky, Elizabeth Parisi, Baily Crawford, Olivia Valcarce, Rachel Gluckstern, Melissa Schirmer, Cheryl Weisman, and Christy Damio.

I have been with my agent Andrea Cirillo forever, and no wonder. I am thankful to her for everything. The Jane Rotrosen Agency is my other family, including Meg Ruley, Annelise Robey, Christina Hogrebe, Amy Tannenbaum, Rebecca Scherer, Kathy Schneider, Jessica Errera, Christina Prestia, Julianne Tinari, Michael Conroy, Donald W. Cleary, Hannah Rody-Wright, Ellen Tischler, Danielle Sickles, Sabrina Prestia, and Jane Berkey.

Amelia Onorato, the graphic novelist and comic artist, is incredibly wise about story, characters, dialogue, and the dark side of fictional families, and I am grateful for her generosity in discussing writing with me.

Molly Feinstein's compassion, wisdom, and support mean so much to me. Every time we speak on the phone, I feel as if we're taking a walk on the beach, looking for sea glass, talking about life as we go along.

Madelene McDuff Grisanty views the world, even the painful moments, with humor and perspective. She keeps me laughing. In her own words, spoken when she was ten years old, "I care so much." She does.

Twigg Crawford is, as always, an inspiration. He's my friend of longest standing. Knowing each other's history so well is a great gift, and it has helped me weave friendships with old friends into my novels, including this one.

Teachers are everything. I'm so thankful to Laurette Laramie. She taught history but also social justice and the need to look beyond the lessons for a deeper truth. She introduced us to the *New York Times*'s feature, "The Neediest Cases Fund." We read them in class. She helped me imagine other people's lives, to care about their suffering, to want to help.

Librarians provide a place to read, learn, and imagine. I am thankful to all, especially Amy Rhilinger of Attleboro Public Library, Beverly Choltco-Devlin of Tacoma Public Library, and my first librarian, Virginia Smith of New Britain Public Library. Mrs. Smith told me I could get a library card as soon as I could write my name, and she gave me one, even though the "ce" of "Rice" trailed off the line. She handed me the key to the world of books, and I'll never forget her.

ABOUT THE AUTHOR

Luanne Rice is the *New York Times* bestselling author of thirty-four novels, which have been translated into twenty-four languages. The author of *Dream Country, Beach Girls, The Secret Language of Sisters, The Beautiful Lost,* and others, Rice often writes about love, family, nature, and the sea. She received the 2014 Connecticut Governor's Arts Award for excellence and lifetime achievement in the Literary Arts category. Several of Rice's novels have been adapted for television, including *Crazy in Love* for TNT, *Blue Moon* for CBS, *Follow the Stars Home* and *Silver Bells* for the Hallmark Hall of Fame, and *Beach Girls* for Lifetime. Rice is an avid environmentalist and advocate for families affected by domestic violence. She lives on the Connecticut Shoreline. Visit her online at luannerice.net.